KEEP *me* SAFE

SARAH ELLISON

To all the girlies who love to want what they can't have, this one's for you.

trigger warnings

This book deals with some heavy topics including:

an emotionally abusive parent - remembered

victim blaming - remembered and on page

sexual assault - remembered/show on page, but not too graphic

a taboo age gap relationship

If any of these are deal breakers for you, I completely understand. It's important to take care of your mental health. I will say that as a SA survivor myself, this story helped me through a lot of the trauma related to that.

-Sarah

playlist

Dylan's Dad - Geena Fontanella

Messy - Lola Young

Anyway - Noah Kahan

Sweet Child O' Mine - Guns N' Roses

7 Years - SkyDxddy

I Was Made For Lovin' You - Kiss

Slow Burn - Kacey Musgraves

Invitation (feat. Kodie Shane) - Ashnikko

Brown Eyed Gril - Van Morrison

Golden Hour - Kacey Musgraves

Finally // Beautiful Stranger - Halsey

Night Moves - Bob Seagar & The Silver Bullet Band

Wondering Why - The Red Clay Strays

Eurydice - Vincent Lima

scan here to listen <3

chapter one
KIRA

"This is a serious accusation. If we find out you're lying, you could get into real trouble," the stout officer warns, his mustache twitching as he frowns.

The stale stench of coffee and cigarettes clings to him, turning my stomach. I've been sitting in this cold metal chair for over an hour, shaking so badly my teeth nearly chatter. Tears streak my face as I stare at him, pleading silently.

He isn't listening to me.

"I tried to tell him no—he wouldn't listen," I say more to myself than to him.

"Are you sure?" he asks, accusation clear in his tone.

I drop my head into my hands, taking a deep, quivering breath. I've told him the entire story three times, but it doesn't matter. He thinks I'm lying. My heart sinks in my chest as I look up to my mom. Her eyes don't meet mine as she sighs, looking more annoyed with the situation than concerned.

"Listen," the officer drones, "from what I'm hearing, there's no case here. You willingly put yourself in the situation. He didn't threaten you. He didn't hurt you." His voice lowers. "Not to mention, you were drinking—which is illegal. You're lucky I'm not charging you for that. I suggest you go home and clean yourself up." His gaze drags over me, making bile rise in my throat.

What is happening?

These people were supposed to help me. That's what we're told as kids, right? Cops protect you? My vision blurs as I stand and make my way out of the police station.

"I told you," is all my mom says.

THREE YEARS LATER, IT PLAYS IN MY HEAD LIKE IT WAS yesterday. I push down the memory, locking it away as I turn my key in the old deadbolt.

The scent of strawberries and vanilla fills the room from the wax warmer in the kitchen, and the sun shines through the windows, painting a golden hue over the space. The bed is made, albeit sloppily, and all I want to do is climb into it.

This place has been my home for nearly an entire year now. The apartment is small and fits only the necessities: a queen-sized bed, a purely functional kitchen, and a bathroom the size of a closet, but I love it. It's mine. I signed the lease the minute I turned eighteen and was legally able to, needing to escape my mother.

She never loved me. I'm convinced of that now.

Still, some small, foolish part of me thought that night—something that serious—would force her to show a sliver of compassion.

I was wrong.

Sinking onto my comforter, I let out a slow breath.

That's over now.

I haven't spoken to her since I left, and I don't plan to.

I need to focus on the present.

I graduated today.

I actually did it.

After everything that happened freshman year, I wasn't sure I'd make it to sophomore year, let alone graduate. The thought fills me with a hint of pride. He didn't win.

Prying my stare away from the cracks in the yellowed ceiling, I sit up, knowing I have to start getting ready to head to work. My job at the local grocery store isn't anything fancy, but I'm beyond grateful for it. Without that income, I wouldn't be where I am today.

Lake Ann is tiny—barely three hundred people live here year-round—which explains why our grocery store is the size of a storage shed. The building's wooden siding and deep green trim make it look like something out of an old Western, but don't let its size fool you. Somehow, it's packed with everything a person could need.

I drop my bag behind the counter and head toward the back, searching for Rob. He's always here, stocking shelves or chatting with customers. I find him crouched in the snack aisle, stuffing bags of chips onto a shelf.

Rob is in his sixties, silver-haired and round like a teddy bear, with a permanent twinkle in his eye. He grins up at me.

"Good afternoon, *graduate*. How does it feel?"

I return his smile, loving that he cares.

"Honestly, not much different. I'm just glad I don't have to enter that godforsaken school ever again," I laugh.

For me, high school was miserable. I had no friends besides Jared. The only thing that kept me going was ceramics.

Mrs. Johnson—Darla, now that I'm out of school—was the closest thing I had to a real parental figure. She owns a pottery studio and lets me use it for free. Without her, I don't know where I'd be. She's the reason I still believe I can open my own studio someday.

"You say that now, but you'll miss it eventually," he says.

I highly doubt it, but maybe it's true for him.

"Do you think you could handle the register? I'm going to finish stocking," he adds.

"Of course!"

I take a seat on the tall wooden stool behind the counter. Thankfully, today is warm, with the sun shining brightly through the old windows and almost no clouds in the sky. Michigan is one of the gloomiest states, so I'm happy that we tend to get a lot more sun during the summer. It makes the cloudy winter days worth it.

A jingle sounds, and the front door flies open, breaking me out of my thoughts.

Jared.

He barrels toward me, his face split into a grin. Before I can react, he wraps me in a crushing hug, lifting me off my seat.

"I can't believe we did it! We're officially adults now!" he exclaims.

Jared has been my best friend since middle school, and this—this joy, this energy—is exactly why I love him. He's sunshine in human form.

I roll my eyes, but I can't help but smile. He smells like fresh laundry and summer heat. His sandy blond hair flops into his bright green eyes, making him look like an overexcited golden retriever.

"We did," I giggle.

"Are you ready for the bonfire tonight?" He puts his hand by the side of his mouth and lowers his voice, "Jake's bringing the booze, and of course, I've got the bud. Plus, my dad works, so he'll be at the station and out of our way until tomorrow."

I shake my head, grinning at him.

Jared's dad is a firefighter, so his shifts are typically overnight. This has given us plenty of time over the years to make some questionable decisions at his lake house.

We're still alive, though, so that's a plus. Although, there were some close calls. A specific memory of too much tequila and a boat comes to my mind.

The door chimes again as it swings open. This time, however, Jared's dad walks through the door.

I take in his broad frame. He's wearing his typical ensemble: a faded black t-shirt that hangs over his ink-covered arms, worn blue jeans, and old brown work boots. He's the picture of masculinity. He scans the store, presumably looking for Jared, but his eyes land on mine instead. I quickly drop my focus to the floor, hoping he missed my staring.

Noah Keller is probably the hottest man I've ever seen, but he is entirely *off-limits*.

His eyes linger on me briefly before shifting to Jared leaning over the counter. "I hope you're not getting Kira into any trouble."

"Of course not. In case you forgot, I'm congratulating her on our literal graduation today."

"I was there," he responds, his eyes landing on me again. "Congratulations, Kira."

Heat rushes to my cheeks under his attention. Ever since Jared and I became friends, Noah has been there for us when he could. I can only imagine how hard it must be doing it all alone. He and Jared's mom split up before I met them, and I've always wondered what happened. But I never got the nerve to ask Jared, and he's never volunteered the information either.

"I just needed a snack before I have to head into the station," Noah says as he opens the clear doors and grabs a cream-filled long john, placing it in one of the parchment bags and onto the counter. My heart races at his eyes on me.

"And, of course, Jared wanted to come too," Noah chuckles as Jared tosses a bag of jerky onto the counter. I ring them up, smiling to myself. I don't know what I would do without these two.

The rest of my shift goes by without much struggle, and Rob even lets me leave a little early, citing my "big day" as an excuse.

Of course, it's going to be chilly tonight. It's Michigan in May. I throw on a cropped sweater and some thicker jeans before grabbing my phone from my dresser.

A new message.

Jared

Are you on your way yet?

I don't wanna start without you

Kira

Miss me already?

I'm finishing getting ready, then I'll head out

Jared

Okay, well hurry bc I've already got a shot waiting for you ;)

I roll my eyes. He knows I'm not a big drinker, but that never stops him from trying.

I pack an overnight bag, fully aware I'll be staying over, and grab my keys from the counter. Double-checking that the door is locked behind me, I make my way to my car. The drive to Jared's is only about fifteen minutes out of town, a route I've taken countless times over the years. It's familiar. Comforting. Like going home.

When I pull up to the house, cars are already filling up the front yard. *Great.* I was hoping that there wouldn't be this many people yet. I don't mind parties, but a large group of people getting wasted makes me a little anxious, especially when it's people I don't know.

I park in my usual spot in the driveway, right behind Jared's silver Mazda, and take a deep breath. I'll be fine. At least, that's what I tell myself as I step out of my car and head toward the backyard.

Jared's house is a white, two-story craftsman overlooking Lake Ann. While the front of the house is beautiful and well-landscaped, the back is the selling point. It features a large deck that leads down to a grass patch with a gorgeous view of the lake. Beyond that stands a worn wooden dock extending into the water.

The entire space is lit with warm string lights, and the fire is already blazing by the lake. Jared stands beside it with a red solo cup in hand. Sensing my presence, he glances up, and his bright eyes meet mine. He smirks as I saunter to the fire to stand with him.

"Kira, you finally made it."

"Yes, and *somebody* promised me a shot." I look up at him, mostly kidding, but some liquid courage would help ease the anxiety filling my chest.

"Well, let's go get it then," he says, mischief playing in his features.

He grabs my hand and leads me to the porch, where we pass a folding table set up for beer pong.

I shout over the music, "We are so doing that later!"

Sliding the door open, we step into the kitchen. Jared starts pouring what looks like tequila into a red solo cup, handing it to me.

"Starting out strong, are we?"

He laughs, "Go big or go home, am I right?"

The liquid burns on the way down, spreading a welcome warmth through my chest. I don't drink much anymore, but sometimes it helps quiet the noise in my head. When I glance up, I catch Jared watching me.

"What?" I ask. He hesitates for a moment, shaking his head.

"Nothing, let's make some drinks and go play some beer pong."

I tilt my head in confusion but push it away.

Typically, I prefer wine, but that's not an option, so I make myself a tequila soda, and he pours himself a jack and coke. Grabbing my hand again, he pulls me back to the porch.

"We play winners!" Jared announces.

While we're waiting for the current game to end, Jared and I sit on the wicker chairs on the porch, sipping our drinks.

"I can't believe high school is finally over," I sigh.

"Me either. It felt like it was never going to end," he responds. "I can't wait to start at Michigan State this fall."

"I'm so excited for you! I'm going to miss you, though," I whine.

"I know," he says, his smile soft. "But I'll come home as much as I can."

The game wraps up, and we're up next against Jake and Ava. Jake is one of Jared's best friends—they met when Jared joined JV football freshman year and have been inseparable ever since. Ava is Jake's girlfriend.

I've only met her a few times, but she seems nice.

"Kira and I are basically beer pong legends. You two don't stand a chance," Jared teases.

I laugh. I wouldn't call myself a legend, but I've had plenty of practice on this porch. Memories of sneaking a six-pack from Noah the summer before freshman year flash through my mind.

Now, we're down to one pesky red cup. Jake and Ava still have two on the table. Jared misses his shot. It's my turn.

No way I'm making this. Pressure makes me choke every time—especially a few drinks in.

"Come on, Kira, you got this!" Jared cheers.

"No, you don't," Jake smirks, throwing me a wink.

I take a deep breath and line up my shot, tossing the ball with a perfect arc and landing directly into the center of the cup. Shouts erupt from behind me. Jared brings his arms around me, lifting me into a big hug. I squeal, giggling as he puts me down.

"See, I knew you could do it. Who's next?" Jared asks.

More people step up to the other side of the table, and we play a couple more rounds until we finally lose to some guys that I can only explain as looking like their names are Brad and Chad. Accepting defeat, Jared shrugs and heads inside to grab another drink, not that he needs it. I follow, making my way down the hall to the bathroom.

Washing my hands, a knock sounds on the door.

"One sec!" I announce, turning off the water.

The door swings open anyway.

Jake looms over me, the dim light casting shadows across his face. He shuts the door behind him. The click of the lock is deafening. My stomach knots, my breath catching in my throat.

I've been trying to get you alone all night," he slurs, the stench of alcohol strong on his breath.

Panic claws up my chest. I force myself to stay still, to breathe, but my heart pounds against my ribs. I glance past him, calculating the distance to the door. Too far.

Then, without warning, he's on me. An arm snakes around my waist, pulling me into him.

Suddenly, I'm fifteen again.

The air is too thick. The room is too small. I can't breathe.

Jake's breath is hot against my cheek. "I couldn't help but notice how you were looking at me earlier," he murmurs, his eyes dragging over me like I belong to him. His fingers brush the hem of my sweater, just beneath my ribs. My skin crawls. My pulse roars in my ears.

I need out. Now.

"Jake, what are you doing?" My voice is barely above a whisper, too strangled by fear.

He smirks. "Relax."

I jerk back, but his grip tightens.

"I like the top," he says, his fingers grazing the bottom of my chest.

My throat locks up. My body shuts down. The memories slam into me like a wrecking ball. I'm trapped. No one can hear me. No one can save me.

Except me.

Time stops. I force my mind to catch up with my body. This is now. I am not fifteen. I am not powerless.

I lift my chin and meet his eyes, steel sharpening my voice.

"Let. Go. Of. Me."

His body locks up. He stares at me as if seeing me clearly for the first time. The moment stretches, suffocating. Then, finally, his hands fall away.

"Shit," he mutters, raking a hand through his hair. "I— I thought you wanted it. My bad."

His bad.

I stumble back, bile burning my throat. "You have a girlfriend!" My voice cracks. Tears sting my eyes, but I won't cry. Not here. Not in front of him.

I lunge for the door, fumbling with the lock.

"Please don't tell Ava," he pleads, reaching for me again.

The moment his fingers graze my wrist, I snap.

"Are you kidding me?" I wrench myself free.

Jared's nowhere in sight. My chest is caving in. I can't be here.

I shove through the back door and gasp for air. The cool night stings my burning cheeks as I stumble down to the lake, barely seeing where I'm going.

The hammock.

I sink into it, curling in on myself, pressing my forehead into my knees. The weight of everything crashes over me, a tide I can't fight.

Was I looking at him a certain way? I wasn't trying to.

This outfit shows too much skin.

I should have known better.

I press my foot against the ground and start swinging myself, rocking through the nausea, the dread. I press my nails into my palm, grounding myself.

I am okay. I am safe.

I repeat it until I almost believe it.

The moon glows on the water's surface, its reflection rippling with the waves. The party hums behind me, a distant blur of voices and music. I catch sight of Jared on the porch, laughing, passing a joint around a circle of carefree faces.

I envy them. I used to be them.

I stare up through the leaves, blinking rapidly. Then I break. Silent, shuddering sobs slip free, my shoulders shaking.

I don't know how long I've been lying there when Jared stumbles up beside me.

"Kira! What are ya doin' over here?" he asks, plopping down beside me and wrapping his arm around me. The scent of alcohol hits me like a slap.

I flinch. My breath hitches. My body tenses.

For one terrifying second, I am not here.

But then, reality snaps back into place. This is Jared. He's not Jake.

I exhale sharply, forcing a smile through the tears.

Jared frowns. "Kira?"

I don't answer. Instead, I reach up, cupping his cheeks with both hands, anchoring myself.

"Oh, Jared, how drunk are you?"

His brow furrows. "Have you been crying—?" He stops mid-sentence, his attention snapping toward the house.

"Uh oh."

I glance up, following Jared's line of sight and the man storming across the lawn in his work uniform. He does not look happy. He stops about two feet away and looks down at us. Slowly, I bring my gaze up to meet his dark eyes, my stomach knotting at the fury there.

"What's going on here?" Noah demands.

Shit.

I thought he was supposed to be at the station tonight. His eyes move to Jared's arm around me and dart back to mine, his features hardening.

He is pissed.

chapter two
NOAH

"Don't make me ask again," I say through gritted teeth.

Tearing my gaze off Kira, I look over to Jared. They're lying in the hammock, his arm around her waist. His droopy eyelids tell me he's already three sheets to the wind, and the pink tint in Kira's cheeks makes me wonder. Is there something going on between them?

"Don't worry, Dad, everyone's leaving," he slurs.

"You're right about that one," I agree, turning toward what's left of the party. "Party's over, go home," I bark.

The guests scramble to gather their things, a few engines revving to life before fading into the night. I exhale sharply. Why didn't Jared tell me he was having people over? I wouldn't have said no. I just prefer a heads-up when there's underage drinking on my property.

"Let's get you inside, big guy," Kira says as she rises to her feet, grabbing Jared's arm and pulling him with her.

I *should* help her. Instead, I pivot and stride toward the house, anger simmering beneath my skin. But why? I don't fully understand it. I pull open the sliding door—not a complete asshole, after all—and hold it as she guides Jared inside. I even help her steer him into his room.

As she leans down to tuck him in, I catch myself watching.

Her long, wavy brown hair spills over her shoulders, cascading down her back, stopping just at her waist. Her jeans fit snug, hugging her curves—

What the fuck am I thinking? This is Kira. I've known her since she was in seventh grade.

Jaw tightening, I force my eyes to the floor, sighing as I turn and leave the room.

Sinking onto a barstool at the kitchen island, I drop my head into my hands. What the hell is wrong with me? I wasn't even supposed to be home tonight. I should be at the station, covering for Dave. His husband had planned a surprise for their anniversary at the last minute, but his work called him in, so Dave ended up taking his shift back. I should've just stayed there.

A door clicks softly down the hall. Footsteps pad into the kitchen.

Kira stops when she sees me, her eyes wide.

"Kira," I say, my tone edged with warning.

What were they thinking?

She turns toward me and immediately starts to apologize. "It won't happen again, I promise," she says, worry written in her features.

I sigh, my voice softer now. "I know, it's okay. I'm not upset with you, but I am a little irritated with Jared."

She lets out a breath, visibly relaxing. "He can definitely be a handful sometimes," she laughs.

"About that," I say. "Are you two…like a thing now?" I'm not sure why I ask. I shouldn't care. They would be great together. She's good for him.

"No, we're definitely just friends," she answers, a soft chuckle escaping her lips.

"Could've fooled me," I reply, grabbing a glass from the cupboard and turning to the fridge for water. Closing it, I turn back to face her and catch her eyes on me. She instantly drops her gaze, her cheeks flushed.

"Listen, I'll talk to Jared in the morning about the party, but I understand you guys had a reason to celebrate," I say, my tone softening. "Now, go to bed, it's already late."

She looks at me and rolls her eyes, "Yes, sir."

My body tenses at those words. She moves to walk away, but I add, "Hey, I'm proud of you. For graduating today, I mean. That's a pretty big deal," I tell her. She simply smiles and continues up the stairs to the guest room.

It feels like Kira has always been at Jared's side.

She brings out a version of him I don't always see—lighter, less guarded. I watch the way she can nudge him into laughter, the way he turns to her instinctively, trusting that she'll always be there. He needs that.

Maybe more than he'd admit.

I lean against the counter, rubbing a hand over my jaw. His mom left when he was two. I never told him the worst of it—how I'd fought for her to stay, how I spent years chasing something that was never real. She never wanted this life. Not with me. Not with him.

By the time he was old enough to ask why she was gone, I'd run out of answers.

And maybe I should've let it go, but there was always that flicker of something in his eyes, a question he never voiced: Why weren't we enough?

I exhale, pushing off the counter. It wasn't just the party that upset me. I wasn't really mad at Jared for drinking with his friends. He's grown now.

So why the hell had I snapped at him?

I WAKE UP TO THE SUN STREAMING IN FROM THE CURTAINS IN MY room. The smell of coffee tells me that I'm not the first one awake. Pulling on some sweatpants and a T-shirt, I open my bedroom door and head downstairs to the kitchen. As I approach, Kira sits at the island, gazing down at her mug. She's wearing a faded, oversized shirt and tiny pink sleep shorts, her long hair in a knot at the top of her head.

"Morning sleeping beauty, how're you feeling?" I ask as I walk over to the coffee pot to get my cup, adding a splash of creamer.

"Not too bad," she responds, smiling up at me, her chestnut eyes meeting mine. "I only had a couple of drinks."

"You shouldn't have had any," I assert, taking a sip.

"I know, I know," she retorts, her eyes playful.

She's beautiful like this.

"You hungry for breakfast?" I ask, distracting myself from my thoughts. I already know her answer.

"I'd like my eggs over medium, please!" she squeals as she gets up to help me. I start on the bacon as Kira grabs the bread to make toast.

This is almost a tradition for us. Jared isn't an early riser, so any time Kira stays over, she helps me make breakfast.

So, why is it that now I can't seem to keep my eyes off her?

When we finish cooking, I make her plate with her special eggs, buttered toast, and a couple of pieces of bacon—*still oinkin'*, as she calls it. I hand it to her, where she's seated on top of the counter.

"So, I wanted to say that I really am sorry about last night," she explains, a frown marring her face.

"Kira, I'm not upset with you," I step in front of her, resting a hand on the counter, my fingers grazing her leg. A slow heat spreads up my arm. I know I shouldn't be this close, standing between her open thighs, but she doesn't pull away.

Her gaze lifts to mine. Lips parting. A sharp inhale.

"I promise, I'm not mad—"

"Oh god, I feel like death," Jared groans from the hallway.

I exhale sharply, stepping back, severing the moment. Jared stumbles into the kitchen, wearing only his plaid pajama pants. Did he see that?

No—he's too hungover to notice. He looks like hell and probably feels worse. Not that anything was happening anyway.

"Have too much fun last night?" I ask.

"Oh, shut up."

"I'd watch that tone if I were you," I warn.

He drags himself over to the medicine cabinet, grabs two Tylenol, and pops them into his mouth.

I take my plate and sit on one of the barstools away from Kira, "Food is ready if you want some."

Jared ignores me and moves over to her, leaning into her embrace. She wraps her arms around him, holding him where I was moments ago. Turning her head, she faces me as her eyes meet mine. I glance at where her leg is touching his bare torso. He doesn't know how lucky he is to have someone like her.

"Okay, I need to get going now. I'm sure you'll survive the rest of the day without me," she says, lightly pushing Jared off her.

"Fine," he groans.

Kira goes to the guest room to collect her stuff, leaving Jared and me alone in the kitchen.

"Listen," I turn to look at him. "I don't appreciate you inviting half of the town over to my house without even giving me a heads-up last night."

"I can't do this right now. It wasn't even that big of a deal," he says as he picks up his plate and turns to head for his room.

"Don't walk away from me when I'm talking to you," I scold.

He keeps walking anyway, a door slamming down the hall. I could go yell at him, but it won't do anything. Not when he's like this.

I sigh and gather the plates, dumping them in the sink. As I start loading the dishwasher, Kira strolls back in, her bag slung over her shoulder.

"Good luck with that one," she tells me, a smile appearing on her face before she walks out the front door. My thoughts drift back to her on the counter, me between her legs. I wanted to touch her, wanted to run my fingers over her thighs.

No, that's wrong, and it's never happening.

But the way she looked at me.

I need air.

I haul open the garage door, greeted by my black '70 Nova SS. It doesn't run yet, but it will. I've had this car since Jared was little—it's my pride and joy. When he was growing up, I never had the time to work on it. Now, with him older, I can finally devote the attention it deserves.

Popping the hood, I get to work, losing myself in the familiarity of the task. Hours slip by. The clock on the wall reminds me I have an actual shift at the station today.

When I arrive at the station, I toss my bag into my locker, settling in for what's likely to be a long night.

"Noah," the commissioner greets.

"Hey, Al, long time no see," I joke.

"Dinner ready yet?" he asks.

Rolling my eyes, I head for the kitchen. I've been a firefighter for fifteen years. Al's been the fire commissioner even longer. He's a no-bullshit kind of guy, which makes him damn good at his job. He's retiring this year. I don't know what we'll do without him.

I usually handle the cooking when I'm on shift—none of the other guys can manage much beyond frozen pizza. Tonight, it's sloppy joes. When the food's ready, I let everyone know, and we settle in to eat.

"Thanks for being willing to cover my shift yesterday. Sorry, I didn't end up needing it," Dave tells me, his mouth full of sloppy Joe.

"That's fine, I don't mind."

"How's your boy doing?" Jeff asks.

"He's fine, a handful as usual," I laugh, thinking back to Kira's comment.

The rest of the shift goes relatively smoothly. We only have a couple of calls during the night, so I am able to get some sleep.

Today, I spend most of my time training and performing preventative maintenance on the trucks.

By the time 6 o'clock rolls around, I'm more than ready to go home, but I need to stop by the store first to grab some groceries for the week. The fridge is looking pretty empty at home.

I push the door open, and a bell rings as I enter the small store. I grab some milk and eggs and place them in the cart. Turning the corner,

I notice a familiar mess of long caramel hair stocking the bread aisle.

"Hey, princess."

A loaf of sliced white bread hits the floor.

"Jesus, Noah, you scared me!"

Chuckling, I pick it up and hand it back to her, but she scowls at me.

"I'm sorry, I didn't mean to startle you," I say.

She sighs, "It's fine. I'm just tired. My shift is almost over, and I honestly can't wait to climb into bed."

"Well, I hope the rest of it goes by fast then," I say as I grab a loaf of bread and set it in the cart.

"Thank you," she looks up at me with exhaustion in her beautiful features. I feel for her. She's doing everything on her own at such a young age.

I don't know how she does it.

chapter three
KIRA

I was not expecting Noah to stop by the store today, but I'm glad he did. After working an extra-long shift to make up for the time I missed for graduation, seeing him made the exhaustion a little easier to bear.

By the time I get home, I'm drained, my muscles aching from hours on my feet. I run a bath, adding a generous pour of lavender-scented bubbles, and peel off my clothes. The moment I sink into the warm water, a soft moan escapes me.

I needed this.

My mind drifts to Noah. I wonder what he's doing tonight. With the way the storm clouds were rolling in, he's probably sitting out on the porch, a beer in his hand, watching the sky. Then, unbidden, a memory sneaks in—his hand grazing my leg, the heat of his body so close.

It was barely a touch, but I wanted more.

I've always had a bit of a crush on him. Who wouldn't? He's tall, gorgeous, and always looking out for me. But I know it only goes one way. He sees me as Jared's friend, nothing more.

I pull on my pajamas and crawl into bed, burrowing beneath the blankets. Grabbing my favorite book, I read until my eyelids grow heavy, letting the words lull me to sleep.

A SHARP VIBRATION YANKS ME FROM SLEEP.

I fumble for my phone, knocking half the contents off my nightstand. Squinting at the screen, I see two missed calls and a text from Jared.

Jared
Wanna go do something today?

Kira
YES! I have today off, so I'm free whenever

Shooting off a quick response, I head to the kitchen to make my coffee when I notice a folded piece of yellow paper on the floor in front of my apartment door. Bending down to pick it up, I carefully open it. As I skim the contents, my entire body stiffens.

"Due to increasing demand and higher operating costs, we have decided to increase your monthly rent to $950."

My heart drops as I glance at the following line.

"This change will be implemented on your next billing cycle."

That's in two weeks! This can't be true. I can't afford that. It's almost double what I'm paying right now. How can they do that?

"If you are not renewing your lease, you will be expected to vacate the premises before that date."

What am I supposed to do?

I see a number at the bottom of the paper and dial it without a second thought.

"Hello, this is Jan."

"Um, hello. I just received a note saying that my rent is increasing?" I ask, my heart racing.

"Oh, yes, we just increased the monthly rent on all of our units. It was well overdue. We haven't increased our pricing in years," she explains.

"Well, I don't think I am going to be able to afford it. Is there anything you can do? Anyone I can speak to?"

"Unfortunately, no, ma'am. This has already been decided and is not up for negotiation. It states in your lease that the landlord can increase rent at any time. Is there anything else I can help with?"

Are you kidding me?

"No, I guess not." I hang up, my breathing uneven.

What am I going to do?

I've already cut every expense I can to stay here.

My vision blurs as a tear slips down my cheek. My legs give out, and I sink to the floor, arms wrapped around my knees. A sob wracks my chest, then another.

Maybe my mom was right.

Maybe I can't do this on my own.

Maybe I was an idiot to think I could.

I stare ahead, unfocused, trapped in the spiral of my thoughts. I don't know how long I sit there on the cold tile floor, but eventually, the dull ache in my bladder pulls me back to reality. With a deep breath, I grip the counter and force myself to stand.

Out of the corner of my eye, I catch my reflection in the mirror—swollen face, red-rimmed eyes. I barely recognize myself.

No.

I take another breath, staring into my own eyes.

I will be okay. I will figure this out. I am not giving up.

I spend the rest of the day in bed, scrolling through rental listings, but every search only makes my anxiety worse.

There's nothing. Nothing even close to what I can afford.

A tear splashes onto my pillow.

I feel utterly helpless.

My phone rings next to me, and I jump. Looking at the caller ID, Jared's name fills my screen. Shit, we were supposed to make plans today. I answer, trying not to sound like I've been crying.

"Hey, Jared."

"Kira! Still want to go do something tonight?" Jared asks hopefully.

"I don't know. I'm pretty tired," I explain, but there's a slight shake to my voice.

"Hey, what's wrong? Have you been crying?"

I don't respond. What am I supposed to say?

"Kira, tell me what's wrong," Jared demands. I'm silent for a moment. I don't know how to answer him without breaking down again. A sob escapes my lips.

"I'm on my way. Stay where you are."

I'm startled by the sound of the lock turning as my apartment door swings open ten minutes later. Jared stands there in the doorway, looking around the apartment for me. I gave him a key because he's the only person I trust with it. When his eyes land on mine, he shuts the door and strides toward me, scooping me into his arms.

"Kira, please tell me what's going on," he pleads.

I look up at him, a tear sliding down my face. I don't want him to know I failed, but he will find out eventually anyway, and I don't have anyone else to talk to.

"I'm losing my apartment," I explain.

"What? Why?" Jared asks, confused.

"They're raising the rent, and I can't afford it. I've already looked, and there's nowhere else in my budget. I don't know what I'm going to do, Jared." My voice cracks.

He rubs my back, comforting me. Jared has always been there for me. Even when he doesn't know what's upsetting me, he's there to keep me from falling apart.

I look up at him and see his eyes are already fixed on me. Emotions war in his eyes as he runs his fingers over my hair.

"Why don't I ask my dad if you can move in with us? We have the space, and you're already like part of the family. Plus, you're there half of the time anyway."

I shake my head. "I couldn't ask you to do that. I don't want to cause any more stress for him."

"Don't worry, you won't. I'll talk to him."

He grabs his phone and walks out of my apartment into the hallway. I hear his muffled voice and hope that Noah isn't upset. I don't want him to be disappointed in me. I wanted to be able to do this on my own.

The door opens, and Jared steps back into the room.

"He's on his way," Jared tells me.

"Here? Right now?" I ask.

"Yep, all I did was tell him that you needed a place to stay, and he said he was leaving now and hung up."

Oh god, is he mad? Is he coming so he can tell me no face-to-face? He wouldn't do that, would he? He's going to be so disappointed. Jared notices the shift in my mood and grabs my arm.

"It's okay, it'll be fine," he assures.

A knock at the door pulls me from my thoughts, and Jared moves to open it, letting Noah in.

As soon as he enters the room, his gaze meets mine, taking me in. I must look like a mess, sitting on my bed, still wearing my sleep shirt from last night. My face is undoubtedly red and splotchy from crying, and I have not brushed my hair today.

"Jared, go get Kira some dinner," he orders.

Jared looks at me as if asking for permission, and I nod slowly. He turns for the door and walks out, closing it softly.

"Talk to me," Noah says, sitting on the bed beside me.

I can't think, especially with his warm body this close to mine. All I want is for him to hold me and tell me that everything is going to be alright.

"Kira,"

I let out a shaky sigh.

"I don't know what to say. I'm losing my apartment. I failed."

"Don't say that. This is not your fault," he asserts.

When I don't respond, he brings his hand to my chin, guiding me to look at him. My stomach flips, heat radiating from his touch.

We've never been this close before.

"You're moving in with us," he says firmly.

I shake my head, "No, you don't have to do that. I'm not your responsibility."

"Princess," his knuckles graze my jaw before he drops his hand.

"You'll always be my responsibility."

A soft knock sounds at the door, and Noah stands to get it. Jared emerges from the doorway, carrying two large bags of what looks like Chinese food. I chuckle to myself. That's going to be way too much.

The three of us sit cross-legged on my bed, takeout containers spread out between us. Jared put on *Married At First Sight*—one of our favorites—and he's completely immersed, nodding along as if he were part of the drama unfolding on screen. I push a noodle around with my chopsticks, my appetite coming and going in waves.

Noah glances at me more than once, and every time, my stomach tightens. I can't shake what he said earlier. I don't want him to think I'm some helpless girl who needs to be taken care of.

Eventually, the boys gather their things. Jared gives me a reassuring squeeze on the leg before heading for the door. "You can move in tomorrow if you want," he says with a grin.

I let out a small laugh. "It'll take me more than a day to pack up my entire life."

But not much longer than that.

A WEEK PASSES, AND MY APARTMENT LOOKS NOTHING LIKE IT ONCE did. The walls are bare, the counters empty, my life compressed into a handful of worn-out boxes. It turns out I don't own much.

Today's the day. By sunset, I'll be at the lake house.

Jared and Noah are supposed to be here soon to help me finish moving, and I remind myself, again, that this is temporary.

Just a stepping stone until I get back on my feet. But no matter how many times I repeat it, the bitter taste of failure lingers. My mother was right. I couldn't do it on my own.

A knock at the door pulls me from my thoughts. Jared bursts in, energy buzzing off him, and within minutes, we're loading the last of my things into Noah's truck. It happens too fast, too smoothly. Before I know it, the place is empty.

I linger in the doorway, fingers tightening around my key. Shame presses against my ribs like a vice. Turning back, I let my gaze sweep across the apartment one last time as if searching for some proof that this wasn't all for nothing.

I find none.

With a slow breath, I lock the door behind me.

The drive to the lake house is quiet, just the hum of the engine and the rhythmic beat of my own thoughts. I follow behind Noah, my hands tightening on the wheel. Despite everything, a small part of me is relieved. Excited, even.

The lake house has always felt more like home than my mother's ever did. It's where I spent summer nights wrapped in a blanket on the dock, where laughter echoed against the water, where I felt—safe.

Carrying the last box up the narrow staircase, I step into the guest room. Warm afternoon light filters through the large eight-pane window, casting golden streaks across the wooden floors. The sloped ceiling makes the space feel tucked away, almost like a secret. The four-poster bed dominates the room, draped in soft, ivory linens. Matching nightstands frame either side, and the vanity sits in the corner, waiting for me.

For the first time in days, my chest loosens.

I set the box down gently and run my hand over the smooth surface of the dresser. Then, with a quiet sigh, I start unpacking.

chapter four
NOAH

When Jared called and told me Kira needed somewhere to stay, I dropped everything. There was no way I'd let her go back to her mom. I don't know the full story of what happened between them, but I know it was bad. She's staying with us, and that's final.

But seeing her like that? It killed me.

Kira is one of the strongest people I know. She handles so much on her own, and I understand how exhausting that can be. So, when she blamed herself for losing the apartment, I couldn't stand it. There has to be a law against jacking up someone's rent with that little notice.

This morning, when we showed up to help her move, I expected to find the same shaken girl from last week. But she wasn't. She had already piled all her boxes by the door, greeted us with a smile—determined, almost stubborn. But underneath that, I still saw it. That flicker of doubt.

Upstairs, her door is open. As I pass, I glance inside. She's sitting on the floor next to the dresser, unpacking a box of clothes, carefully folding each item before tucking it away.

"How're you feeling?" I ask.

"Noah, you have to stop sneaking up on me!" she yelps.

I laugh and look down at her, still waiting for a response to my question. After a moment, she seems to realize and answer.

"I'm okay, I think. It's obviously not easy, but you guys really helped. I appreciate you letting me stay here."

"Of course, you're always welcome. You know that," I tell her. I tried to get her to stay with us when she was first looking for an apartment, but she wanted to be able to find one on her own, and I understood that.

"Well, thank you anyway. I don't know what I would have done if you had said no."

I can't believe that thought even crossed her mind. She looks up at me, her russet eyes speckled with gold from the sun coming from the window. There's pain there, but something else too. Something more intense. Glancing down at her mouth, I try not to imagine how she would taste. Clearing my throat, I push away the thought.

"How do you feel about steak for dinner?" I ask.

"I would love that."

"Medium rare?"

"You know me so well," she says. "Do you have lemons? I could make lemonade!" she adds, smiling up at me.

"We do," I say with a soft laugh.

Leaving her to finish organizing, I head for the kitchen. My jaw tightens. I *need* to get my head on straight.

I drag a hand through my hair, exhaling slowly as I grab the steaks from the fridge. Focus. Dinner. That's all.

"Steak? Hell yeah!" Jared exclaims as he walks through the kitchen to the living room.

I add all the seasonings and marinade to the steaks before returning them to the fridge. The lemons on the counter draw my attention, so I grab a cutting board, a knife, and the juicer and set them right next to the fruit. It takes me a few minutes to find our pitcher, but when I do, I put it next to the cutting board right as Kira comes jogging down the stairs.

"Thank you!" she coos with a big smile, noticing the supplies.

"No problem. I thought it'd be easier than you asking me where everything is," I answer.

She rolls her eyes at me, moving to grab a lemon and place it on the wooden board. I leave her in the kitchen and take the meat out to the patio.

Dropping the steaks on the grill, I glance at the horizon, where the sun is setting. Pinks and oranges paint the sky, and the smell of spring still lingers in the air. When I look back to the house, Kira emerges from the slider with a pitcher full of... is that pink lemonade?

"Oh my god, they look so good! When are they going to be done? I'm so hungry!" Kira whines.

"Soon, princess," I reassure her. "What happened to the lemonade?" I gesture over to the pitcher on the table.

"You had some strawberries in the fridge, so I added them to it and made *strawberry* lemonade," she says with a grin.

Of course, that's something she would do.

I remove the steaks from the grill, place them on a platter, and do the same with the potatoes. Then, I set them both on the patio table. Kira puts out three plates and silverware, and we dig in.

"Hey, Kira," Jared says with his mouth still half full of food. "Jake is having a party tonight. Do you wanna come with me?"

She hesitates for a moment, "Um, I don't know. I'm tired from the move, and I would kind of just like to relax tonight." Her eyes shift downward, and I can't help but feel like there's something else to that.

"Please?" Jared begs.

"Jared, she said she didn't want to go," I catch myself saying.

"Fine," he whines as he eats another bite of his steak.

"I'm sorry, Jared, maybe another time," she assures with a small smile.

She has been through a lot this past week and deserves time to rest. If I were Jared, I wouldn't even go to the party, let alone try to get Kira to go.

When everyone finishes their food, I grab the dishes to bring them to the sink, but Kira slaps my hand away.

"No, you cooked everything. I can handle the dishes."

"You don't have to do that. You did a lot today. Go sit down," I say.

"No, I want to help, especially because I know Jared won't," she demands. I hadn't even noticed that he had already left the room.

"Okay, you win this time. Let me at least help you carry everything to the sink?" I suggest.

"Deal," she says as she nods.

Setting the dishes in the sink, I grab the sponge, scrubbing the first plate before she sees me.

"No!" she screams. "Unhand that dish!" She runs up to me and tries to wrestle the sponge out of my hand. I'll give her credit. She's putting in a great effort, but she's no match for my strength or height. I dangle it in the air above her head, and she tries to reach it.

Looking down at her, I notice a smear of bubbles on her cheek from the sponge, and I laugh.

"What?" she asks.

"You've got something right…" moving my hand toward her face, I add, "…here," wiping the suds off with my thumb. Her gaze lingers on mine for a moment. Without warning, she takes advantage of my distraction and snags the sponge, hiding it behind her back.

"I'm doing the dishes. Go sit down," she orders.

I raise my hands in the air, "Alright, I surrender."

"Good." She stares at me, probably making sure I won't try anything else, as she scrubs the next plate and loads it into the dishwasher.

Pouring myself some lemonade, I take a sip.

"Do you like it?" she asks quietly.

"I do, actually, it's delicious."

She beams at me before turning back to the dishes. She is so gorgeous without even trying. I don't understand why Jared hasn't ever made a move on her. They've been close for years. I'm honestly surprised that they've never dated.

Speaking of the devil, Jared emerges from the hallway.

"You sure you don't want to come, Kira? It's gonna be a lot of fun!" Jared asks.

"I think I'm good. Thank you, though," she answers with a forced smile.

"Alright, I'm gonna head out then."

"Drive safe!" she calls.

"Don't do anything stupid," I add.

After Jared leaves, we settle into the living room, planting ourselves on opposite ends of the couch. The soft hum of the TV fills the space as Kira grabs the remote, flicking through channels before landing on some kind of reality show. The screen flashes with over-the-top arguments— two women in cocktail dresses gesturing wildly at each other over a candlelit dinner.

I steal a glance at Kira. She's completely absorbed, her brow furrowed in concentration.

"You know this is fake, right?" I tease.

"Of course I do," she says without looking away.

A little impressed, I ask, "Then why do you watch it?"

"Because it's an escape."

"What do you mean?"

She repositions herself, facing me, our legs almost touching. Her gaze meets mine, steady and sincere. "Their lives are so exaggerated and unrealistic, their problems so minuscule, that it takes me out of my reality for a bit. It's nice."

I hadn't thought about it like that, but it makes sense. She's already been through more than most thirty-year-olds. I can see why she would want to forget about life for a while.

"I have a question, but you don't have to answer if you don't want to," she says, looking over at me.

I tilt my head. What could she ask that I wouldn't want to answer?

"Of course, anything."

"What happened with Jared's mom? I've always wondered, but I didn't want to push him," she explains.

Oh. *That's* her question. I sigh, readjusting in my seat. I haven't talked about Angie to anyone in years, and I'm not sure I want to start now.

"That's a long story," I tell her, silently hoping she drops it.

"I have time. Unless you don't want to tell me, that's okay," she says, her eyes soft.

I could tell her it's not her business, that I don't want to talk about it, but something in her gaze begs me to be honest with her.

"We were young when Angie got pregnant with Jared. We had only been together a couple of months, but her parents were very traditional. They pretty much forced us to get married when they found out.

I wanted it to work so bad. I had always wanted a family, and this was my opportunity to have one. We tried, or at least I did, but she was never truly happy with us. She wanted more.

It wasn't long before I found out that while I was at the station, she was sleeping around with other guys. When I confronted her, she blamed it on my work schedule and left. Jared was only two."

Her brows knit together as her russet eyes meet mine, understanding swirling in them.

"I'm sorry, Noah. You didn't deserve that."

I shake my head, shrugging. "We're better off, but it has always been a soft spot for Jared."

I ignore that it's a soft spot for me, too. I wasn't enough. We weren't enough. I haven't had a serious relationship since, and I tell myself that's because I needed to prioritize Jared, but I think deep down, I couldn't handle that rejection again.

We sit there in mutual silence for a few minutes, neither of us knowing what to say. That answer was heavy and probably more than she was bargaining for.

"I've also been meaning to ask," she almost whispers, "How much would you like me to pay for rent? Or maybe I can take on some of the utility payments?"

"No," I reply abruptly. "You're not paying me to stay here."

"Noah, I'm not going to stay here and not contribute. I can't do that."

"You can and you will," I insist.

"I'm going to pay you," she says, eyeing me.

Sighing, I drop the subject for now. She can try all she wants. I am not taking any money from her. While I admire her desire to help, that money would be better spent elsewhere. She can use it to help cover college expenses in the fall.

When I look back at Kira, she has her eyebrows scrunched together, and she's chewing on her bottom lip.

"What's on your mind?" I ask.

Snapping out of her thoughts, she shakes her head, her eyes shooting up to mine.

"It's nothing. I'm fine," she shrugs, looking away from me.

"Don't do that. You can talk to me," I say.

Her eyes soften as she lets out a shaky breath. "I just feel like my mom was right. I failed like she said I would," she admits, her voice breaking at the end.

Tears gather in her eyes, and she bites down on her lip, trying to hold them back. But I see the way her jaw tightens, the way her shoulders tense. She's fighting it—fighting the hurt, the weight of everything pressing down on her.

Fuck. I can't just sit here.

Without thinking, I reach for her, pulling her into me. She doesn't hesitate. She climbs onto my lap, curling into my chest as though she belongs there. My arms fold around her, holding her tight, and I swear I feel her finally let go. A quiet sob escapes her, muffled against my shoulder, and I stroke my hand down her back, letting her know I'm here—that I've always been here.

"Hey," I murmur, my lips near her hair. "It's okay. This is *not* your fault. The landlord was an asshole for giving you barely any notice." I squeeze her just a little. "You're doing so damn well, Kira. You have your shit together way more than I did when I was 18."

She pulls back just enough to look at me, her lashes damp, her cheeks flushed. "You're lying," she sniffs. "There's no way. In case you haven't noticed, I'm a *hot mess.*"

I reach up, brushing a strand of hair from her face, trying to ignore how soft her skin looks, how close her lips are.

"I was an even hotter mess, I promise you that."

A small laugh breaks through her tears. It's quiet, but it's there. Progress. I keep rubbing slow, steady circles on her back, feeling the way her breathing evens out, the way her body relaxes against mine.

She rests her head against my chest, and I exhale, setting my chin gently on top of her head. I shouldn't hold her like this. Not this long. Not like I don't want to let go.

But I *don't* want to let go.

She smells like warm vanilla, something sweet and soft, and it's messing with my head. My entire body is burning with the awareness of her. I need to shut this down before—

She shifts just a little, trying to get comfortable.

And her ass presses right against me.

I go rigid, sucking in a sharp breath. *Shit.*

She immediately pulls back, eyes wide. "I'm sorry!" she squeaks, scrambling to lift off me. "Did I hurt you?"

Jesus Christ.

"No, princess," I say, my voice rougher than I'd like. "You're fine."

She looks at me, really *looks* at me, her cheeks flushed, her lips parted like she's about to say something. And that stare—fuck, she needs to stop looking at me like that. Like I'm something safe. Like I'm something *more.*

I clear my throat, desperate for an escape. "Do you want to get ice cream?" I ask, grasping at anything. "If we leave now, we can make it before they close."

Her face brightens just a little, and relief sweeps through me.

Good. We need to not be alone right now.

chapter five
KIRA

Did that just happen? Noah Keller held me in his lap while I cried. Oh my god.

His strong arms wrapped around me, warm and steady, like the world outside didn't matter anymore. For a few moments, I forgot everything else. It felt so… safe. So *right*. I don't think I've ever felt that safe before. Maybe I've never let myself feel safe. But now, the thought of him letting go of me—of this fragile calm—frightens me more than it should.

I didn't want him to pull away, but then… I shifted, and suddenly, I could feel his body under me—strong, *hard*—and oh my god, *did I just ask him if I hurt him?*

My face is burning with embarrassment. I want to bury my head in the seat. Noah clears his throat, dragging me back to the present moment. Looking up at him, I see his patience—like he's waiting for me to catch up with him. Right. He asked if I wanted ice cream.

"Oh, yeah, that would be nice," I mutter, still blushing.

We climb into his truck, and the silence between us fills the space.

The engine hums to life, and then he flicks on the radio. I watch him, his hands steady on the wheel, eyes locked on the road ahead. There's something about the way he drives—easy, like he's in control of everything around him. And I can't help but notice how *massive* his hands look, gripping that wheel like it's the only thing holding him together. His tattooed arms strain against the fabric of his shirt, and I can't stop myself from staring.

My thoughts tumble, and suddenly, guilt creeps in. He didn't deserve to be part of my breakdown. I shouldn't have unloaded all that on him. He's just… a guy who's trying to be kind. And here I am, making him shoulder my mess.

"I'm sorry for losing it a little tonight. You didn't deserve to deal with that," I say. He glances over at me. His eyes moving down my body before shooting back to the road ahead.

"Don't apologize."

Before I can say anything else, we turn into the parking lot of the ice cream shop. There's a pretty long line, but it doesn't take long to get to the front.

"What can I get for you guys?" the lady asks.

I feel him behind me, the warmth of his body comforting me.

"I'll take a chocolate milkshake, and she'll have…Kira, what would you like?"

I look at the menu. Mom would have told me to get the sorbet.

You don't need the extra calories.

Screw that.

"I would like a medium strawberry hard serve in a cone, please."

Before I can get my wallet out, Noah hands her his card.

"You don't have to pay for me," I say.

"I invited you out for ice cream, which means I pay for the ice cream," he replies.

Grabbing my cone, I stride back to the truck.

"Why don't we eat here?" Noah asks, gesturing to all of the empty picnic tables.

"It's cold outside. I wanna eat in the truck," I whine.

"It's sixty degrees, it is not that cold."

I look him dead in the eyes and climb into the seat, shutting the door and taking a lick of my ice cream. He looks at me exasperated and opens his door.

"You can be a brat when you want to be, you know that?" he laughs.

"I know," I say, shrugging.

Why do I feel like that wasn't a complaint?

After we finish our ice cream, Noah looks at me, his expression tight and serious. He hesitates for a second as if he's not sure how to say what's on his mind. Finally, he speaks, his voice careful. "Listen, Kira, about earlier... that was completely inappropriate of me. It didn't mean anything. I just saw you upset, and I wanted to help."

His words hang in the air, heavy, almost like he's trying to reassure himself more than me. I sit there, the weight of his tone settling uncomfortably in my chest. I swallow down the lump that suddenly forms in my throat.

"Oh, it's fine," I say, too quickly, trying to sound casual—normal. But there's a pinch in my voice I can't hide. I don't know why I expected anything different, but hearing him distance himself like that stings. "I shouldn't have climbed onto you like that. It's my fault, really."

I force a laugh, but it feels hollow. What did I think he was going to say? I know he doesn't see me that way, and that should be a relief, right? But something about his words makes my chest ache, and I can't quite shake the feeling that I've crossed some line I didn't even know existed. He's Jared's dad. This was never supposed to happen.

"No, I'm the adult in the situation, and I should have stopped it."

A small, irritated spark flares up inside me, sharper than I expected. "I'm an adult too, in case you haven't noticed," I snap, trying to keep the edge out of my voice but failing. His tone makes me feel small—like I'm some kid who needs protecting. I'm young, sure, but I'm not oblivious.

Noah doesn't reply, and the silence that stretches between us feels even heavier now.

He shifts the truck into gear, and we head back toward the house, but the air in the cab feels suffocating. The tension in the truck feels like it's been thickened with every mile. I don't know if I can stand it.

Each second feels like a reminder of everything I'm not supposed to be feeling. I'm too aware of every little movement he makes, the way his jaw tightens when he turns the wheel like he's bracing himself against something. Maybe it's me.

As soon as he parks, I'm out of the truck before he can say anything else, walking briskly through the house and to my room, the door clicking shut behind me.

I climb into bed, but my mind races. I try to shut it down, to push away the image of us on the couch—him holding me, his body warm and solid around mine—but it doesn't go away. I can still feel the press of his chest against my back, the way his arms felt around me, safe and strong.

The memory makes my skin burn, even now, as I lie in the dark.

And somehow, despite what he said, the silence between us feels louder than before.

When I wake up, Noah isn't home. I check inside Jared's room, and he's nowhere to be found either. He probably stayed at Jake's. I shudder at the thought of him. Yes, I was exhausted last night, but I also didn't want to see Jake again after the party.

I finish unpacking the rest of my boxes, putting everything away, and placing some of my sculptures throughout the space. The room is starting to look like mine, making me feel a bit better. I have to remind myself, though, that I don't plan on staying here forever. This is temporary.

The last box contains all the mugs I've made at the studio. They're all a variety of colors, mostly neutrals. Some sport floral patterns, others mountain landscapes. These are my babies. I line them up on a wooden shelf above the bed, saving a couple to bring downstairs to use for coffee. With how busy my life has been this last week, I haven't had time to go to the studio. I miss it.

Well, I know what I'm going to do today.

I throw on comfy clothes and run downstairs, grabbing coffee and my keys.

Darla's pottery studio, Lakeside Pottery, is only about twenty minutes away in a historic building smack in the middle of Traverse City. I step inside, and the peace I usually feel here washes over me. The space is divided into two sections: the store, where artists sell their finished pieces, and the workshop, where all the wheels and kilns are located.

I look past the shelves of ceramics for sale to the counter, and a tuft of gray hair with a small section dyed purple peaks out. As soon as she sees me, she lights up.

"Hey honey, I haven't seen you in a while! How have you been?" Darla asks, her voice sweet and warm.

"How much time do you have?" I ask with a sad laugh.

"That bad? Come on, hun, let's go over to the wheels."

After wedging our clay, we sit at the wheels facing the large front windows. My favorite spot. The sun shines through them, illuminating the potted plants that line the sill. The view of downtown Traverse City is unmatched, and I sigh as I throw my clay down on the wheel and center it. Darla does the same on hers.

"Alright, baby, tell me what's going on," she says.

I do. I tell her everything except the part where I sat on my best friend's dad's lap and how he may or may not have enjoyed it. I tell her about losing the apartment and moving in with Jared. She doesn't make me feel ashamed or like I failed, and I love her for it.

Talking to someone who isn't directly related to the situation is refreshing. She knows exactly how to comfort me, reassuring me that everything will be okay, and distracts me by telling me about what's been going on with her life. She talks about her grandkids and how they're getting too big, earning a smile from me. I love how easy it is to talk to her.

When I finish throwing the vase I've been working on, I remove the bat from the wheel and set it on the shelf to dry.

"Oh, I've been meaning to talk to you about something," Darla says, "I want to get the community more involved here, and I was wondering if you would like to start teaching some classes on the weekends? You would obviously get paid."

"Seriously?" I squeal. "Of course! I would love to do that!"

"Perfect! How does once a week sound?" she asks.

"Works for me! Just let me know when, and I'll make sure I have the days off."

Grinning like an idiot, I look through the shelves of the recently fired pottery, looking for the dish I've been working on. Finding it, I bring it over to the table and get out all the different colors of glaze.

I spend a few more hours there, working on several projects. I can't believe I will be able to teach classes here. Before I leave, I meet with Darla to plan our first workshop.

The sun is about to set when I return to my car and head back to the house. It's a weird feeling not going back to my apartment. I find myself wondering if Noah is home now or if he had to go into the station.

Where was he this morning?

Pulling into the driveway, I see that his truck isn't there, but Jared's car is. When I open the front door, he is sitting on the couch on his phone, the TV on in the background. Hearing the door close, he looks up at me and smiles.

"Hey Kira, where have you been all day?"

"The studio," I reply. "Have you had dinner yet?"

"No, I only got back home like thirty minutes ago," he explains.

"I'll go see what there is to cook," I tell him.

I eventually decide on a simple one-pot pasta. I don't feel like making anything too complicated and am in the mood for carbs. Scooping some out onto two plates, I carry them into the other room, handing one to Jared.

"This looks so good," he says. We both devour our pasta while we get sucked into the drama of the show he was watching. Once we're both finished, I grab a blanket off the back of the couch and get comfy.

"Can I have some?" Jared asks, gesturing to the fuzzy throw covering my lap.

"I guess," I say playfully, lifting the covers to let him in.

He scooches in closer to me, pulling me into him. We cuddle up like that for a while, watching the show's main character solve crime after crime.

"Kira," Jared mutters, pausing the show.

"Yeah?" I ask.

"Are you and Jake…" he trails off.

My heart stops.

"Why?" is all I can get out.

Hurt flashes in his eyes at my response. He thinks there's something going on between Jake and me. The thought turns my stomach.

"Well, Ava broke up with him, saying she saw you two together. When I talked to Jake about it, he said you were all over him the night of the party." His words feel like an accusation.

Of course, that asshole lied. My heart rate spikes as I remember what he tried. I ground myself and try to take deep breaths, but it doesn't help. *I can feel his hands on me, holding me down onto the mattress. No, I—*

"Kira, are you okay?" Jared grabs my arm.

I snap back into the present, a tear falling down my face. I quickly wipe it away.

"I'm fine," I say, breathless.

"You are obviously not fine. What is going on?"

What if he doesn't believe me? Jake is one of his good friends. I wouldn't be surprised if Jared just took his word for it—if he didn't believe me.

I feel the words pressing against my chest, threatening to spill out, but when they finally do, they sound rushed, too fast. "He's lying," I say, the weight of it making my throat tighten. "What he said isn't what happened. I was in the bathroom, washing my hands, and then he came in and locked the door. He tried to make a move on me, and I freaked out. He wasn't forceful, not like that, but I did not want him to touch me. I promise you that."

Relief washes over him as his body relaxes.

Then he speaks, his voice low and tight with frustration. "That fucker. He didn't want to get in trouble with his girl, so he threw you under the bus. I'm going to have a word with him next time I see him."

I let out a breath, some of the tension easing out of my shoulders. I think I can relax. Maybe I was wrong to doubt him, but there's a nagging feeling in my stomach, a small part of me that isn't entirely convinced.

"I'm sorry, Kira," he says softly, pulling me into a hug. "I know you would tell me if you were seeing someone."

He says the last part as almost a question.

I nod into his chest, but I can't shake the feeling that he's still unsure—like he's still thinking there's more to the story. Maybe I'm just imagining it. I try to brush it off, but the thought lingers.

"Let's get back to our show," he smiles, puts down a pillow, and lies his head on my lap. Laughing, I adjust my body and get comfortable as he hits play on the remote.

I run my fingers through his sandy brown hair to reassure myself. He isn't mad at me. I am okay. I've made a lot of progress when it comes to the anxiety and flashbacks, but they aren't totally gone. That night three years ago still haunts me. Eventually, light snores sound from my lap. He must have fallen asleep.

The front door swings open, causing me to jump a little at the noise. Surprisingly, the movement doesn't wake Jared. Looking up, I see Noah emerge, his eyes meeting mine. He glances down at Jared, asleep in my lap. He gives a slight nod of understanding, staring back up at me.

"Hey," I say, my voice soft.

The dim light of the TV illuminates his face as he looks at me for a long moment before responding.

"Where did you go this morning?" he asks, his voice bordering on demanding.

My brows scrunch together at his tone. Is he mad at me?

I can't help but pick up on how his gaze lingers where my fingers are buried in Jared's hair.

"Everyone was gone when I woke up, so I went out."

"Out where?"

He definitely sounds mad.

Why does he need to know?

"Out," I say, refusing to give him what he wants. He isn't my parent. He doesn't need to know everything I do.

Wrong answer.

Noah's jaw ticks as he glares at me, frustration thick in his tone. "Kira. Where were you?"

Irritation builds in my chest at the absurdity of his anger.

"Why do you care?"

chapter six
NOAH

WHY *DO* I CARE? I STAND THERE FOR A MOMENT, SILENT, TRYING to find a response. I can't. My gaze drifts back to Jared, lying in her lap, and something inside me tightens. There has to be something going on between them.

"I care because you live under my roof," I say, but I know there's more to it than that. I shake my head, heading into the kitchen.

When I got back this morning, I wanted to talk to her. I wanted to apologize. I don't want her to think I see her as some helpless kid. But when she didn't come home all day, and the guys invited me out to the bar, I figured, why not? I don't usually go out, and a few drinks didn't sound so bad. Now, though, I regret how much alcohol is still in my system.

She's irritated with me, and I get it. I was an asshole. She should be able to come and go as she pleases. I shouldn't care that she wasn't here this morning. So, why the hell do I?

Quiet footsteps sound from the hall. I glance up and see her, her body framed in the doorway. She eyes me before heading straight for the fridge, trying to reach for a bottle of wine that's just out of her grasp. She lets out a frustrated breath.

What do you think you're doing?"

She ignores my question. Walking over to the counter, she hoists herself up onto it, her ass now at eye level. My hands fist at my sides. It's taking everything I have right now not to touch her.

"You're too young for that," I scold.

"Bite me," she says, smirking, grabbing a bottle, and jumping down.

My mind goes to imagining exactly where I want to bite her. God, I shouldn't be alone with her right now. Grabbing a glass off of the rack, she pours herself a hefty serving and brings it to her lips.

"Don't worry, I know it's my bedtime," she says, turning away from me and sauntering up the stairs. She stops momentarily and looks back, "Oh, and I was at the studio."

I'm starting to think her staying here will be more difficult than I first thought.

When I go downstairs the next morning, Kira stands at the stove in her pajamas and fuzzy socks, cracking eggs into a pan. Her hair sits in a low ponytail. My eyes trail down to the hem of her cropped sleep shirt. A sliver of skin is exposed above the waistband of her bottoms, and my hands itch to trace it.

Prying my gaze off her, I open the cabinet above the coffee maker. My hand reaches for a mug but stops when I notice a few I've never seen before. They each have a distinct design and color theme.

"Did we get new mugs?" I ask primarily to myself.

"Good morning to you, too."

"Sorry, good morning, Kira. Did we get new mugs?"

"They came from my apartment. I made them," she says, pulling her bottom lip between her teeth.

I finally put it together. She mentioned that she went to the studio last night. I completely forgot she's into ceramics. I pick one up, inspecting it. It's a speckled cream color with a landscape of different blues, greens, and browns. It's beautiful. Flipping it over, I see a signature on the bottom.

"You are *really* good at this."

Looking over at me, she smiles as her cheeks flush.

"I guess I'm not too bad at it. Darla actually asked me to teach some classes at her studio. You can use that cup if you'd like," she shrugs, nodding to the mug in my hand. "You don't have to, though."

"I want to, princess."

I pour coffee into the mug, grab the creamer from the fridge, and add a splash.

"Want some?"

"Oh, sure, thank you!"

Reaching up, I find another of her mugs. This one boasts flowy coral and fuchsia flowers with deep green stems. After filling it, I place it on the counter next to her.

"Still like it black, right?"

She nods, smiling, as she dumps the scrambled eggs onto a plate and hands them to me. The food is even more delicious because I didn't have to make it.

The rest of the morning passes by relatively quickly. After breakfast, Kira has to go to work, so it's just Jared and I left in the house. In true Jared fashion, he doesn't get out of bed until sometime after noon, and by that time, I'm already getting ready to leave for work.

When I first step into the station, I know today will be a hectic shift. Half the crew is already out on calls and the air reeks of anticipation. Hurrying to the kitchen, I work to finish dinner as soon as possible. The guys will be thankful for it when they get back. Dave strolls into the kitchen as I pull the pot off the stove.

"Howdy partner, whatcha cookin'?"

"Does it matter? You'll eat it regardless."

"You are not wrong."

Dave is somewhat of a black hole. He'll eat anything you give him without complaint, which makes my job easier.

"You know how Al is retiring soon?" Dave asks.

"Yeah."

"Well, I wonder who's going to replace him as commissioner."

"I have no clue. Al is a great boss. I don't know anyone that could fill those shoes."

"I think you could, but you'd have to admit that first," he deadpans.

Before I can respond, a voice barks over the intercom.

"Fire spotted at 479 North Grace Street, possible victims trapped inside."

Dave and I break into action, racing down to the garage. I pull on my suit and climb into the truck. Dave hoists himself up, joining me in the passenger seat. The rest of the guys file in the back. As the garage door opens, the flashing lights reflect off the windows. We pull out onto the street, sirens blaring.

"Update: there is known to be a child still in the home. The fire seems to have started in the basement."

I glance over at Dave, his face hardening. Pressing on the gas, I maneuver the truck through traffic. We're only about a minute or two out, but some cars refuse to get out of the way. Nothing pisses me off more than when people don't pull over for us. Is your destination really more important than someone's life?

When we pull up, the house is engulfed in black smoke, flames licking at the sides. As soon as we're parked, I jump out. Running toward the house, a panicked woman approaches me.

"Please, we can't find our son!"

"I'll find him, don't worry. What's his name?"

"Brendan, he's only five!"

My stomach drops.

I turn to Dave, "Call for backup and get the hose ready. I'm going to go get the kid."

The front door is wide open, smoke heavily flowing out of it. I push through, scanning my surroundings. The fire has started migrating from the basement, turning the walls black. What looks like the living room to my right is almost totally consumed.

"Brendan, are you in here? I'm here to help!"

I'm finding this kid, and he's going to be okay. There's no other option. I'm not losing another kid.

Not seeing anyone on this level, I climb up the stairs and call out again. Searching each room one by one, I realize they're all empty. Suddenly, I hear a cry off to my left. The smoke makes it almost impossible to see more than a couple of feet before me, but I see him. He's crouched in the corner of the last bedroom.

"I'm here, Brendan, don't worry!"

I rush over to him, scooping him into my arms. His eyes are tear-soaked and terrified.

"It's okay, buddy, I've got you."

I start back down the stairs. The blaze has gotten worse. When I reach the end of the steps, I notice the flames almost wholly blocking the front door. Debris plummets from the ceiling in front of us. We need to get out now. Pulling him tight to my chest, I move to the back of the house, hoping to find another door. Relief floods me when I see one. The knob won't turn, and the lock is broken. Stepping back, I slam my heel into it, knocking it off its hinges. Finally outside, I look down at

Brendan, checking him over.

"Are you okay?"

He just cries, shaking his head.

When I round the house, I hear a scream come from his mother. She runs up to me, gasping for air.

"Brendan, oh my god, are you okay?"

"I'm going to bring him to EMS so they can check him over to be sure, but he seems to be alright." She's on my heels as I take him to the ambulance.

"He looks okay, but we're still going to take him in to be sure," the paramedic says.

I let out a breath. Thank god. His parents climb into the truck with him as they leave for the hospital. We get to work on putting out the flames. It takes us a while, but we get it done. The home is a shell of what it once was. This isn't going to be easy for the family, but at least they all made it out. I shudder at that.

"Hey, are you doing okay?" Dave asks me.

"I'm fine," I reply a little too quickly.

He looks at me like he doesn't quite believe me but shrugs it off.

"Well, good work, son. You took the initiative and saved that kid's life," Al says from behind me. He must have shown up while I was still inside.

"It was what had to happen. Any one of the guys would have

done it."

"That may be true, but they didn't. You did."

When we return to the station, I head straight for the showers. Stripping off my clothes, I twist the knob, and the water sputters to life. I let the stream hit my face, the coolness grounding me. Today was rough, but he made it. He's going to be okay.

My mind drifts to Kira. What is she doing right now? Probably home from work, maybe lying in bed in one of those oversized shirts she loves, her nose buried in a book. I think back to how good she felt on top of me the other night, her soft body pressed into mine. I can feel myself stir at the thought. Fuck, what am I doing? I slam my fist against the tile, and the water instantly turns ice-cold.

By the time I leave the station, I'm more than ready to get home. My fingers glide over the steering wheel as I turn down the driveway. Kira's car is in its usual spot, but Jared's is gone. I throw my truck into park, hop out, and head inside.

The windows are open, letting in the fresh air. Michigan in the spring—warm during the day, cool at night, and in the mornings—is one of my favorite times of year. The slider's open, but the screen's closed. As I move toward it, I spot Kira on the deck. She's sitting at the patio table, earbuds in, molding clay into what looks like a hand. Her legs are covered in smears of clay, and she looks like a mess.

She's so gorgeous like this. Nothing else matters to her right now outside of that sculpture. She looks happy and more relaxed than I've seen her in a long time.

Like she can sense my presence, she looks up, jumping when her eyes notice me. Pulling her earbud out, she asks, "How are you always sneaking up on me?"

"It's my house," I say, stepping onto the porch. She rolls her eyes. "What are you working on?"

"It's just a little project."

Now that I'm closer, the details are more evident. I was right. It's a hand positioned to look like it's waiting to receive something. It's so realistic, and the proportions are perfect.

What's it waiting for?

Feeling her eyes on me, I look over at her. She wants a response, to know what I think of it.

"It's amazing," I say, not taking my eyes off her. Her freckled cheeks heat as she looks up at me. Images flash through my mind of her looking up at me like that for other, more sinister reasons.

"How was your shift?" she asks.

"Not great. I'm glad it's over," I answer.

Concern grows in her features as she turns to me.

"Why, what happened?"

I can't put that on her. She doesn't need my problems right now.

"Nothing, it's fine," I say, wishing I hadn't said anything in the first place.

"It's not good to keep those things bottled up," she says softly.

I want to tell her that it's not anything she needs to worry about—that I can handle it myself, but something in the way she's looking at me makes me comply.

"There was a house fire today. A kid was trapped inside," I explain. "He's fine, I got him out, but it just brought up a lot of shit that I wasn't ready to deal with."

I pause, looking away, trying to steady myself. My throat feels tight, the words hard to push through.

Her eyes soften, and she steps closer, her gaze gentle, like she's trying to reach something buried deep in me.

"What do you mean? What happened?" she asks, her voice barely above a whisper.

I swallow hard, the memory clawing at the edges of my mind. I haven't told anyone about him—not since it happened. Afterward, I shoved it down, locked it away in some dark corner of my mind, hoping it would stay buried. But it doesn't. It resurfaces at the worst moments. Like today.

My chest tightens, the weight of it threatening to crush me, and I try to breathe through it.

"Noah," she says again, her hand reaching out, fingers brushing my arm like a lifeline. "You can tell me."

I flinch at the touch, the hesitation hanging between us thick enough to choke on.

chapter seven
KIRA

The pain in his eyes tells me that there is more to this than he's letting on. The gears turn in his head as he decides how much to tell me, and I get it. Everyone has their demons, but I can't bear the idea that he's hurting with no one to lean on.

"There was a fire early on in my career that was very similar to the call today," he starts, and I think he's going to stop there, but he sits in one of the chairs and continues. "There was a little boy stuck inside, around the same age as Jared at the time. He must have heard his parents yelling for him and thought he was in trouble because he hid."

Noah sucks in a breath, and tears well in his eyes. My heart breaks for him and for where this story is going.

"I was the one who was sent in to find him, and I searched as fast as I possibly could, calling his name. By the time I found him, it was too late. He wasn't breathing."

A tear slides down his cheek, but he wipes it away.

"All I could think was I should have found him sooner. I could have saved him."

I can't take it anymore. I kneel in front of him, wrapping my arms around his torso as he sits in the chair. He freezes at the contact, his body tense. I ignore his hesitation, nuzzling my head into his chest.

"That wasn't your fault," I tell him, needing him to believe me.

He gives in, hugging me back, his chest expanding as he sighs.

"Logically, I understand that. I did what I could in that moment, and it wasn't enough, but that doesn't stop the guilt."

I relate to that more than he will ever know.

We sit like this for a while, neither of us ready to let go.

A FEW WEEKS HAVE PASSED SINCE I MOVED IN WITH JARED AND Noah. I'm still adjusting, but something about this place feels like it could eventually be home—though I can't shake the feeling of being an outsider. I'm careful not to overstay my welcome, so I've been putting as much into savings as I can, but it's a struggle, the balance between feeling at home and not wanting to impose.

Today is my first class at Lakeside Pottery, and nerves twist in my stomach. I've been doing pottery for four years now, but teaching? That's new territory.

I arrive at the studio an hour early, hoping the time alone will give me a moment to collect my thoughts. The smell of fresh clay and the quiet hum of the room help me center myself. But the flutter of nerves is still there, gnawing at the edges of my calm. I take a deep breath, reminding myself that I've done this thousands of times on my own; now, I just need to guide others through it.

I glance around, taking in the space—workstations lined up with neatly arranged supplies, the pottery wheels gleaming under the soft lighting. Satisfied, I head over to the refreshment bar Darla set up, grabbing my favorite mug and filling it with coffee. It's warm against my hands, the familiar comfort of caffeine working its way through my veins.

Ten minutes before the class begins, people start to trickle in. I smile, greet everyone, and introduce myself. The group is a mix of ages, from a young girl who can't be older than ten, to a woman in her sixties. It's a little overwhelming, but I'm excited too. This is exactly what I wanted—a chance to teach and share my passion with anyone who's interested.

"Okay, everyone," I say as the last student takes their seat, "Let's get started."

I demonstrate the first step, wedging the clay, then move on to centering it on the wheel. Some of the students get it right away, but others struggle. I move between them, offering gentle corrections, my voice steady even though my heart races. Watching their bowls start to take shape, I can't help but smile. This is what I love—guiding them through the process, seeing their progress.

Among the group, one girl, maybe a little older than me, finishes her bowl first. She steps away from her wheel and wanders over to my workstation. Her platinum-blonde hair shines in the soft light, and her cerulean eyes are bright with curiosity. I catch her eye, and she flashes a smile.

"You're really good," she says, leaning over to look at my piece in progress. "I'm Maddie by the way."

I'm about to say something when we're interrupted by the last student finishing their bowl. I show everyone how to remove their pieces from the wheel, and we set them aside on a shelf to dry before trimming them next week.

"Thank you, everyone, for coming. This was so much fun! I will see you all in a week for trimming."

As they're all packing their things and leaving, Maddie stops in front of me.

"We should hang out sometime," she says. I let out a small laugh at the abruptness of her statement.

"You know, I think I'll take you up on that. Do you want my number so we can plan something?"

"Of course, girl!"

I smile to myself. I've never had many friends other than Jared, and it would be nice to have a friend who isn't a boy.

Before I head out, I check in with Darla.

"How did I do?"

"You were wonderful, dear. Oh, speaking of, here's your portion of the profits from the class," she says, handing me cash. It's more than I expected, and I almost feel bad taking it.

"I really had fun doing this. Thank you for letting me be the one to do it."

"Of course, honey."

I don't think that class could have gone any better. I was so nervous at first, but it was perfect. I love showing people something that they've never seen or done before. When the concept clicks, the look in their eyes is the best feeling.

Turning down Noah's road, I smile. Today was amazing. I finally feel like I'm succeeding with something. Putting my car in park, I climb out, and Jared greets me at the door, a popsicle in his hand.

"I want one," I whine.

"There's more in the freezer."

Giving him my best puppy dog eyes, I stick out my bottom lip. He folds immediately.

"I can never say no to you," he tells me with a smile.

While he's doing that, I run upstairs to drop off my stuff and grab the book I'm currently reading. I plan on relaxing for the rest of the day. Jogging back down the stairs, I'm met with a stunned Jared holding a blue popsicle—my favorite flavor.

"Thank you!" I say, pushing past him and heading for the slider. I'm going to plant my happy ass in the hammock and read for as long as I can. It's a beautiful day. There are no clouds in sight, and the sun heats my skin. It's about seventy degrees, the perfect temperature to lay out in. The sound of the birds chirping comforts me as I swing lazily.

Opening my book, I pick up where I left off. The enemies are right about to become lovers. Those classic, wonderful words, *who did this to you?* She's about to tell him when I'm interrupted by a voice.

"I'm bored," Jared groans, standing in front of the hammock.

I look at him over my book, "Find something to do then."

"I want to do something with you."

Closing my book, I sigh. "Fine. What do you want to do?"

"Maybe we can go get gas station hot dogs and then come back and have a fire?"

"I don't know if I'm in the mood to socialize with anyone else."

"No, just you and me. We can roast marshmallows?"

I ponder it for a moment. I'd rather read, but I do need to eat something, and he's asking so nicely.

"Let's do it."

I hop into his car, and we head to the local gas station. Hands already full of other snacks, we grab our hot dogs and get in line.

"Hey, Jared, I see that you brought the whore out of the house."

Turning toward the voice, I recognize the man as one of Jake's friends. His eyes move over my body, and I feel dirty. I want to throw up. Or punch him. Either option works.

I can help who's next, please!"

I rush over to the counter, needing to escape the situation. Glancing over, I see Jared still talking to him. His voice is low, so I can't hear what he's saying. I hope it's not nice. Setting my items on the counter, I hand the cashier my card. I'll meet him in the car.

What is that guy's problem? It's not like that's a new insult for me, but I wasn't expecting it to come out of some random person's mouth like that. Jared's door swings open, and he climbs inside, words already spewing from his lips.

"I am so sorry about that. I don't know why he said that," he says, worry in his eyes.

"It's fine. I can handle it. Let's just go home."

I try to turn my head away, but he reaches up to cup my cheek, making me look at him. His fingers are so gentle.

"Don't listen to him, okay? He's an idiot."

I nod, looking away as we pull out of the parking lot.

When we get back to the house, Jared works on getting the fire started. It's not quite dark yet, the sun sitting right above the horizon. I'm in my room. The temperature has dropped significantly, and I need layers. Slipping on a hoodie and some leggings, I try to ignore the feeling seeping in from our interaction with that guy earlier. He's wrong. I'm not a whore. It wasn't my fault. Taking a deep breath, I head downstairs, pushing myself to smile. I grab the bag of marshmallows and head outside.

We sit by the fire for a while, each of us in our own folding chairs. We talk about college and how excited he is to go. I'm happy for him. He deserves it. Glancing up, I notice him staring at me.

"What, do I have marshmallow on my face?"

His eyes hold mine, the fire reflecting in them. He smirks as his eyes trail down my body.

"No, you're just beautiful."

There's more emotion in those words than there should be.

"I know," I laugh, winking at him, needing to distract from the gravity of his statement.

Disappointment flashes in his eyes, and he looks at me like he has more he wants to say, but instead, he sighs, shaking his head.

"I think I'm going to head inside. It's getting late," he tells me before standing and turning away.

"Oh, yeah, I guess I should too."

What was that?

Stepping out of the shower, I dry off quickly and toss my damp hair into a towel. Guilt wraps itself around me like a heavy blanket. I don't understand why Jared reacted like that, but it feels like it's my fault. I pull back the comforter and slide into bed. The cool sheets against my skin do little to soothe the knot in my chest. I stare at the ceiling, thoughts swirling in every direction. What's going on with him? Why did that asshole earlier feel the need to say those things?

I try to push the thoughts away, but they linger. I'm exhausted, my body begging for rest, yet my brain refuses to cooperate. After what feels like hours of tossing and turning, I throw off the covers and slip out of bed.

The stairs creak beneath my feet as I tiptoe down. A glass of water is all I need to clear my head. The cabinet door opens with a soft groan, and I pull down a cup, filling it with water from the fridge. I'm about to turn back when I hear footsteps behind me.

"Couldn't sleep?" Noah asks, his voice low.

In the soft moonlight streaming in from the window, I see him standing in the doorway, shirtless. I've seen him like this countless times before, but tonight, it feels different. The air between us is thick with something I can't quite name. His muscular torso is covered in tattoos, one of which—a raven perched on a branch—I recognize. It's one of my favorites.

I feel my gaze slip lower, unable to stop myself. His sweatpants sit low on his hips, highlighting the V of his abdomen. My eyes wander further, catching the outline of something I shouldn't be looking at. Something impressive. My pulse picks up.

"Eyes up here, sweetheart."

I bring my gaze up to meet his, my cheeks heating. Oh my god, he just watched me check him out. I brush it off, mostly because I don't have another option. Choosing to ignore his last comment, I answer his question.

"No, I couldn't sleep. I came down to get some water," I mumble, gesturing to my glass, now sitting on the counter.

"How did your class go this morning?" he asks, stalking toward me.

His eyes move down my body, darkening when they reach the tops of my thighs. Following his gaze, I realize that I forgot to put on bottoms. I'm standing here in a T-shirt and panties. Leaning over me, he reaches up into the cupboard above my head.

He's so close now, the scent of patchouli and something sweet invading my senses. As he leans into me, I reach my hand up, placing it on his bare chest. His warm, hard body towers over me, and I feel him take a deep breath. I know I shouldn't be touching him, but I don't move. Slowly, he brings his eyes down to mine, his gaze heated. I study his face as his jaw tenses.

"Kira," he rasps. He grabs my wrist with the lightest of touches and takes my hand off him.

"My class was great. I had a lot of fun," I say, dismissing the rejection. I know it was the right thing to do, but it still stings. I try to move away from him, but I'm stopped by his hands dropping to the counter on either side of me, pinning me to him.

"I knew you could do it. I'm proud of you."

My heart jumps, and I look away, smiling at myself. He notices my reaction and places a hand on my jaw, making me look at him.

"You like it when I say that, don't you?"

My eyes widen, and I hesitate. He's right. I love it when he says stuff like that to me, but I can't tell him that. There's no way I can let him know what his words do to me. *Nothing can happen between us*, I remind myself. Our bodies are touching now, his hips pressing into me.

"Use your words, princess," he orders, brushing his thumb against my bottom lip. I take in a sharp breath, my lips parting. The touch fuels an ache deep in my core. His eyes are dark and hungry as they look down into mine.

"Yes," I whisper. "I like it."

I reach up to touch him again, needing to feel his skin on mine. As soon as my hand grazes his chest, he winces. Closing his eyes, he lets out a breath.

"Don't."

But I don't listen. I let my hand glide down his torso, feeling the strength of his taut muscles.

chapter eight
NOAH

OF COURSE, SHE LIKES PRAISE. THAT MAKES SO MUCH SENSE.

But she needs to stop touching me like that. Every time her fingers brush against my skin, I feel myself react. I'm already hard, and the weight of it is becoming impossible to ignore. My self-restraint is crumbling, and the worst part? I don't know how much longer I can hold it together.

This—*this*—is not okay. There is no scenario where me being this close to her, feeling the heat of her body against mine, is appropriate. She doesn't know what this is doing to me. I don't know if I can keep pretending like it doesn't matter.

Noticing my hesitation, Kira looks up at me, her eyes burning with something I can't quite read. Her fingers trail lower, grazing the waistband of my sweatpants, and I hiss, my whole body reacting against my will.

"Kira," I warn.

Tilting her head, she argues, "What, you can touch me, but I can't touch you?"

Her hand slides up my chest, following the lines of my tattoos. Each gentle stroke makes heat coil in my stomach, and I'm losing control. It's taking every ounce of willpower not to press my lips to hers right now.

We're inches apart. I can smell her—soft, intoxicating. The weight of her body pressed against mine is almost too much to bear.

I need to walk away. I need space. But my feet are rooted to the floor.

She darts her tongue out, wetting her lips, and the sight makes my breath catch in my throat. *God,* what I wouldn't do to feel that mouth on mine. She laces her fingers into the hair at the back of my neck, pulling me closer. My body reacts before my mind can catch up, and I groan, my hands instinctively tightening around her hips.

No. No, this can't happen. I can't let it. My head screams at me to stop, to think about Jared, to stop making everything more complicated than it already is.

"Kira, stop," I bark.

She jumps back, startled, dropping her hand. Her eyes are wide, and for a split second, she looks… scared? I regret it immediately. I didn't want to hurt her, but the reality is, she doesn't know how far I'm teetering on the edge.

My hands clench at my sides before I reach for her, but I stop myself. Taking a deep breath, I exhale slowly, letting my emotions settle before I shake my head, stepping away.

I need to get out of here. I need to walk away before I do something I can't take back.

But I can't stop the thoughts racing through my head. The way she felt in my arms, the way her body seemed to call to mine. I wanted to turn her around and bend her over the island. *What the fuck is wrong with me?*

I'm thirty-six years old—old enough to be her father. There's no reason for me to be thinking like this. She needed somewhere safe to stay, and here I am, getting lost in fantasies. I'm the one who should be protecting her, not... *wanting her.*

Yanking open my bedroom door, I collapse onto the bed. Nothing like that is ever happening again. I'll make sure of it. Kira needs a safe space right now, I'm not going to fuck that up for her.

I don't understand why I can't control myself around her. It's been a long time since I've gotten laid, that's it. She just happens to be an attractive woman living in my house who also just happens to walk around half-naked sometimes. Rolling over, I ignore my aching cock, forcing myself to try to sleep.

In the end, I only get a couple of hours. When I wake up, Kira has already left for work. Jared's gone, too, although I have no idea where he went. He's starting to worry me with how much he's partying.

I eat a small breakfast and spend the morning doing some chores. Jared helps sometimes, but the majority of the cleaning falls on me. Or at least it did. Now that Kira's been staying here, she's been helping with a lot of the housework.

The scents of grease and oil mix together, invading my nose as I step into the garage. It's one of my favorite smells. This is my happy place. It's me and the car, nothing else. I open the garage door, letting in the warm, almost summer air, and move the arms of the lift under the body of the

Nova. I had it installed about a year ago, wanting to get serious about getting her running.

I slot the new fuel pump into place, tightening the bolts surrounding it before replacing the fuel tank. Sliding out from under the body of the car, I go to start it. After a couple of tries, the loud purr of the engine fills the space, resonating through my body. Grabbing a red rag off my workbench, I wipe my hands off, trying to remove all the grime.

"Hey, McDreamy!" I'd know that voice anywhere, not to mention the nickname that I haven't been able to rid myself of since we were in high school. I maneuver around the car. Keith is standing at the entrance to the garage. Looking past him, I notice his old beat-up Chevy parked in the drive.

"Runnin' yet?" he asks.

"Soon, hopefully," I tell him.

I've known Keith since we were in elementary school. We've always been friends, and he lives across the street. He doesn't look much different from when we were younger. He still has bright blonde hair, but now a beard covers his face, and he's filled out a bit. He used to be so goddamn skinny. I chuckle at the thought.

We chat for a bit, talking about work and life. I tell him about the commissioner retiring and how I have no idea who will replace him. He's a contractor, so he explains his most recent job, a deck for one of our neighbors.

"I'm telling you, man, she was hitting on me. She even invited me to stay for drinks!" he exclaims.

"And did you?"

"I couldn't. I had the girls that night."

I nod, laughing.

My phone goes off in my pocket, and I pull it out.

Jared

I won't be home tonight. Staying over at Jake's

I'm not surprised. He's over there more than he's home.

I shoot him a short response, letting him know it's fine with me.

I invite Keith for dinner, but he mutters something about having to take the girls to town before leaving.

It looks like it'll be Kira and I for dinner then. We haven't spoken since last night. I don't know what's gotten into me. I should have stopped it sooner. I shouldn't have touched her to begin with. She's way too young, and I'm pretty sure Jared has a thing for her. The way he looks at her and touches her. The thought makes my stomach twist. There has to be something between them.

After a quick shower, I get started on dinner. Tonight's menu features homemade chicken fettuccine Alfredo. The aroma of garlic, cream, and seasoning fills the kitchen, making my stomach growl. The garlic bread is toasty in the oven, and I've set the table for two. Kira should be home any minute. She usually gets off work at five, and it's already fifteen minutes past.

I should apologize. Last night was inappropriate. I shouldn't have let things go that far. I need to reassure her that it won't happen again. The pasta slides onto two plates as I scoop it from the pot. By five-thirty, I begin to feel a knot of concern tightening in my chest. Maybe she got held up at work.

I pull out my phone and shoot her a quick text.

Noah

Dinner's getting cold.

By six-thirty, my concern turns to irritation. She hasn't replied. Wouldn't she have told me if she was going to be late? I dial her number. No answer. My stomach tightens. Something doesn't feel right.

I pack up the food and toss it in the fridge, then grab my keys. I try to avoid imagining the worst. The drive to the store is short, though the speed I'm driving at seems to make it even shorter.

When I arrive, her car isn't in the parking lot. My pulse quickens, but I force myself to stay calm. Maybe she's with Jared and his friends. Still, something feels off. I don't think she's fond of his friends. I redial her number—straight to voicemail. Where the hell is she?

I text Jared, but he doesn't respond either. I hesitate for a moment before deciding to head back home. She's probably fine. I tell myself that over and over, but it doesn't stop the dread gnawing at me.

The drive back feels like it takes an eternity. My fingers tighten on the wheel, the silence in the truck amplifying my thoughts. When I finally turn onto our road, I see her white Pontiac Grand Am parked in its usual spot.

Relief floods through me. I exhale sharply, slamming the truck into park and jumping out. My feet hit the ground, and I move quickly toward the front porch.

"Is your phone broken?" I ask, throwing the door open. She's there, sitting on the couch in the living room. Relief washes over me. She's here. She's safe. That relief, however, quickly turns into irritation when I remember that I've been looking for her for over an hour, and she hasn't responded to any of my texts or calls.

"Um, no?" she responds, raising an eyebrow. She looks upset, a frown playing on her face. I hesitate for a moment but choose to ignore it, pressing on.

"I texted and called you, but you didn't answer. Where were you?" I question, moving toward the couch. She stands to face me, tilting her head to look at me. I stop feet away from her, her face hardening.

"You're not my dad. I am an adult, and I don't have to tell you where I am at all times," she retorts, with a clear attitude in her tone.

"Trust me, I am well aware that I am not your father, but you do live under my roof, and that means I deserve to know when and if you're coming home."

Staring up at me, her hands on her curved hips, she laughs, "You're kidding, right?"

She can be a real brat when she wants to be. She's always been like that. She won't take anyone's bullshit. But this isn't bullshit. This is valid. She needs to tell me if she isn't coming home.

"Something could have happened to you. All you had to do was text me."

"I'm sorry, *Daddy*, I'll be sure to tell you next time," she mocks. My eyes widen, heat rising in my chest. "And not that it's any of your business, but I had to stay late at work. I didn't even see that you called." I must have just missed her when I drove to the store. I feel like an idiot. She tries to turn away, but I grab her by her wrist. She twists back to look at me, anger in her features.

"Don't call me that," I say, my voice low.

Her eyes are dark as they bore into mine. This is about more than just this argument. She's mad about something else. Defeated, I let go of her.

"Just go to your room."

"Gladly," she says, stomping up the stairs. I can't help but appreciate the curve of her ass as she disappears up them. She's hot when she's angry.

No, she's not.

Pulling my eyes away, I sink onto the couch.

What am I doing?

chapter nine
KIRA

I don't know what I was thinking. It's been a few days since Noah and I were in the kitchen. When he touched me, I could have sworn there was something there. But of course, there wasn't. There can't be. I know that. The way he just left me standing there still makes me feel like an idiot. Why did I even touch him like that? I know why: he was shirtless, warm, and pressed so close to me. For the first time since that night when I was fifteen, having a man that close didn't scare me.

That's one thing I love about Noah—he could never scare me. He can definitely piss me off, though, and that's what happened tonight. Rob asked if I could work later because someone else called in sick. I wasn't going to turn that down—I need the extra hours. Should I have told Noah? Probably, but it doesn't justify him throwing a fit like that. He's not my dad. He doesn't need to know everything I do. I don't like it when he treats me like a kid. I'm almost nineteen, and I've been caring for myself for years now.

He was genuinely upset, though. When he walked through the door, I saw that flash of concern in his eyes, quickly masked by irritation. He was worried about me.

I push the guilt aside and focus on the view outside my window. The sun sets over the lake, painting the sky with pinks, oranges, and purples, reflecting off the still water.

I wish I could stay here forever. I love this house—there are so many memories here. It's the one place I ever felt truly wanted as a kid. Noah being upset with me is his way of showing he cares about me, and I get that. But he could've gone about it in a kinder way.

The next morning, my alarm yanks me out of a deep sleep. I really don't want to go to work today. Still half asleep, I pick out a comfy outfit and shuffle toward the bathroom. But as soon as I reach for the door, it turns by itself, swinging open to reveal a wall of man in a towel.

I take my time sliding my gaze up to Noah's. His towel hangs low on his hips, his body still damp from the shower.

What I wouldn't give to run my hands over those tattoos again.

"Excuse me, princess," he says as he steps past me. It takes me a moment, but I finally head into the bathroom for my own shower, trying to remind myself that I'm mad at him.

I'm opening today, so it's only me until ten when Lexi comes in. She's been working here for about two weeks and seems to be doing well. She's a little older than me, probably twenty or twenty-one, and I like her.

We don't typically get that many customers this early, so I start by stocking some of the shelves. It's relaxing. I like being by myself, and the predictability of the task is comforting. I lose myself in it, letting my brain wander.

My phone rings in my pocket, and I pull it out to see Maddie's name on the screen. We have plans to hang out later today, and I know I shouldn't answer at work, but what if it's important?

I roll my eyes and smile as I swipe, Maddie's face filling the screen.

"Hey girl!"

Her blonde hair is styled up in a messy bun, and it looks like she just rolled out of bed. I'm jealous.

"Hey, I'm at work right now, so I can't really talk."

I set the phone on the shelf as I continue organizing the candy section.

"Is it just you there?"

"Yeah, until ten," I answer.

"You're fine, then," she laughs.

My mouth drops open at her audacity as we both devolve into giggles. She's probably right; no one will be in for another hour, and this is no different than listening to music.

"What is it you called to tell me, then?" I ask, feigning annoyance.

"I just wanted to talk to you," she says. "And I may have met a girl last night, and I was too excited to wait to talk to you until later."

"Oh my god, tell me about her *now*," I squeal.

"She's tall and pretty and confident. I'm almost one hundred percent sure she likes girls, but it's always hard to tell, you know?"

I can't say I do, but I reassure her anyway.

"I bet she does."

The door jingles before I know it, and Lexi walks in carrying her purse and coffee.

"Gotta go," I mutter to Maddie as I tap the red end-call button and shove my phone back into my pocket.

Lexi gives me a wave before heading to the back to punch in. That was close. I finish putting away the chocolate bars I've been working on and head to the register.

It's almost time for me to leave when I glance out the window onto the street and see Jake walking toward the store with a group of his friends. It looks like it's him, some tall blond dude, and…my heart stops.

Not him, it can't be him. I thought he left town. But he's there. Zach is on his way into the store. I haven't seen him since—Suddenly, I'm back there. That night. It plays in my head like a fucking movie. I try to control my breathing, my heart racing.

"Uh, Lexi, can you watch the register?" I ask, my voice shaking.

She looks shocked, maybe worried. I don't care. I need to get away. Where am I going to go? The back room, that's it. I rush to the door, slamming it shut behind me. I lock it, sliding to sit on the floor. I try to take deep breaths.

In.

Out.

In.

Out.

A sob racks my chest, and I try to hold back the tears. I'm okay. *I'm safe.* I hear them enter the store. Loud voices, laughing. I hear *him,* and bile rises in my throat. I focus on my breathing, but the memories still come. *Zach throws me over his shoulder and then onto the bed. Where is Jared? What is happening?*

A soft voice from the other side of the door coaxes me back to reality. How long have I been here?

"Kira, are you okay? Can I come in?" It's Lexi.

I force myself to stand, opening the door for her. Her eyes are filled with concern when she takes me in.

"Are they gone?" I whisper.

"Who, that group of guys? Yeah, they left," she says. "What happened?"

"It's nothing. I'm fine."

I pull my phone out of my pocket and check the time. I was technically done with my shift ten minutes ago. Thank god, I'm ready to leave. My hands still shake as I slide my phone back into my pocket. Lexi notices.

"Are you sure you're okay?"

"Yeah, I'm fine. I'm going to head out now."

I would ask her if she needs any help, but I can't stay any longer. I need to get out of here. I walk out to my car, terrified, studying my surroundings. As soon as I get in I hit the lock on the door and quickly shoot over a text to Maddie.

Kira

Hey girl, I'm not going to be able to hang out tonight. I have to work late :(

I hate lying to her, but I don't know if I can handle telling her yet.

Taking a deep breath, I turn the key and pull out of the parking lot.

I reassure myself the entire drive home. I'm not fifteen anymore. He can't hurt me again. *I won't let him.*

When I get home, I go straight to my room, barely registering the warmth of the house around me. My chest feels tight, my hands cold despite the heat outside. I need to be alone.

Noah looks up as I rush past him, his brows pulling together in confusion. He opens his mouth like he might say something, but then he hesitates and lets me go. I can feel his gaze lingering, but I don't stop. We haven't talked since our argument, and he probably assumes that's why I'm upset. Maybe that's easier for him to believe.

He doesn't know what happened that night.

Hell, even Jared doesn't know what happened. I never told him, never told anyone. After the cops blamed me, after they looked me in the eye and said it was my fault, I lost the courage to say another word. Maybe if I had, someone would have believed me. But I hadn't, and now it's too late.

My room is dim, the late afternoon sun casting long shadows across the floor. I close the door behind me and press my back against it, exhaling shakily. My heart is still pounding, and I don't know if it's from the memories clawing at the edges of my mind or the effort of keeping them at bay.

I need a distraction.

I grab the book from my nightstand and force myself to focus on the words. The familiar rhythm of the story, the certainty of its structure, pulls at me like a lifeline. Unlike real life, fictional stories follow rules and patterns. There's always an answer, always a resolution. Always a happy ending.

If I can just sink into the pages, maybe, for a little while, I can pretend everything is okay.

But it's not. And I know it.

A soft knock startles me. My pulse jumps, and I clutch the book tighter, my fingers pressing into the worn cover.

The door creaks open slowly, and Jared stands there, watching me.

"Dad and I are going to watch a movie if you want to come down," he says. He notices my lack of reaction and adds, "There's pizza."

I give him a small smile. I should go down there. I haven't eaten anything since this morning.

"I'll be down in a bit," I assure him.

After climbing out of bed, I grab my favorite big sweater, also known as my emotional support sweater, and throw it on. It has a bunch of small holes in it, but I love it anyway.

Walking down the stairs, I can smell the pizza in the kitchen, and my stomach grumbles. I'm so hungry. I take three slices of pepperoni and head into the living room.

Noah is on one side of the couch, a beer sitting in front of him on the coffee table. Jared is on the opposite side, holding a fuzzy blanket. I plop down between them, sitting noticeably closer to Jared. He throws the blanket over me and presses play on the movie.

Vin Diesel pops onto the screen, and I know we're watching the first *Fast & Furious* movie. Classic Noah and Jared. This series is one of their favorites. Over the years, it's become one of mine too. I settle in next to Jared, leaning my head on his shoulder.

I can feel Noah's eyes on me as I glance up, meeting his gaze. His face is tense, his brows knitted. Is he still mad at me? I don't have the energy to deal with that right now. Ignoring him, I sigh and turn back to the movie, snuggling into Jared. He wraps an arm around me, his other hand holding his phone.

We stay like that for the rest of the movie. When the credits roll, I don't want it to end. My anxiety almost completely disappears when I'm with them, and I need that right now.

"Wanna watch the second one?" I ask, hopeful.

"Oh, I can't, I'm sorry! I have plans with Jake tonight."

My face falls. I know they're friends, and Jake's stunt in the bathroom doesn't change that, but it still doesn't feel good. Noah's eyes meet mine, and there's recognition there.

"We can still watch it if you want," he says softly.

I think about it. The last time we were alone, things happened when they shouldn't have. But I don't want to be alone right now, and he's offering, so…

"Sure," I reply.

After Jared leaves, Noah looks over at me.

"I'll be right back," he says.

I wait patiently, snuggling up with the blanket. I listen for sounds in the kitchen, and I distinctly hear the door of the microwave close. Oh, he better come back with popcorn.

Minutes later, he re-emerges from the kitchen with a popcorn bowl in one hand and a glass of white wine in the other.

"Legally, I do not know you have this," he says as he hands it to me.

My heart melts a little as he sits down on the couch. He's pressed against the armrest, as far as he can get from me. I let out a laugh, and he looks over at me.

"What's so funny?"

"Nothing."

He scowls, grabs the remote, and puts on the second movie. The popcorn smells delicious, and I want some. The only problem is there's an ocean between us, and he has a death grip on the bowl. I crawl over the cushions to sit by his side and feel his body tense.

"Relax, I just want some popcorn," I explain, reaching my hand into the bowl. He softens a little, but not completely.

"Kira, I've been meaning to talk to you."

My heart skips a beat as I look up at him. Is he still mad at me?

Before he can say anything, I apologize.

"I'm sorry about the other night," I blurt. "I promise I'll let you know if I'm not coming home in the future."

He shakes his head, "That's not what I'm talking about."

"What do you mean?"

"That night. In the kitchen. That should have never happened." His voice is low but firm.

My heart sinks.

"Don't worry, I understand. You don't see me like that, and why would you? I don't know what I was thinking. I'm sorry."

"What?" he asks, sounding confused.

"I get it. I'm Jared's friend to you. It's fine, really," I don't know if I'm telling him that or myself.

He's looking at me like I'm crazy, disbelief playing in his eyes. His jaw flexes, and he seems like he's trying to find the right words. I don't need this rejection right now, not on top of everything today.

"God, Kira, I wish it was that simple."

He sounds frustrated, and the look in his eyes tells me he's fighting himself.

"What does that mean?"

"It doesn't matter," he says. "Watch the movie."

I don't argue because I don't know what to say. What does he mean by that?

I lean my head on the back of the couch, looking up at the TV. I know that nothing can happen between us, so why does it bother me so much?

He's Jared's dad and almost twenty years older than me. I let out a long breath and sink further into the cushion. My leg brushes Noah's, and he takes a sharp breath.

He doesn't say anything, but I feel him pull away. Ignoring the sting of rejection, I grab a throw pillow and lay down with my head on the opposite end of the couch. I cover up with the blanket. I try to straighten my legs, but he's in the way, and my foot brushes his thigh.

"Sorry!" I say, tucking my legs away from him.

He looks down at me, his eyes soft.

"It's fine," he sighs, picking up my feet and laying them in his lap.

As we watch the movie, his thumb traces lazy circles on the arch of my foot. I'm not sure he even realizes he's doing it, but it feels incredible, so I don't say anything. I don't want him to stop.

chapter ten
NOAH

I know I shouldn't be touching her. What I'm doing isn't inherently inappropriate, but the look of pure pleasure on her face makes it feel that way. Her eyes flutter closed as she lets herself relax. It's so tempting to move my hands up her legs, but I don't.

This I can control myself.

After a while, her breathing evens out, and soft snores sound from the other side of the couch. Her face is so peaceful like this. I think back to what she said earlier.

You don't see me like that.

I wish that were the truth. It would make it so much easier. I shouldn't see her like that. She's practically a kid still and doesn't need me looking at her like I want to fuck her. But god damn, she is beautiful, and her strength is incredible.

The movie ends, and the credits roll on the screen. I grab the remote and shut it off. Glancing back at Kira, I wonder if I should let her sleep there. The couch isn't very comfy, but I can't bring myself to wake her up.

Sliding my hands under her, I pull her to my chest, picking her up. She stirs a little, her head nuzzling into my neck.

"Shh, it's okay. I'm just bringing you up to bed."

I ignore the fact that I wish it were my bed. Carefully, I walk up the stairs to her room. She's so soft and smells like strawberries mixed with a warm summer night. I lay her gently into her bed, bringing the comforter up around her. The moon shines in through her window, illuminating the side of her face. I don't think she realizes how stunning she is.

I force myself to leave the room before I can do anything I'd regret. Lying down in my bed, I sigh. I can't believe she would think I'm not attracted to her.

Out of nowhere, a scream pierces the air from across the hall, followed by another. My mind immediately goes to Kira. I shoot out of bed, rushing to the door. What if someone's in there? If they hurt her, they're dead.

I hurl her door open, seeing her still lying in bed. I survey the room, not seeing anyone. Still, I search every corner, making sure no one is there. Kira's body twists on the bed. She's still asleep. Is she having a nightmare?

I slowly move toward the bed and sit down next to her. She pinches her brows together. She looks terrified. I reach out to touch her, grabbing her arm.

"Kira, it's okay."

She pulls away, screaming. Without thinking, I grab both her arms, trying to wake her up. She fights me.

"No, please!" her face twists. "Please, don't!"

"Kira, it's me, Noah," I try to assure her.

Her eyes snap open, and she sucks in a breath. She lets out a sob and looks up at me, fear in her eyes. Pulling her into me, I hold her. She tucks herself as far into my arms as she can.

"It's okay, I'm here."

She's shaking. And I can feel her heart racing. Moving one hand to her back, I run my fingers over it.

"You're safe, princess. I've got you."

Her head tilts up, eyes meeting mine. They're red and swollen. I bring my thumb to her cheek, wiping away the tears.

"You don't have to talk to me if you don't want to. Just know that I'm here."

She nods, more tears streaming down her cheeks. I lace my fingers into her hair, guiding her head to my chest, resting my chin there.

Who did this to her?

If I find out that someone hurt her, I'll end them. The fear in her eyes was so visceral it killed me.

I hug her tighter to me. She feels so fragile in my arms.

"Will you stay?" she whispers so quietly I almost don't hear.

I shouldn't, but I can't leave her like this. She needs me.

"Of course."

She moves to lay back down, and I help cover her with the blankets. Standing up, I sit on the bench seat by the window. I'll stay, but I don't think I can lay there with her.

"What are you doing?" She asks, amused.

"Staying."

"Why are you over there?"

"I think you know why."

"Noah, come lay down. I promise I won't do anything bad."

It's not her I'm worried about. I like to think I have control over my own actions, but it's difficult when she's that close to me.

"Please," she whines.

God, I can never say no to her.

Rising to my feet, I stalk over to the bed and climb under the covers beside her. I make sure to keep some distance between us, careful not to touch her. She rolls her eyes and laughs at me, turning away.

"Thank you."

Surprisingly, it doesn't take her long to fall back asleep. I glance over at her, now lying on her back. The fear from earlier is gone, replaced by a gentle calmness. I'm glad I was here for her, but I can't stop thinking about what could have happened to her for her to be that scared.

Without warning, she rolls, laying her head on my chest, her leg sliding over me. I suck in a breath. I hate how much I want this. I should leave now. She's asleep. Instead, I give in, just for tonight. Wrapping my arm around her, I pull her closer.

I wake up to the sun shining in through the window. It takes a moment before I realize these aren't my sheets. This isn't my room. *Shit*. Glancing down, Kira has wrapped her body around me, and my hand is on her almost bare ass.

Memories of last night flood my mind. Kira had a nightmare and asked me to stay. I was stupid and did. Now, I'm holding her like she's way more than my kid's best friend. Carefully, I slide out from under her, trying not to wake her up.

She stirs a little before rolling over onto her stomach. I step into the hall, quietly shutting her door. Hopefully, Jared isn't home yet, or if he is, he's sleeping. I don't know what time it is, but it has to be after nine. I can't believe I fell asleep in her room. What the fuck was I thinking?

I slowly walk down the stairs, surveying the kitchen as I do. I don't see him. He's probably still asleep. I grab one of Kira's mugs from the cupboard and turn on the coffee maker. It's the same one I used when I first noticed them. It's quickly become one of my favorites, and I won't let myself think about why. It's a nice mug, that's all.

Like she can hear my thoughts, soft footsteps sound from the stairs. She's still wearing her pajamas, and it takes all the control I have left not to look at those soft thighs or how her shirt hangs slightly off her shoulder.

"Mornin'," she says, a shy smile on her face.

"Good morning."

She saunters toward me, her hips swaying with each step. My heart jumps as she stops inches away, her eyes locked on mine. I remember the fear in those eyes last night. What caused it?

Fuck, Jared could walk out here any minute, and there is no reason she should be this close to me. Standing on her tippy toes and reaching her hand up, she swipes a mug out of the cabinet. I let out a breath, looking down at her. She smirks and pours herself some coffee. She's an entirely different Kira this morning.

Jared chooses this exact moment to amble into the room.

"When did you get in?" I ask.

He was here while I was with her, in her bed. Jesus, I need to get it together. If he had seen us… I can't let myself think about what would've happened.

"Late," he responds, moving to get a glass of water.

"Are you hungover?"

He ignores my question, chugging the water. I look over at Kira, and she shrugs.

"Jared, it's a Tuesday."

"And?" he says.

"I wanted to go to town to go shopping today, do you want to come with me?" Kira asks Jared, trying to change the subject.

"I can't, I'm sorry. I promised Keith I would mow his lawn today. Maybe Thursday?"

"I work. It's okay. I'll just go by myself."

Yeah, that's not happening.

"Have fun," Jared says before wandering back into his room. How is he okay with that?

"You're not going downtown alone."

"I will be fine. I've done it before."

"Yeah, that doesn't make me feel any better," I say, eyeing her. "I'll go with you." She looks up at me, an exasperated expression on her face.

The drive into Traverse City is quiet but not tense, not like I expected. Neither of us brings up last night, but something lingers between us, an unspoken shift. I can't stop thinking about how scared she was. The look in her eyes. The way she shrank into herself.

I grip the wheel a little tighter and focus on the road.

Finding parking downtown is a nightmare, and parallel parking this truck makes it worse. I mutter a curse under my breath as I maneuver into a tight spot along the street. Kira doesn't comment, just waits for me on the sidewalk, her arms crossed loosely.

When I finally climb out, I round the front of the truck and meet her gaze.

"Where to?" I ask.

"I need to find some new shorts. I don't really have any good ones for summer."

"Lead the way."

We fall into step together, weaving through the late-morning crowds. Shops and boutiques line the street, some sleek and modern, others homey and cluttered with knickknacks meant to lure in tourists. The warm breeze carries the scent of sunscreen and lake water, a mix that's so familiar it tugs at something deep in my chest. This place has always felt like a second home.

Kira veers off the main strip into a small consignment shop, and I follow. The space is tight, racks of clothes packed into every available corner. She heads straight for the back, where a modest rack of women's shorts sits against the wall.

I watch as she flips through them, her fingers skimming over denim and cotton. She's wearing those same jeans—the ones that hug her ass in a way that makes it impossible not to notice. This time, she's paired them with a cropped short-sleeve shirt, the fabric loose but just short enough to tease.

She reaches up to rifle through the hangers, and her shirt lifts, exposing more of the soft curve of her waist.

I swallow, my fingers twitching at my sides.

I shouldn't be looking at her like this.

But I can't help but picture my hands there.

"I'm going to go try these on," she says, pulling me out of my thoughts. I nod and follow her.

There's a bench there, so I sit down. She disappears into one of the fitting rooms, the lock clicking. After a few moments, the door opens, and she's now in a pair of high-waisted denim shorts. If I thought the jeans were tempting, fuck, these are sinful. They fit her perfectly.

"What do you think?" she asks me.

"They look nice."

Her face falls a bit, and she turns to look in the mirror. Now I can see her ass in them. *Jesus.* I look away, focusing on a wall of purses in the distance.

"You should get them. They fit you really well."

She turns back to me with a smile on her face. She mutters something about having to try the rest on and goes back into the room. In total, she tries on five pairs of shorts and likes two of them. We make our way to the front of the store and get in line at the register.

It's our turn to check out, and Kira sets her items on the counter. The cashier greets us and starts entering the prices into the machine.

"You did a good job with this one. She's beautiful," she says, a smile on her face.

Does she think I'm Kira's dad?

Kira quickly gestures between us, "Oh, he's not—we're not related."

The lady looks up at us, confused, but then her eyes widen in realization. Great, now she thinks we're together, and there's judgment in her eyes. Kira senses it, too, looking up at me. I shrug, letting her know that it doesn't matter. She relaxes and hands the lady her card.

We step out of the shop, and Kira immediately starts laughing.

"Well, that was weird. At first, she thought I was your kid, but then she thought I was your girlfriend."

I laugh with her as we wander back toward the truck. Before we can get there, though, Kira stops and looks up at an old building. It's a bookstore. Her eyes move to mine, and I know exactly what she wants.

"Go ahead, we have time."

chapter eleven
KIRA

I've always loved this bookstore, the warm wood tones and books lining every wall. It's cozy. Noah follows behind me as I browse through the sections, making my way to one in particular.

"You can go look at stuff too, you know?"

"I'm good."

He asked for it.

I find the sign that says "Romance" and head right for it. It's in a secluded area toward the back of the store. I can't afford to buy anything right now, but I still love to look. I pick up one with a shirtless man on the cover and hear a quiet laugh behind me. I turn around to glare at him.

"What's so funny?" I ask.

"Nothing, nothing," he says, waving his hands in the air.

My cheeks heat, and I turn back around, grabbing another book. I feel him come up behind me. Reaching over my shoulder, he takes a book down. It has an alien on the cover, and he looks at me inquisitively.

"You wouldn't get it."

His eyebrows shoot up, and he shoves the book back on the shelf. He glances down at the one I'm holding. I flip it to the back and read the description. I make it to the end when I see the words.

I want him, but I can't have him.

He's my best friend's dad.

I look up at Noah, a smirk on his face. I hurry to shove the book back where it came from.

"I think you should get that one," he teases.

It honestly sounds like something I would read, but I'm not telling him that. I'll make a mental note to add it to my TBR.

He chuckles and wanders to another shelf. I ignore my embarrassment and continue looking through the books. There are a couple more that I find interesting, so I pull out my phone and make a list in my notes app.

When I tell Noah I'm ready to leave, he gestures to my empty hands, asking why I didn't grab anything. I tell him that I don't have the money right now.

"Let me buy them for you then."

"Absolutely not."

"Why?" he asks, genuinely confused.

"Because you're already letting me stay with you rent-free, I'm not going to have you buying me things too."

He protests but eventually gives in. As the sun sets on the horizon, we make our way back to the truck.

"Thank you for coming today," I tell him.

"Of course, I wasn't going to let you wander down here by yourself."

When we get home, Jared is sprawled out on the couch, looking utterly miserable. His shirt is half off, and his shoulders are an angry shade of red.

I drop onto the cushion beside him, eyebrows raised. "What happened to you?"

He groans. "Keith failed to mention that mowing his lawn meant *all* two acres of it." He shifts, wincing as his sunburn protests. "Took me three hours."

I bite back a laugh. "Please tell me you at least put on sunscreen."

Jared glares at me. That's a no.

I shake my head. "At least you know for next time?"

"There *will* be no next time," he grumbles. "Not unless he pays me."

Noah walks in from the kitchen, an easy smile on his face. "Damn, that's rough," he says, nodding toward Jared's shoulders.

Jared mutters something under his breath.

I go to grab the aloe vera from the bathroom, and when I come back, I squeeze some onto my fingers and start gently rubbing it onto his shoulders. He flinches at first but then sighs as the cool gel soothes his scorched skin.

While I work, Noah flops down onto the recliner, stretching out like he owns the place. "We should go out tomorrow night," he says casually. "There's live music at the brewery in town."

Jared perks up slightly. "That actually sounds fun."

Noah smirks. "Yeah, it'll be a good family outing."

I make a face. I'm not sure I love that phrasing.

Noah just winks, and I roll my eyes, but my stomach does a stupid little flip anyway.

LATER THAT NIGHT, I'M LYING IN BED, STARING AT THE CEILING.

I *should* be thinking about work tomorrow. Or, hell, *anything* else. But all I can focus on is what happened in the kitchen with Noah.

There was something there. I *know* there was. The way he looked at me when I touched him—there's no way he didn't feel it, too.

But in the end, it doesn't matter.

He's Jared's dad.

The cashier at the store today thought he was *my* dad, and when I corrected her, she looked like she was about to call the cops.

I exhale, curling the blankets tighter around me, forcing my mind to go blank.

I can't let myself think about Noah like that.

I close my eyes and push him out of my thoughts.

No, please, no!

He doesn't listen. Can he hear me?

I try to stop him, but I'm not strong enough, the alcohol slowing me down. He hoists me up over his shoulder, a grin plastered on his face.

Let go of me!

His grip tightens around me, and he opens a door. No, no, no. I know how this ends. I have to get out of here.

I need to fight back!

I'm pulled back to reality by Noah's strong hands on me.

"Kira, it's okay, I'm here," he whispers.

I haven't had nightmares like this in over a year. I thought I was past it, but seeing Zach must have triggered them. I can only imagine what Noah thinks. Tears stream down my cheeks as I look up at him.

"Kira, what is going on?"

"Can you just stay with me again? At least for a little bit?"

Reluctantly, he nods, sitting on the bed. Before, when I would have nightmares alone at night, I wouldn't be able to fall back asleep afterward. I was too afraid of going back into the nightmare. With Noah last night, it was different. He made me feel safe.

He lays back on the bed beside me, and I look up at him. I want him to hold me so I can sleep, but I don't know how to ask. He seems to realize, holding his arm out so I can cuddle closer.

"I really shouldn't be in here," he says.

"I know, but I'm glad you are."

His body is warm and hard beneath me. Wrapping his arm around me, he pulls me into him. His touch causes my skin to heat, and I try my best to keep my thoughts PG.

He's here because he wants to make sure I'm okay, not because he wants anything to happen between us. I make it all ten seconds before I bring my hand up and place it on his chest, slowly tracing down his abdomen. He sucks in a breath, grabbing my hand.

"Kira, don't start."

I whimper, "Why not?" But I know the answer. We are already crossing a line here.

"Go to sleep," he says, running his fingers through my hair.

The feeling is nearly orgasmic. I let out a little moan, instantly regretting it. He stops, looking down at me.

"Jesus, Kira, you can't do that," he groans.

Glancing down, I gasp, taking in the impressive bulge in his sweatpants.

He's hard.

For me.

A hand comes down and grasps my chin, directing me to look back up at him. His gaze is heated, but there's something else there, like he's barely holding himself back. Our faces are so close now I can feel his breath on my lips. Fuck, I want him to kiss me. His jaw tightens.

"Last warning, princess. Go to sleep, or I'm leaving."

I look up at him, trying to read the emotions playing on his face. His eyes narrow, and I give in, lying back down on him. If this is all I can have, then I'll take it.

When I wake up, he's gone, and the smell of coffee from downstairs tells me he's probably already awake. It's the beginning of June, and it's finally starting to feel like summer, so I throw on one of my new pairs of shorts and a T-shirt and head downstairs.

Jared is seated at the kitchen island, and I'm surprised he's up. He usually sleeps in. Noah is standing by the stove, his eyes fixed on me.

"I should probably get going soon," Jared says.

"Oh? Where are you headed off to so early?" I ask.

"I completely forgot, but I have an academic advising meeting at MSU today. I should still be home in enough time to go to dinner, though."

"Well, that's exciting!" I tell him.

I'm happy for him. He's always wanted to go to Michigan State ever since he was little.

The late afternoon sun casts long golden streaks across the yard as I work on my sculpture. The warm air wraps around me, thick with the scent of grass and clay, and a soft breeze teases the strands of hair escaping from my messy bun.

I glance down at my piece, brushing my fingers over the smooth, cool surface. What started as a shapeless lump of clay has taken on the delicate form of a cupped hand, fingers gently curled like it's meant to hold something. *But what?* I tilt my head, studying it from different angles, but the answer doesn't come.

Frustration prickles at me, but I force myself to set it aside. Sometimes, ideas need time to settle before they make sense.

Deciding I'm done for the day, I gather my tools, wiping my hands on an old rag before carrying the sculpture inside. In my room, I carefully wrap it in a plastic bag to keep the clay from drying out too quickly and place it on a shelf above my dresser. It's safe there—waiting, like me, for whatever comes next.

A small thrill of excitement runs through me as I turn to my closet. I don't go out much, and even though it's just dinner, I want to dress up a little. My fingers skim over worn t-shirts and denim before landing on my favorite sundress. Cream-colored, with brown flowers and soft green leaves, it ties in the back, the hem brushing mid-thigh. Simple but pretty.

I slip it on, smoothing the fabric down before making my way to the kitchen. As I step inside, I catch the tail end of Noah's phone call.

"It's fine. Just be safe. We'll do dinner another time. Love you too, bye." He hangs up, looking up at me, his eyes trailing down my body.

"What was that about?" I ask.

"Jared isn't going to make it. He made some friends, and they convinced him to hang out tonight."

"Is he still coming home, though?"

"He's not sure," he says, frustration in his voice. "We'll get dinner another time. It's fine."

My face falls, "Why can't we still go? I was kind of looking forward to it."

"Do you really want to go with just me?" he asks, seeming genuinely surprised.

"Why wouldn't I?"

"Fine, let me get dressed," he says, disappearing upstairs.

When he comes back down, he's wearing dark jeans and a faded black Metallica shirt. It hugs his muscled arms in a way that should be illegal. He looks good.

He clears his throat. "Ready to go?"

We pull up to the brewery, and it's packed. There's almost nowhere to park, so we end up across the street. Noah stays behind me until we reach the door, opening it and gesturing for me to head inside.

The interior of the building resembles a cabin, with wood paneling and warm lighting. It's not too busy in here. Most of the people are likely already out back. We order two pretzels, and Noah gets a beer.

Almost all of the tables are full as we step through the back door. Some people even brought lawn chairs that they have perched up in front of the small stage. Scanning the space, I spot an empty two-person table and head straight for it, Noah following closely behind.

Looking around, I take in the sheer amount of people here.

"This place is popular tonight," I say, setting down our food. The tables are all lit with a single candle in the center. Paired with the string lights wrapping around the fenced-in yard, the ambiance is immaculate.

"Well, yeah, it's the only thing to do in Lake Ann," he says with a chuckle.

The sun is dipping below the horizon as the band walks up on stage, each member grabbing their instrument. The crowd starts to cheer as they begin playing. I immediately recognize the opening riff to "Sweet Child O' Mine."

"I love this song!" I squeal.

"A bit before your time, isn't it?" Noah asks, a smile spreading across his face. I roll my eyes at him and sing along with the band.

He laughs, looking at me with curiosity in his eyes.

"Who sings it then?" he asks, trying to trip me up.

Not happening.

"Guns N' Roses."

He raises his eyebrows, surprise on his face.

"There's a lot you don't know about me," I tell him.

"I'd say so! First those books at the bookstore and now this?" he teases. My cheeks heat as I bring my hands to my face. Of course, he would bring that up.

"Listen, I didn't know that's what that book was about when I grabbed it."

"Sure you didn't," he says, winking at me.

Fuck, I like that. He makes it so hard not to want him. Well, I can play that game too. I lean across the table, my breasts pushing out of the top of my dress the slightest bit. His eyes move down, taking them in.

"So what if I did?" I ask.

His dark eyes shoot up, reflecting the candlelight. A flurry of emotions shows there, and I can't tell if he's mad or about to kiss me.

I'm about to take it back, but I'm silenced by his rough hand brushing against my thigh under the table. His jaw tightens as he sucks in a breath.

"I'll be right back," he says before standing up and walking back into the bar.

I shouldn't have pushed him. Nothing can happen between us. I know that. It would kill Jared, but I love his hands on me. Not to mention, he's hot when he gets all grumpy. I glance up, watching the band play, when someone sits in Noah's seat.

"Oh, sorry, that spot is ta—"

My heart stops in my chest when I see who it is.

It's *him.*

chapter twelve
KIRA

I haven't been face-to-face with him in almost four years, but he looks exactly the same. Like a nightmare dragging itself into the daylight.

His tall, thin frame leans over the table toward me, close enough that I catch the sharp scent of cologne and something bitter underneath—alcohol, maybe. His dark eyes, nearly black, bore into me, and my stomach twists violently.

I can't breathe.

The air feels thick, pressing against my lungs, but I force myself to sit up straight. *Do not cower. Do not let him see.*

"You two looked cozy." His voice is the same, too—oily, smug, curling around me like a chokehold.

He's here. He's right here.

"Leave me alone, Zach," I manage, but my voice is tight, barely containing the tremor threatening to break free.

His smirk widens. "So you're fucking Jared's dad now? How am I not surprised? A slut like you wants all she can get, right?"

My skin turns to ice. I can't move. I can't blink. The bar around us fades into nothing—just muffled voices, blurred shapes, a faraway hum. *Not real, not real, not real.*

"What do you want?" I whisper. *Hadn't he taken enough already?*

My heartbeat slams against my ribs, fast and uneven. *Where is Noah?*

Zach leans in closer, his breath warm against my face, and I flinch. "From you? Nothing right now." His teeth flash in a grin, predatory and cruel. "But I know where to find you when I want a whore."

His words hit like a slap, like hands pinning me down, like darkness swallowing me whole.

He straightens, turns, and walks out as if he didn't just rip me open all over again.

The bile rises so fast I barely swallow it down. The bar is too bright, too loud, spinning around me as my breath shatters into pieces. I grip the edge of the table, my nails digging into the wood, trying to ground myself, but it's useless. I can't be here. I can't be *anywhere* he might find me.

Someone sits down across from me, and I jerk back so hard the chair wobbles. *He came back—*

"Kira."

Noah's voice cuts through the static, low and steady. I blink, vision tunneling until it lands on his face—concerned, steady, real.

"Are you okay?"

I look up at him, and he instantly recognizes something is off. I'm shaking, and I can't catch my breath. I've had anxiety attacks before, but this one takes the cake.

"Let's go," he says, moving toward me to help me stand.

His arm wraps around me, supporting me. Guiding me back to the truck, he opens the door, helping me climb in. I'm lightheaded, and I still can't breathe. As he shuts his door, I finally let myself cry.

"Hey, what happened?" he asks.

"Listen, I need you to breathe with me, okay?"

I try to stop hyperventilating, holding my breath.

"Look at me," he demands.

I listen, my eyes meeting his hazel ones. Concern fills them as he reaches for my shoulders, holding me in place.

"*In. Out. In. Hold it. Out.* There you go. You're okay, I promise. I'm here."

My breathing has slowed now, my heart following suit.

"Can you please just take me home?" I beg.

"Of course," he says, resting his hand on my leg for reassurance, but I don't know if it's me or him that he's reassuring. I put mine over his, squeezing it. His grip is tight on my thigh. As we drive, he glances over at me every once in a while, probably afraid I'm going to break down, but I don't. I push it down like I always do.

Noah pulls into the driveway and immediately rounds the truck, opening my door and helping me down. He guides me into the house, but I keep walking through the slider and onto the back patio. I need air.

I'm so tired of being scared all the time, and now it's worse. There's a reason to be afraid when I go out. He could be anywhere.

The slider glides open as I sit down on the swing, and Noah steps out onto the porch. He sits in the chair across from me, and his eyes meet mine.

"Kira, I'm going to need you to talk to me."

No.

There's no way I can tell him what is going on. He won't believe me. Or even worse, he'll agree with the cops and say it was my fault. I can't handle that right now.

"I promise I'm here for you. I hate seeing you like this and not being able to help. What happened?"

He's been there for me through my nightmares. He kept me from crumbling tonight. He deserves to know. I take a deep breath and pray that he listens.

Crickets chirp outside as I get ready in my room. It's a warm summer night, and anticipation is thick in the air. Jake's parents are out of town this weekend, and he's having a party tonight to celebrate the end of the school year. I can't wait. He even said he invited some upperclassmen.

Mom isn't home. She's working late tonight, like every other night, so she probably won't even realize I'm gone. I grab my phone and house key right as I hear a car pull into the driveway.

I peek out the blinds to make sure that it's my ride, and I see the beat-up red charger idling loudly. It's them. I head out the door and run up to the car, sliding into the front seat. I glance in the back seat, seeing Jared on his phone.

"Took you long enough," Zach complains.

"I'm sorry."

"Whatever," he says, pulling out of the driveway.

We're swerving down the road, going way too fast, and I grip the seat, my knuckles turning white. I don't like riding with Zach, but none of our other friends can drive yet. Zach is eighteen, so he has had his license for a while now.

When we get to the party, there's already a lot of people. Jared disappears almost instantly, leaving me alone. I hear someone call my name, and I glance up. Zach is walking toward me, holding a plastic cup in his hand. Reaching his hand out, he offers it to me. I'm no stranger to alcohol, having broken into my mom's stash more times than I can count.

"Come on, you'll like it. Don't be boring."

I take the cup from him, downing it to prove a point. It burns as the liquid glides down my throat. I hand the cup back to him and wander back into the living room, looking for Jared. He's still nowhere to be found, so I take my usual place on the couch, quietly observing the party. I'm watching two guys shotgun when Zach sits down beside me, handing me another drink. I take it, choosing to sip on it this time.

It goes on like that for a while. Zach brings me drink after drink. I've honestly lost count of how many I've had. I'm definitely drunk, and I should probably stop, but I'm having fun.

The rest of the party blurs together. By two a.m., most people are either gone or passed out. From the living room, I see Jared in the kitchen with Jake, passing a joint between them. I try to stand and make my way over to them, but I stumble, and a hand grabs my wrist.

"Where are you going?" Zach asks, a crooked smile on his face.

I try to explain, but he ignores me, talking over me, "No, you've been teasing me all night. Time to put out," he says, throwing me over his shoulder.

What? What is he doing? I don't like this. "Zach, no, please put me down."

"Not tonight. I'm getting what I want tonight."

"No, please, let go of me!" I slur out, but the music is too loud. No one is going to hear. The alcohol is still running through my system, making it hard to do anything.

I hear a door open.

He carries me inside, dropping me onto a mattress.

The door closes.

And locks.

No, no, no.

"Please stop, Zach,"

He ignores me as he hovers over me, a sick grin on his lips. I want to throw up. I squeeze my eyes shut as he unbuttons my shorts and yanks them down my legs. A tear falls down my cheek.

I am all alone.

There's no one to stop him.

With each touch from him, I lose more pieces of myself until I'm a shell of the girl who stepped into this house.

It feels like forever, the violation, the pain.

When he finally finishes, he shoves off me.

"Fucking slut," he says as he heads for the door.

He leaves me there.

Trembling, I move to find my clothes. I need to get dressed so I can leave. I need to get out of here. I try to hold back my sobs as I pull my clothes on.

I open the door a crack, looking into the living room. Jared is out there with Jake and Zach. They're all laughing at some joke Jake told. My stomach twists. I can't go out there. I need to go home.

My mind is still slow from the drinks earlier, and my hand shakes as I reach for the handle to the back door. The temperature has dropped, and I'm still only in shorts and a tank top. Shivering, I start the long walk home. It's probably only a few miles, but it takes me over an hour. Mom's car is in the driveway when I get there.

"Where have you been?"

Words refuse to come as a sob racks my chest. She looks up at me, the faintest hint of concern in her eyes.

"What did you do?"

I tell her what happened, needing her to be a normal mother, just this once. She sits for a moment, sighing.

"Well, look what you're wearing. I mean, what did you expect?"

The cops end up sharing the same sentiment.

Noah looks up at me, his expression unreadable at first—then shifting, darkening, a storm brewing behind his eyes.

This is it.

My chest tightens. My fingers curl into fists on my lap, nails digging into my palms. I already know what's coming. The judgment. The words I've heard before, spoken in different voices but always meaning the same thing—*You did this to yourself. You were reckless. You should have known better.*

I brace for it, for the disappointment, for the blame that will turn my shame into something unbearable. I *deserve* it, don't I?

But it doesn't come.

Noah shifts closer, lowering himself beside me, and when he speaks, his voice is nothing like I expected. No accusation. No anger. Just quiet certainty.

"Kira, what happened to you was not your fault."

The air leaves my lungs in a sharp exhale. *Not my fault.*

I don't move at first. I can't. The words don't make sense. *Not my fault.* I stare at him, searching his face for doubt, for hesitation, for *anything* that will prove he's just saying what he thinks I need to hear.

But there's nothing. Just unwavering belief.

He believes me.

The realization slams into me so hard my whole body trembles with it. A single tear slips down my cheek, followed by another. I don't wipe them away.

Noah watches me carefully, his voice softer now. "Tell me what happened tonight. What triggered that?"

For a second, I think about not telling him. I hate admitting that Zach still has that much effect on me.

"He was there. When you walked away, he came up to me," my voice is still shaky as I speak.

His jaw tightens as he takes in a breath. He's upset. I shouldn't have told him. He doesn't need this extra stress.

"If he ever comes near you again, I'll personally end him," he promises.

His thumb comes up, wiping away what's left of my tears. The weight that has been crushing me for years feels lighter.

He actually believes me.

We're inches apart now, his hand still cupping my cheek. My eyes dart to his mouth, and I pull my bottom lip between my teeth. I would give anything to feel those lips on me. He catches the shift in my gaze, tightening his grip on my jaw. My heart pounds in my chest for a completely different reason this time.

"Kira," Noah warns.

Before he can say anything else, I press my lips into his, my hand sliding up his chest. A groan escapes him as he kisses me back, pulling my lip between his teeth.

"We can't do this," he says, breaking the kiss. "This is not what you need right now."

But I do need this. I need to know what it feels like to not be scared—to be with someone I know won't hurt me. He eyes me, his gaze heated but his restraint visible.

"Please," I whisper.

He lets out a ragged breath as his fingers trace up my neck, gripping my chin.

"Are you sure about this, princess?" he asks.

I nod, and his eyes darken. He grips the hair at the back of my head, angling my face up to his. His lips brush over mine, and I can't wait any longer. I need more.

"I need you," I breathe out.

The last cord of his control snaps as his lips devour mine, hungry and ravaging. He kisses me with such force that a whimper escapes my lips, fueling his fire.

He pulls me up onto him, and I straddle his lap, his hands sliding up my waist. I can feel him—already hard against me. Reaching up, I lace my fingers in his hair, tugging. He groans, smirking into our kiss.

He wants this just as much as I do.

chapter thirteen
NOAH

This is fucked up. I know that. But I can't bring myself to stop.

She feels too good—too damn good—rocking against me, her body molding to mine like she was made for this. Her breath hitches as I tug at the hair at the nape of her neck, angling her mouth to mine. I devour her, lips sliding over hers, teasing, tasting. When I break away, I trail slow kisses along her jaw, down the column of her throat, sucking just enough to earn a soft, shivering moan.

I slip my hands under the hem of her skirt, fingertips skimming over soft, warm skin. Fuck, she's all curves, sinful in this dress, and when I squeeze her ass, she presses closer, grinding down on me. Through the thin fabric, I can feel how tight her nipples have gotten, and I shouldn't— but I *love* how her body responds to me.

I dip my head, capturing one in my mouth, teasing through the fabric with my teeth. Her sharp inhale sends heat straight to my cock.

"Noah," she breathes out.

Her hand slides down my chest, trailing all the way to my aching cock. She palms it, squeezing lightly, and I hiss, looking at her.

"Fuck, princess," I groan. "We shouldn't do this."

She doesn't stop. Her palm moves, pressing, teasing. Just as I suck in another breath, the sound of tires crunching over gravel shatters our bubble.

Kira gasps, freezing. Her wide eyes snap to mine.

"Shit," I mutter, the weight of reality crashing down. "It's probably Jared."

Guilt slams into me as she scrambles off my lap, straightening her dress with shaking hands.

"Hello, anybody home?" I hear from the house.

I stand up, moving to sit back across from Kira. I'm still hard, so I readjust myself in the chair. He's going to know. There's no way he won't.

"We're out on the porch," I call.

Kira straightens her dress, tucking her hair behind her ear. Following the movement, I see a dark spot on her neck. Did I leave a fucking hickey on her? What am I, sixteen? I gesture for her to put her hair back, and she does, a little confused. Jared pulls open the slider, peeking out the door.

"I just wanted to check-in. I'm exhausted, so I'm going to head to bed," he says. "I'm sorry I couldn't make it to dinner."

"It's okay. I'm glad you had fun," Kira assures.

"Well, goodnight, guys," Jared says as he spins around, disappearing into the house.

What the fuck just happened?

"Go upstairs," I tell her.

For once, she doesn't argue, rising to her feet and heading inside. That was too close. What if we didn't hear him? If he wouldn't have gotten home when he did... Why do I wish he didn't?

Easing open the door to her room, I close it behind me and make my way over to her. Kira is sitting on her bed, her feet dangling off the side. She looks up at me with those warm brown eyes, an undercurrent of worry filling them. I move her hair to the side, barely touching the red mark at the curve of her neck. I wince.

"Yeah, good job on that one," she says, a small laugh escaping her lips.

"Kira, that never should have happened," I say, my fingers trailing her jaw.

"What, the hickey? Yeah, probably not the best idea."

"You know what I mean. That can never happen again."

Her face falls, eyes dropping to the wood floor.

"I should have known better. I mean, fuck, Kira, I'm old enough to be your dad. There is no reason I should be touching you like that. You're still just a kid, and after what you told me..."

"Noah, I wanted that—needed it, really, and I'm the one that kissed you. I practically forced myself on you," she says.

My eyes trail down to her lips, my thumb brushing over them. I want to kiss her again, feel her body on mine, but I can't. Nothing more can happen between us. I'm not what she needs.

"Trust me, you didn't force anything, but it doesn't matter. It won't happen again," I tell her. "Goodnight, princess."

Turning around, I step out of her room, shutting the door behind me.

THE FOLLOWING DAY, I DON'T SEE MUCH OF KIRA, WHICH IS probably for the best. I can't seem to control my actions when it comes to her.

Tonight, she's somewhere with Jared, so I have the house to myself, which gives me plenty of time to sit with my thoughts. I can't believe I kissed her last night. Not even twenty minutes after she told me what was likely the most significant trauma of her life, I was pulling her on top of me. What does that say about me?

If Jared hadn't come home, would I have stopped?

I need a drink.

Grabbing my phone, I dial Keith's number.

"Hello?" he answers.

"Do you have the girls tonight?"

"Nah, they're with their mom. Why, what's up?"

"Wanna go to Dillinger's and grab some beers?"

"Meet you there in fifteen," he chuckles before hanging up.

I throw on a clean T-shirt, grabbing my wallet and keys. I need to get out of this house and get my mind off of her.

I pull up to the pub, seeing Keith's car already there. I walk inside and see him sitting at the bar, a tall beer in hand.

"Damn, you're quick," I say, sitting down beside him.

"What can I say? I missed you," he says with a chuckle.

"Or maybe you missed the cold beer."

"The world may never know."

I flag down the bartender and order a tall kölsch, glancing around the bar as I wait. It's busy for Thursday night. Nearly all of the tables are full. "Any Way You Want It" by Journey blares through the speakers, barely audible over the shouts and laughter.

A hand taps my shoulder, and I turn to look at Keith.

"I think you've got an admirer," he says, gesturing over my shoulder. I follow his gaze to a brunette across the bar. She looks to be about thirty, and she's pretty. Keeping her eyes on mine, she saunters up to the bar, an added sway in her hips. She's wearing a tight red dress that hugs her curves with bright red lips to match. She leans on the bar next to me, a smirk on her face.

"Hey, handsome, you gonna buy me a drink?"

I let out a laugh and look over at her. She's the kind of woman I should want. She's beautiful and *my age*. I don't want to be rude, so I oblige.

"What would you like?" I ask her.

"I would *love* a vodka cranberry," she says, sitting beside me.

"I'll be right back," Keith says.

Great, he's leaving me alone with her. He probably thinks he's doing me a favor. The bartender hands over her drink, and she brings it to her lips, taking a sip.

"So, what's your name?"

"Noah, yours?" I ask, but I don't hear the answer as the door to the bar swings open and Kira steps through it, followed by Jared and his friends. She looks up at me, and our gazes meet. She's wearing a dress similar to the one she wore the other day, but this one is solid black. It fits her in all the right places. My mind flashes back to her on top of me, my hands up her skirt.

Fuck, I can't think about that.

Kira's eyes shoot to the woman next to me, then to her hand on my thigh. When she looks back up at me, there's a flash of hurt in her eyes, but it quickly hardens into anger. She drops her gaze, moving to follow the boys to a booth in the corner.

I look back at the woman, and she seems to sense something is up.

"What, did I say something wrong?"

I tell her I'm not in the place for anything more than a conversation, and she takes the hint and returns to her group of friends. Noticing her absence, Keith reappears at my side, plopping beside me.

"What happened? Thought you two were hitting it off."

"She was nice, but I just wasn't interested," I tell him.

He shrugs, looking at me like I'm an idiot. I barely register it. My focus keeps drifting to Kira, but she won't even glance my way.

She's playing pool now, effortlessly sinking shot after shot, beating every one of Jared's friends like it's nothing. The guys are eating it up, laughing, egging her on. She lines up for the final shot, leaning over the table, her back to me.

The hem of her skirt barely covers her ass. She knows it, too—shifting just enough to make it worse.

What the hell is she thinking?

I glance around. Every man in this damn bar can see her. My jaw tightens, and just as I'm about to get up and say something, one of Jared's friends beats me to it.

He strides over, leaning in behind her like he belongs there, one hand braced on the table beside hers. His voice is low, murmuring something about lining up the shot, but I don't hear it. All I see is how close he is, his chest nearly flush with her back, his hands too damn familiar.

My fists curl against my thighs.

Keith notices. "You good?" he mutters.

I ignore him. My chair scrapes against the floor as I push back and stand, striding toward the pool table.

"I doubt she needs your help. She's fully capable of hitting the ball on her own."

The kid looks up at me, not recognizing who I am.

"Jeez man, what's your problem?" he asks, backing away from her.

Glancing down, I see that her hand is shaking under the stick.

"Let her try on her own and show you assholes who's boss."

Kira, Jared, and I used to come down here and play pool all the time when they were younger. She's good, and I don't doubt she will make this shot.

"Go ahead, Kira."

She focuses in on the cue ball, pulls the stick back, and sends the eight ball right into the corner pocket. She looks up at me, a hand on her hip.

"I could have handled that myself. Go back to your date," she bites out.

I lower my voice so Jared and his friends don't hear, "She isn't my date."

She ignores me, turning back toward the group.

"Ready to go, Kira?" Jared asks.

Before she can respond, I cut in, "No, I'm going to take her home. She was just telling me how she wasn't feeling very well." I look down at her, her eyes shooting daggers at me, but she doesn't say anything.

"Okay, well, I'll see you later then?"

She nods at Jared, and the group heads out the door.

"What the fuck, Noah?"

"I don't trust them, especially after that asshole grabbed you like that."

She looks up at me. Tilting her head, she moves a step closer.

"What if I wanted him to?"

Yeah, right.

"I know you didn't. I know what you want, and it's not him." Her eyes widen at my statement.

"You have no idea what I want."

"You sure about that?" I ask, and she eyes me.

On our way out, I stop by Keith and tell him Kira isn't feeling well, so I'm taking her home. I can tell he knows there's more to it, but he doesn't push.

Kira doesn't speak a word the entire drive. She's pissed. I couldn't let her go with them, not with the way that guy was touching her. It was for her safety. At least that's what I tell myself, ignoring that seeing anyone else's hands on her makes me want to bring her home and show her who she belongs to. But that's just it. She isn't mine, and she never will be.

When we pull into the driveway, she throws the door open before I can park the truck. She climbs out and heads to the front door, but I jump out and am on her heels before she can open it.

"Kira, stop."

She spins around to face me, and her eyes harden.

"I'm sorry for stopping you from going with Jared, but I did it for your own good."

She lets out a cynical laugh, "Honestly, Noah, I don't care about that. I didn't really want to go anyway."

"Then why are you stomping off like a toddler?"

"Are you kidding me?" she starts, "You know what, it's fine."

I reach out and cup her jaw, making her look at me.

"What's wrong?" She gazes up at me, anger in her eyes.

"Nothing, it's stupid. It makes sense. She's someone who you could and *should* be with."

What? Fuck, is she jealous? If only she knew that I was staring at her ass in that dress the entire night, not the woman that was sitting next to me.

"That's what this is about?" I start. "Kira, I told her I wasn't interested."

"Why? She was beautiful, your age, and ready to climb you like a tree."

I let out a sigh, my jaw tightening. She doesn't get it.

"I don't want her."

chapter fourteen
KIRA

I don't want her.

His words play over in my head as he looks at me. His eyes are heated, and his hand on my face makes it hard to think straight. He should be allowed to pick up women at bars. He's a single man. I shouldn't be jealous. But I'll be damned if that statement didn't just make my heart skip a beat.

I have no claim over him, but when I walked in and saw him with her, it felt like a betrayal. That's the only reason I let Brennan touch me. I knew it would piss Noah off, and I was right.

He still hasn't taken his hand off of me.

"You know I don't want her," he repeats, his eyes staring directly into mine.

The implication of his words hits me. I know he doesn't want her because *he wants me*, but it doesn't matter because he will never let himself have me. Nothing more can happen between us. It's wrong. I know that, but the way he's looking at me is exhilarating. I need to clear my head, and I can't do that when he's this close. Turning away, I break out of his grasp.

"I'm going to go to bed. Goodnight, Noah."

At first, I think he'll stop me, but he doesn't. He stays silent, watching me as I walk away.

THE NEXT MORNING, I WAKE UP TO THE SOUND OF A DISTINCT KNOCK at my door. Before he even enters, I know it's Jared. A second later, he barrels into the room and launches himself onto my bed, wrapping his arms around me.

"Happy birthday, Kira!"

His voice is bright, full of unfiltered excitement, and it tugs something deep inside me. As my eyes adjust to the soft morning light, I blink up at him. His light brown hair is a mess, sticking up in wild angles, and he's still in his pajama bottoms. He must have come straight here the moment he woke up.

His gaze drifts down, pausing where his hand rests on my hip. I follow his eyes and realize—one of my legs is kicked over the comforter, and my shirt has ridden up in my sleep, exposing more skin than I intended. A rush of warmth creeps up my neck as I quickly tug it down. Jared lets out a small sigh but says nothing, just giving my leg a quick pat before pushing himself off the bed.

"Come downstairs. Breakfast is ready," he says, already heading for the door.

"I'll be down in a minute."

"Don't take too long. It's gonna get cold," he calls before disappearing into the hallway.

I stare at the ceiling for a moment, letting the quiet settle around me. *Nineteen.* It doesn't feel any different. It never does. Just another day.

I used to dread my birthday. Growing up, all the other kids got parties and presents. My mom thought those things were frivolous, and cake was always out of the question.

But the smell of bacon and coffee drifts in from the kitchen downstairs, pulling me out of those thoughts. My stomach tightens in response, and I finally push myself out of bed.

It's not like that anymore.

I have people who care about me now.

I throw on a pair of shorts and head downstairs, running a hand through my hair to shake off the last traces of sleep.

As I step into the kitchen, the sight stops me in my tracks.

Jared is perched at the island, happily digging into his plate, and Noah stands by the coffee pot, pouring coffee into one of my mugs. He hands it to me without a word, like he's done this a hundred times before. My fingers curl around the warm ceramic as I glance down at the counter—and freeze.

Eggs, toast, crispy bacon, fluffy pancakes, even a carefully arranged fruit platter.

An entire breakfast spread.

For me.

My chest tightens, something hot pressing against my ribs.

"You guys did all this?" I ask, my voice softer than I intend.

"Happy birthday," Noah says softly.

"Oh my god, thank you guys so much!"

"This was all him," Jared says, gesturing toward his dad.

Meeting Noah's eyes, he shakes his head, waving me off.

"It's nothing. I just thought you deserved a good breakfast before you went to work this morning."

My heart warms at his gesture. He's always taking care of me, always making sure I have everything I need. Filling my plate with one of everything, I take a seat next to Jared at the island.

"So, what are your plans today?" Jared asks.

"Nothing really, just work."

"Good, because you're busy tonight."

Oh god, what is he planning? I don't think I'm in the mood for any kind of massive party, and I was looking forward to having some time to relax tonight, just me and my book.

"Please tell me it's nothing crazy," I tell him.

"It's nothing crazy."

Somehow, I don't believe him.

My shift goes by without any significant issues. It's super slow, and I can't help but wish that I would have taken the day off.

By the time 7:30 rolls around, I'm ready to leave, but I'm not excited to see what is waiting for me at home. Every year, I tell Jared that I don't want a big party, and every year, he outdoes himself. He has good intentions, so I can't bring myself to stop him. Before leaving, I change into one of my favorite dresses that I brought with me, knowing I would likely come home to a full house.

The drive back takes longer than usual, probably because I'm going five under. I use the time to mentally and emotionally prepare for the night.

Maybe Jared listened and planned a movie night? That thought disintegrates as I pull up to the house. Cars line the driveway, spilling onto the street. Not very sneaky of them. At least they left my spot open. I park behind Jared and make a mental note that Noah's truck is parked up by the house. He's here somewhere, and for some reason, that eases my nerves.

Stepping up to the front door, I take a deep breath and turn the handle. Swinging it open, I barely have time to step into the room before Jared pops out in front of me.

"Surprise!"

I take in the crowd in the room. Most of the people are acquaintances at best. Thankfully, I don't see Jake.

Right then, I see Maddie emerge from the sea of people, a smile growing on my lips. We've been able to hang out a couple of times since my first pottery class, and we're practically best friends now. It's refreshing having a girl best friend. I love Jared, but there are some things that he doesn't get.

"Happy birthday, girly!"

"Thank you," I say with a laugh as she pulls me into a hug.

"Come on, let's go get you something to drink."

She leads me into the kitchen. Stopping at the counter, I scan the room for Noah before I catch myself. Why would he be hanging out with teenagers? He's probably upstairs. Why am I even looking for him to begin with?

"What does the birthday girl want?" she asks me, breaking me out of my thoughts.

"Surprise me, but make it strong. I'm going to need it to handle this much socializing," I chuckle.

She begins pouring what seems like too many different liquids into the cup.

"Don't look! It's supposed to be a surprise!"

I avert my gaze, instead favoring the slider. The sun is getting ready to set over the water, and it makes me want to go sit on the dock. I feel eyes on me, and I know before I see him that he's there, out on the porch.

"Damn, who is that?" Maddie asks, handing me my drink.

"That's Noah. He's Jared's dad."

"I know I'm not into men, but that is one *fine* man."

I laugh at that, turning back to her.

"I'll be right back."

Her expression turns suggestive, but she nods, waving me away.

Pulling the slider open, I step out onto the porch. The party hasn't yet made its way out here, so it's quiet as I approach Noah.

"What are you doing out here?"

He looks up at me, the warm light highlighting his features. His dark hair is messy as he runs a hand through it. God, he makes it so hard not to want him.

"Just making sure you're alright before I head upstairs."

"Thank you, but I'm fine, Noah. I can handle myself."

He lets out a forced laugh, "So you've said."

Glaring at him, I step between his spread legs, my thighs brushing his. The roughness of the denim shocks my skin. Maybe it's the confidence from the drink, but I lean down to whisper in his ear.

"Trust me, I can handle myself. Can you?"

His eyes darken, and the restraint there is evident. Good. I stand up, turning away toward the door.

"I'll be upstairs if you need me," he growls.

I don't turn around. Instead, I open the slider and step inside. Maddie meets me at the door, a confused look on her face.

"What was that about?" she asks.

"Oh…nothing."

Her eyes narrow, and a smirk appears on her face.

"Mmm, sure, nothing," she responds.

We spend the next couple of hours wandering around the party, socializing. The music is loud, and the people are louder. I'm surprised Noah is putting up with it.

Maddie doesn't bring him up again, but I can tell she senses something is up. I look up to see her making her way back over from the bathroom.

"I hate to do this, but I have to get going. I've got tons of homework that I need to do," she says.

"That's completely fine, I understand. Thank you for coming."

"Oh, and about that DILF upstairs–"

"Maddie, it was nothing," I interrupt.

"Just know you can talk to me, okay?"

"Okay."

She grabs her bag and heads for the door. I trust her and know she wouldn't say anything, but it still makes me nervous that she can tell something is going on. If Jared ever found out, he would never talk to me again. I need to be more careful.

Looking around the room, I suddenly have no desire to hang out with any of these people. Jared is off, god knows where, and I don't have the energy to find him. I take my chance to sneak upstairs to my bedroom. Maybe no one will notice that I'm gone.

Stepping into my room, I close the door softly behind me, muffling the sounds of the crowd downstairs. I grab my book off my dresser and climb into bed, the plush comforter surrounding me. This is what I wanted to do for my birthday: to lose myself in a fictional world where, for a moment, I can pretend this one doesn't exist.

I'm interrupted by a knock on my door.

There goes my peace and quiet.

"Who is it?" I ask.

"Noah," a gruff voice responds.

What is he doing at my door so late?

"Come in," I tell him.

He does, shutting the door behind him and locking it. Before I can analyze the action further, I notice the shiny gold gift bag that he's holding in his hands, and butterflies gather in my chest.

"I have something for you."

"Noah, you didn't have to do that," I say, standing up to meet him. I'm reminded of his sheer size as my head barely reaches his shoulders.

"I wanted to. Happy birthday," he says, handing me the bag.

It's heavier than I expected, so I set it beside me on my desk. Hesitating for a moment, I look up to him, but he nods, letting me know I can open it. I gently pull the gold and white tissue paper out of the top and glance into the bag, but I can't believe what I see.

They're books.

One by one, I pull them out and begin to realize that they are all the romance books I looked at when we went shopping together. He was paying attention. What am I saying? Of course, he was. He's always paying attention.

This is the most thoughtful gift I think I've ever received. My cheeks heat when I see the one at the bottom of the bag.

It's the dad's best friend romance.

My eyes shoot up to his, and he grins. I pull it out of the bag and hold it up to him.

"Are you trying to tell me something?"

"I saw you writing down the title. Plus, it seems right up your alley," he says, his voice rougher than before. He's close now, so close I can feel the warmth radiating from him.

"This is the perfect gift. Thank you, Noah," I say, pulling him into a hug. It takes a moment, but I feel his arms wrap around me, the sensation causing my heart to jump. His smell invades my senses, warm and masculine.

"You deserve it," he murmurs, his fingers lazily threading through my hair before trailing down to my jaw. With a gentle but insistent touch, he tilts my face up to his.

His eyes burn into mine—intense, restrained. But beneath the surface, I see it. The hunger. The need.

Then his mouth crashes into mine, his thumb sweeping over my cheekbone as he kisses me—deep, slow, intoxicating. His lips are warm, demanding yet tender, and the way he holds me makes my head spin. His other hand slides to my waist, pulling me flush against him. The heat of his body, the hard planes of his chest pressing into me, send a shiver down my spine.

I could stay like this forever.

His touch is both careful and possessive, as if he's afraid I'll disappear if he lets go. My fingers roam over him, slipping under his shirt, tracing the firm lines of his stomach. His muscles tense beneath my touch, and just as I start to push further, he breaks the kiss, gripping my jaw.

His gaze is dark, his calloused thumb pressing against my swollen bottom lip.

"What do you think you're doing?" he asks, not releasing me.

Without thinking, I answer, "Getting what I want."

He shakes his head, "That's not happening, princess, not with Jared downstairs."

"But it's my birthday," I pout.

chapter fifteen
KIRA

His eyes harden, and he hesitates a moment. Is he going to stop this? I get my answer as his rough hands grip my thighs, picking me up, my legs wrapping around him. He drops me onto the bed, leaning over me, his dark hair falling into his face.

"I shouldn't be doing this. You're way too innocent for the things I want to do to you," he says, his knee nudging my legs apart. God, seeing him like this is addicting.

"Trust me, I'm not."

He tenses at that.

"What does that mean?" he asks, possessiveness clear in his tone.

"It just means those books you bought me are dirtier than you think."

He eyes me, a hint of curiosity in his features.

I reach my hand up, feeling him through his jeans. He's thick and hard, and fuck, I want him inside me. A grunt escapes his lips as he grabs my wrists and pins them above my head.

"Not so fast."

His lips find mine again, and he kisses me, more intense this time. I pull his bottom lip between my teeth as his hand trails over my body, down to my hips. His hand leisurely traces up my inner thigh, his fingers brushing the edge of my panties. Anticipation floods me as I arch into him.

"Is this what you want?" he growls.

I quickly nod, not wanting him to stop.

"You have to be quiet. I don't want anyone to hear how you sound when you come for me. Especially not Jared."

My mind quickly goes to my best friend. He would hate me forever if he knew what we're doing right now, but I can't seem to care enough to stop. I want this more than anything.

"Kira," Noah says, waiting for my response.

"I'll be quiet, I promise," I tell him. I need him to touch me. I need to touch him.

He stands up, peeling his shirt over his head. His jeans hang low on his waist, and his defined muscles draw my attention lower.

"Look at me, princess," he says, and I listen. He's gazing down at me with hooded eyes. I can only imagine how I look, cheeks flushed, dress riding up, my hair a mess. "If you want to stop, we stop. Do you hear me?"

I nod, needing his touch.

"Use your words."

"Yes," I say, my voice desperate.

"Good girl," he says, his voice low as he moves toward me.

His hands drop to my knees, sliding up my thighs to push my dress up even more.

"Take this off," he demands.

I do as he says, leaving me in only my black lace bra and panties. The bra is sheer, and I thank my past self for choosing this set. Pushing my legs open, he presses his lips to the inside of my thigh, and I suck in a breath.

His eyes meet mine, a silent request for permission. God, seeing him like this is probably the most salacious thing I have ever seen. I give him a small nod, letting him know I'm okay. His hand slides up my other leg to cover my pussy, his thumb brushing over my clit through my panties. My hips rise off of the bed, a small moan escaping my lips.

"Shhh, princess," he says, repeating the movement. I push into him, needing more friction.

His fingers continue their exploration as he licks and nips up my thigh, each kiss an explosion of sensation. I lace my fingers in his hair, arching into him as he pulls my panties to the side, and his fingers glide over my slick, aching pussy.

"Fuck, baby, you're already soaked for me."

My heart flutters at that, but before I can respond, his mouth is on me, his tongue expertly navigating my clit. I grip his hair tighter, trying to be quiet, but fuck, he knows what he's doing.

"Oh my god, Noah," I moan.

I know he told me to be quiet, but the music downstairs is loud. No one is going to hear us. Still, he pauses, looking up at me. I get the message, covering my mouth with my other hand. He nods before pulling me tighter to him, his hand trailing up my thigh.

"You're doing so good for me, princess," he says, his voice deep, the vibration of it traveling through me.

His fingers play with my pussy, as he kisses up my body, stopping at my breasts. He sucks in my nipple through the sheer fabric of the bra, biting lightly as his fingers push into me. I gasp, and he looks up at me, satisfaction clear in his eyes.

I pull him to me, kissing him slow and deep, his fingers keeping a torturous rhythm. I'm practically panting when he moves back down between my legs, his mouth devouring me. I can feel the tension coiling in my core, white-hot. I'm close, and he knows it.

"Eyes on me. I want to see your face when you come for me," he orders.

With his thumb on my clit and his fingers deep inside me, my orgasm crashes over me. Despite my best efforts, I let out a moan, and Noah's hand shoots up to cover my mouth. He's still pumping into me, and it feels too fucking good.

When he finally pulls his fingers out of me, his eyes are filled with desire. He brushes my hair away from my neck as his lips graze my skin before reaching my ear.

"To answer your question from earlier," he whispers, "I can handle myself everywhere but with you, princess."

I try to form a sentence, but I can't seem to find any of the words. I've wanted this from him for years, and it was better than I could have imagined.

I sit up on my hands and knees, crawling toward where he stands at the end of the bed. I need to feel him, touch him. I want to make him feel as good as he made me. I reach my hand up, feeling his bare chest. His body is beautiful. He sucks in a breath, eyeing me. I trail my hands down his torso toward his jeans.

But before I can do anything, his hand grabs my wrist. He looks down at me, shaking his head.

"Not tonight. Not with Jared right downstairs," he says, his voice low.

I look up at him, nodding slowly. A wave of guilt overwhelms me.

What did we just do?

Noah Keller, *Jared's dad,* just gave me the best orgasm of my life but won't let me reciprocate because I'm best friends with his son. This situation is so fucked up. I don't know if Jared could ever forgive me if he found out, but I want the man standing in front of me more than I've wanted anything else in my life.

As if sensing the turmoil swirling in me, Noah gently tugs me into him, his fingers threading into my hair. He holds me there, not saying a word, his heartbeat steady and grounding against me. He's not rushing this, not treating it like a mistake. He's here with me, in this quiet space between us, and I don't want to let go.

Time seems to slow as his fingers trace small, soothing patterns on my bare back. The warmth of his body against mine is like a balm, easing the ache in my chest. For a brief moment, it feels like we could stay like this forever.

But then, he pulls away. My heart lurches in my chest, the familiar sting of disappointment settling deep in my stomach. Is this really how it ends?

Before my thoughts can spiral, he slides open my dresser drawer and pulls out a pajama shirt. He holds it out to me, pressing a soft, lingering kiss to my forehead. His eyes linger on me for a moment longer, as if trying to say everything he's feeling without words.

"Goodnight, Kira." With that, he leaves the room, closing my door softly behind him.

THE NEXT MORNING, I PULL UP TO LAKESIDE POTTERY, THE SUN just now breaking the horizon. Noah wasn't up yet when I left, and I've decided I won't think about him today. Not the way he looked at me last night or what it could mean. I don't need that distraction right now.

Today is the second pottery class *that I'm teaching*. That's still a crazy thought to me. Ceramics have been such an essential part of my life for the past four years, and being able to give that joy to others is indescribable.

It doesn't take me long to get set up. I'm alone as Darla won't be in until ten, but thankfully, we're only trimming today. Once I'm content with the supplies, I go to find the reason I got here so early.

Walking into the kiln room, I see it on the second shelf, reaching out for me. I grab the hand, pulling it down to examine it closer. I'm so proud of the detail that I put into it. The hand is outstretched, the tendons in its wrist visible, its palm filled with minuscule creases. Now, it's time to create what it's holding. I bring the half-finished piece back with me to my workstation. Placing it on the metal table, I stare at it. It could be holding anything.

A snake?

Sounds cool, but no.

A book?

I like that idea, but it still doesn't seem quite right. My brain runs circles around the topic, not latching on to any one object.

My thoughts are interrupted by a chirping from the other side of the window. The studio is silent otherwise, so it draws my attention. I glance up at the tree outside, not seeing the source. The song continues, and my eyes finally land on a small yellow and black bird.

I know what I want the hand to hold.

Before the class is over, everyone gets their pieces trimmed and ready for their first firing. After most of the students have left, Maddie steps up to my station, her eyes bright.

"You up for some lunch?" she asks.

I'd be lying if I said part of me wasn't excited to go home and see Noah, but I feel like last night changed things. I don't think I'm ready to face the rejection I know is waiting for me.

"You know what? Sure. Want to get pizza at that place down the street?"

"That place down the street" is the best pizza place in the Bay Area. I've been going there with Jared and Noah for what feels like forever. Their wood-fired pepperoni pizza is to die for.

Maddie looks over at me, mischief in her eyes. "Perfect. We've got plenty to discuss."

I tilt my head in confusion, and then it hits me. She's talking about Noah. There's no way she knows what happened last night, but I can't shake the feeling that she knows *something*.

It's tourist season, so when we get to the restaurant, it's busy. There are people filling all of the tables. Thankfully, we don't have to wait long before we are seated at a two-person table on the rooftop. The view from up here never gets old. In front of me, the bay is visible in all of its glory.

"Okay, spill," Maddie says, a childish grin covering her face as our waitress brings us our drinks.

"Spill what?" I feign ignorance. I know what she's getting at. She saw the way Noah was looking at me last night.

"Hmmm, I don't know, what was it?" She raises an eyebrow as if in deep thought, "Oh, yeah. Maybe how you want to fuck your *other* best friend's dad and how he wants to fuck you too?"

I choke on my water. There's no malice in her tone, and I know she would never judge me, but I still don't know how to respond. There's no point in denying it. She'll see right through it.

"Oh, that."

She nods at me, waiting for me to elaborate.

"Fine. I've always had a crush on him but never thought it would go anywhere."

"Until…?"

"We kissed. It was the night I ran into Zach, and I told Noah everything. He made me feel so safe, Maddie. I know I shouldn't be doing this. I know it's a bad idea, and it's bound to hurt Jared, but—"

"Woah, slow down, it's okay." She takes my hand in hers from across the table. "You know that I would never think less of you for something like this. Besides, I'm all for it. He's like, Greek god-level hot, and I don't even like men."

I let out a breath, relaxing my shoulders.

"There's more…"

"Do tell."

"Last night…We may have kissed again, and he may have eaten me out."

A shriek erupts from Maddie's mouth.

"Shhh," I say, raising my finger to my lips.

"Sorry, just, wow. Lucky you!" she says with a giggle.

I let myself smile with her.

"Listen, girl, I support you in doing whatever makes you happy. If and when Jared finds out, it will hurt him, but it will only be temporary. I know he'll forgive you."

I nod, letting her words sink in. It doesn't make me feel much better, but it is the reminder I need.

We leave the topic there, and our discussion moves toward the girl she's been talking to.

"Her name is Lucy. She's the one I was telling you about that day you canceled on me," she teases, but the knowing look on her face tells me she isn't serious.

She knows now what happened that day. And what happened when I was fifteen.

"Are you two a thing, then?" I ask, wiggling my eyebrows.

"Kind of?" It comes out as more of a question than a statement, and I'm instantly hesitant.

"What do you mean, kind of?"

Anyone who is lucky enough to have Maddie would be crazy not to immediately lock her down.

"We haven't put a label on it yet, but we spend all of our free time together," she explains.

I roll my eyes, and she senses the suspicion there.

"It's not like that, I promise."

"As long as you're happy," I tell her, glad she has someone.

Before we know it, it's been two hours, and the waitress has asked us if we needed anything else about four times, so we decide it's time to go.

As we're heading to our cars, Maddie looks over at me, her smile fading.

"Just be careful, Kira. I don't want you getting hurt."

Her eyes are genuine, and I know she cares.

"Same to you," I tell her.

No one is in the living room when I walk into the house. I saw both of their cars in the driveway, though, so I know they're home. The open sliding door tells me they are most likely on the back porch. Grabbing a glass from the cupboard, I open the fridge and pour myself some of the strawberry lemonade I made again the other day.

I step out onto the deck and feel the sun warm my skin as the smell of the water washes over me. My eyes find Noah immediately.

He's shirtless, cleaning out the flower bed next to the house. Maddie wasn't lying about the Greek god comparison. His muscles ripple with his movements, and tattoos only enhance the effect. A thin layer of sweat glistens on his skin as he looks up at me, our eyes locking for a moment before he drops his gaze back to the flower bed.

Arms wrap around me, hoisting me into the air. I instantly recognize them as Jared's.

"Ew, you're all sweaty. Put me down!" I squeal.

He laughs, doing as I ask and turning me around to face him. His white muscle shirt is covered in dirt and grass stains with a distinct rim of sweat around the collar. He must have been helping Noah with the yard work.

"I have something for you," he says, the sunlight reflecting in his emerald eyes. "For your birthday. Let me go get it."

He runs through the slider into the house, and I take the chance to look back at Noah, but his gaze is already fixed on me. His eyes are filled with a mixture of emotions that I can't quite identify. This is it. This is when he's going to tell me that last night was a mistake.

"Here it is!" Jared exclaims as he runs up next to me.

Noah nods toward Jared, and I reluctantly turn to face him. In his hands, he is holding a small gift box with a little green bow. Placing it in my hands, he gestures for me to open it. I untie the bow and open the hinged box, letting out a loud gasp. It's a gold necklace with my name in a scripted font. It's gorgeous.

"Thank you so much, Jared, it's amazing!"

A smile spreads across his face as he looks down at me, his eyes lingering on mine for a beat.

"Want me to put it on for you?" he asks, his voice lower now.

I nod, handing it to him and turning around. Why does it feel like something just shifted? My eyes meet Noah's as Jared's hands brush up my neck, clasping the closure.

"I tried to give it to you last night, but I couldn't find you anywhere," he explains, hurt woven into his words.

My body tenses, a pang of guilt hitting me as images of the night before play in my mind.

Noah focuses on the necklace, his eyes hardening before meeting mine again.

"All done," Jared almost whispers, yanking my attention back to him. I turn back to face him, but at the edges of my vision, I watch Noah put down his tools and disappear into the house.

chapter sixteen
NOAH

I am not jealous of my own goddamn son. I mean, what was he supposed to do, not buy her a gift?

But watching him with her, the way he looks at her. The way she lets him touch her. It makes me want to crawl out of my skin. I don't believe for a second that he doesn't want her as much as I do. He was trying to find her that night, during the party he threw for her, but he couldn't because she was upstairs.

With me.

That was not supposed to happen, but it's all I've been able to think about. The way she responded to my touch, the way she begged me, her fucking taste on my tongue. It's seared into my memory. We haven't spoken much since that night, and at this point, I'm not sure who's avoiding who.

A beeping sound signals that the zucchini bread is ready. Refocusing my thoughts on the task at hand, I pull the bread out of the oven and place it on the hot pad on the counter. The smell of sugar and cinnamon fills the room. Today is Al's retirement party, and he's a huge fan of zucchini bread, so I decided that was a better option than store-bought cake.

Soft footsteps come from the wooden stairs, drawing my eyes to the source. I sense it's her before I even see her. She's barefoot in a pair of denim shorts and a cropped t-shirt, her honey-brown hair in two braids that fall over her shoulders. Her face hardens when her eyes meet mine, but I pretend I don't notice.

"Mornin'. Sleep good?"

I'm asking because I genuinely want to know. She hasn't been having as many nightmares lately, but every once in a while, she wakes up in a panic.

She ignores me, stepping past me to grab a yogurt from the fridge.

"Listen, Kira, I–"

"Just don't. I already know what you're going to say, and I really don't care to hear it," she says, turning away from me.

"And what is it that you think I'm going to say?"

She looks around, probably making sure Jared isn't within earshot, before taking a step toward me.

"You're going to tell me that the other night was a mistake. You're going to tell me that you regret it, and it won't happen again," she answers, her voice low. "Was that close?"

"Kira..." I trail off. I want to tell her that's not the case. I want to tell her that If I could, I would take her upstairs right now and prove it to her, but I know better. We can't do this. It's not fair to Jared or Kira. She deserves far better than me. She needs someone her own age, like Jared.

The way her expression shifts from anger to disappointment crushes me, but it's better this way. I would rather have her think I don't want her than fuck up her life even more than I already have. She doesn't want this, not really.

"You're an asshole," she sighs, grabbing her keys off the counter and heading for the door.

I let her go.

All the guys are there when I get to the fire station. Half of them are on shift. The other half are here for Al's party. He'll still be here for the next month or so, but we wanted to celebrate the occasion as soon as he announced the date. He has been planning this retirement for a while, so it isn't a surprise, but it's still surreal. He's been the fire commissioner since before I became a firefighter. It's hard to imagine what this place would look like without him.

Dave decorates the kitchen with numerous tablecloths, balloons, and a "Happy Retirement" banner. His theme seems to be black and gold.

"Looks good!" I announce, placing the zucchini bread on the counter.

"Thank you, we're about ready. Does someone want to go find him?" Dave asks.

"I will," Jeff answers.

I chuckle, shaking my head at them.

Somehow, we manage to get all the guys into the kitchen before Jeff comes back with Al, and we are all waiting there when they come through the door.

"Surprise!" everyone yells.

The shock is barely noticeable on Al's face, but it's there, and his lips turn up in a small smile.

"Happy retirement, old man," I tell him.

He laughs, thanking me.

"Is that what I think it is?" Al asks, nodding toward the zucchini bread.

"Of course, what else would it be?"

We spend over an hour eating and reminiscing on the memories we've all made here before we're interrupted by a call. Some guys head out to respond, and Jeff and Dave start cleaning up.

"Can I talk to you for a minute?" Al asks me.

"Of course," I say, following him out of the room.

Al steps into his large office, gesturing for me to close the door. Papers cover his desk but in somewhat organized piles.

"Listen, boy," he says, sitting in his chair. "Before I leave, I need to know that this place will be in good hands. I need to know that the person who takes my position will prioritize all these guy's safety above all else."

I nod, not entirely sure where he's going with all of this. Of course, that's what he would want in a new commissioner, but why is he talking to me about it?

"I think that person is you."

I shake my head, a laugh escaping my lips.

"Thanks, Al. I'm flattered that you think I could do that, but you and I both know there has to be someone better for the position than me."

"Don't be an idiot. You're perfect for it. I know you still beat yourself up over what happened a couple of years ago, but that wasn't your fault. You deserve this position, and you deserve to let yourself be happy."

"But—"

"At least think about it. There isn't anyone else who would be better at this position than you."

"I will *think* about it, but I still don't think I'm the best fit."

"Well, I *know* you are."

Al stands up, disappearing out the door and leaving me to sit in my thoughts. There's no way I can be the next commissioner. Al is the glue that keeps us all together, and I don't know if I'm capable of that.

Heading back into the kitchen, I check to see if they need any help cleaning up, but everything is back in its place, and Jeff is wiping down the counters.

"So, you the new boss yet?" Dave asks, teasing me as he pushes the chairs back into the table.

"No, why would you think that?"

"Whatever you say, commissioner."

I roll my eyes, grab the empty plate that used to hold the zucchini bread, and head for the door.

The next morning, I wake up to music playing from somewhere downstairs. Kira. Part of me regrets not correcting her yesterday. The other night shouldn't have happened, but it wasn't a mistake either. I wanted that. I want her.

I run through my mental checklist for the day. We always have a big party for the fourth of July. This year is no exception. Thankfully, all the yard work is done, the lawn freshly mowed, and the garden beds cleaned up, so there isn't much I have to do other than prep the food. Throwing on a pair of sweatpants, I head downstairs.

She must not hear me enter the room. She's facing the counter with her back to me, her hair in a messy knot, tendrils of it falling onto her shoulders. The sun shines through the slider behind us, illuminating her body. She's cutting up some pineapple, swaying to the music in one of her oversized t-shirts that barely covers her ass.

Wait a minute…is that *my* t-shirt?

I step toward her, trying to get a closer look. I recognize the old, worn Chevy logo.

That is my shirt.

As if sensing me behind her, she spins around to face me, the fear in her eyes quickly fading to relief, then irritation.

"What do you want, Noah?"

"Well, coffee for one," I tell her, moving around her to take my new favorite mug from the cupboard. "Oh, and breakfast," I say, taking a piece of pineapple.

"Stop it, this is for later," she scolds, swatting my hand away.

I laugh and can't help but steal another piece, and she glares at me. If looks could kill, I would be a dead man.

"Maybe listen to the person holding the knife," she says, waving the blade in the air.

"Fine, fine. Thank you for doing that, by the way. You didn't have to." She really didn't. Jared never helps with this kind of stuff anymore, so I'm used to doing it alone.

"It needed to be done, plus I was hungry too," she says, popping a piece between her lips.

God, that mouth of hers. I glance down at *my shirt* that she's wearing, her sleep shorts barely visible under it. Did she sleep in it? My gaze follows the curve of her breasts, telling me that she isn't wearing anything underneath. I can't help but imagine bending her over the counter, showing her exactly what she does to me.

Fuck. I close my eyes and rub my hand over my face.

Kira goes right back to slicing the fruit, throwing it all into a bowl for later. This woman is going to be the death of me. Letting out a breath, I pour coffee into my mug and grab the creamer from the fridge.

"Nice shirt, where'd you get it?"

She looks down at what she's wearing, then back up at me, her cheeks flushed. I nod, leaning down to whisper in her ear.

"Careful, princess, you wouldn't want Jared to see you in that," I say, my eyes meeting hers.

"Want me to take it off then?" she asks, her hands moving to the hem.

I haven't wanted anything more in my life.

"Just change into something else before the party."

I turn and head for the garage. I need to get out of this kitchen before I do something I shouldn't.

I'M STILL IN THE GARAGE WHEN KEITH SHOWS UP LATER WITH A BAG of fireworks and a cooler dragging behind him.

"I got the booze and the explosives!"

I let out a laugh, slamming down the hood on the Nova. I take the cooler from him, helping him bring it around the house to the porch. It's probably around four now, and everyone should be showing up soon, so I should probably put on a shirt.

"I'll be right back. I'm gonna go change."

"Alrighty, I'll be here with a beer."

Running up the stairs, I throw on a pair of shorts and a T-shirt. By the time I get back outside, Kira is sitting with Keith on the back porch, *still wearing my shirt*, except now It's tucked into the front of her fitted denim shorts, the strings of her green bathing suit poking out from the top. She notices my eyes trailing over her body, a smirk on her face. She knows what she's doing to me.

"McDreamy, Keith here was just telling me how you used to be quite the party animal. I wonder when that changed."

"Keith," I sigh.

Kira lets out a laugh.

"I've got to go finish the lemonade, but I'd love to hear more about Fun-Noah later," she says, standing and swiping a beer out of the cooler.

"Drop it," I demand.

She groans, opening the cooler and setting the bottle back inside before heading into the house.

I take her spot in one of the wooden chairs facing the porch swing. Memories of that first night play in my mind. Her in that fucking dress. The feel of her body on mine. It felt so right, but then Jared came home, and it reminded me why we can't do that.

"Wasn't that your shirt?" Keith asks beside me.

"Yup."

I have half a mind to go inside and tell her to take it off, but part of me likes seeing her in it.

chapter seventeen
KIRA

I step through the slider, satisfaction coursing through my veins. I took this shirt two nights ago when Noah was on shift at the station. I woke up from a pretty bad nightmare, and I was so used to him climbing into my bed and holding me, but he wasn't there, and I couldn't fall back asleep. So, I wandered into his room, and it was lying there on his bed. It smelled like him, that deliciously warm, earthy scent, so I took it.

I didn't mean to wear it downstairs, and when he saw me, I was half expecting him to ask for it back, but he didn't. Whether or not he regrets the other night, he likes seeing me in it. I won't lie. It hurts the way he's been avoiding me since my birthday. I know I shouldn't have pushed him, but he wanted it too, didn't he?

"Hey, girly!" I hear from behind me.

I turn to see Maddie coming in through the slider. Pulling the wooden spoon out of the pitcher, I set it down and wrap my arms around her.

"I'm so glad you could make it."

"It better be worth it. I'm missing out on the opportunity to be drunk on a boat in Lake Michigan," she says with a giggle.

"It's worth it because you're with me, right?"

She laughs, nodding at me.

I place the lid on the pitcher, setting it aside before searching the freezer for the popsicles I bought the other day. Digging through the pack, I grab a blue one, my favorite.

"Want one?" I say, gesturing to Maddie.

"Pink, please!"

Jared must have already picked through them because only one pink is left. I grab it and hand it to her.

"So, how's it going with your sexy firefighter?" she asks way too loudly.

"Maddie!" I whisper yell.

"What? C'mon, give me something."

"We haven't really talked since my birthday."

She looks at me, her eyes narrowing, "That asshole."

"Leave it alone, Maddie," I tell her. "What about Lucy? Are you two a true couple yet?"

Her cheeks flush as she looks at me, and all she gives me is a small nod.

"Really?" I gasp.

"Yeah, she's *officially* my girlfriend now," she says, excitement bubbling in her eyes. "I asked her last night."

"Oh my god, Maddie, I'm so happy for you," I say as I guide us out of the slider.

There's already a ton of people here, but the anxiety that usually manifests is nowhere to be found. Noah is standing at the grill with Keith, a beer in his hand. They seem to be in a deep conversation about the best way to grill a burger, and I can't help but watch as his muscled arm reaches out, flipping them with ease.

His eyes catch mine before they move down to my shirt—well, his shirt—and his jaw ticks. My body heats at his gaze, but I force myself to look away, turning back toward Maddie.

"God, I want someone to look at me the way he's looking at you right now," Maddie says.

I roll my eyes, shaking my head. "He's just making sure I don't sneak something to drink," I tell her, not entirely believing myself.

"Speaking of..." I look out into the yard.

Jared and some of his friends are standing in a circle, plastic cups in hand. Jared's eyes meet mine, and he gestures for Maddie and me to join them. Grabbing her hand, I pull her with me to the group.

"You guys want to play a round of cornhole?" Jared asks, "You and Maddie versus me and Brennan."

I look up as Brennan approaches. Only a little taller than Jared, he's objectively beautiful. He was the one who was flirting with me at the bar the night that Noah refused to let me leave with them. I glance back at

Noah, his gaze laser-focused on Brennan. I think someone's jealous.

"If you go get me a drink, then yeah. Come on, Brennan. You can stand on my side," I say with a sweet smile.

Jared's jaw visibly tightens as he glances between Brennan and me. What is that about?

"What kind of drink?" he asks, pulling me out of my thoughts.

"Surprise me."

Jared returns with a plastic cup filled with a fruity yet strong liquid, and I grin at him.

"Thank you," I say. "Now, are you guys ready to lose?"

Jared chuckles, seemingly back to normal, "You're on."

Brennan and I head to stand by the board closest to the hammock, which just so happens to be closer to the grill. Noah's eyes are trained on me, a scowl on his face. This is going to be so much fun.

"You can start!" Jared exclaims from the other side of the yard, tossing the bags to us. I roll my eyes, bending over to pick them up off the ground and set them on the board. I can feel eyes on me as I stand up and notice Brennan's gaze gliding up my body.

"You go first," I say, only loud enough for Brennan to hear.

"Don't mind if I do."

His first throw misses, landing at Maddie's feet, and I let out a small laugh. He looks over at me, an eyebrow raised in a challenge. His next two land on the board, although one just barely. As he goes to throw the last bag, I take a sip of my drink, and I watch it go right through the hole at the top of the board. I hear Jared cheer, but I'm distracted as Brennan's hand comes up to my waist.

"You think you can beat that?" he asks, his brown eyes not leaving mine.

My body responds, anxiety filling my chest, but when I look up at him, I don't see any danger there. He isn't going to hurt me, at least not right now. I take a deep breath and plaster on a smile.

"Yes," I answer, taking another sip of my drink before grabbing a bean bag. His hand drops from my hip, and I take a second to look over to the porch. Noah is gone. Keith is manning the grill without him. I glance over the crowd of people on the porch, and that's when I see him. He's leaning against the stairs with his arms crossed and his focus locked onto me. He looks pissed.

Good.

I turn back toward the game and study the board on the other side of the lawn. All I need to do is get more than five, but I'm in the mood to show off a little. Stepping up to the board, I throw the bag with a perfect arc, and it slides into the hole, knocking one of their bags off in the process. I look up at Brennan with an innocent smile.

"I must have just gotten lucky," I tell him, and he laughs.

"Of course, you're good at this."

The rest of the game goes similarly, and Maddie and I secure the win in what feels like record time, finishing as the sun starts to dip below the horizon.

"Alright, I'm not subjecting myself to that again. Let's go swim." Jared says.

Finishing my drink, I wave it at Jared, and he laughs.

"I'll be right back," he says, grabbing my cup.

I'm already feeling a light buzz from the first drink, but hey, it's a party. I see Keith untethering Noah's pontoon boat as we approach the dock.

"Where are you going?" I ask.

"To go blow some shit up," he responds with a grin.

"Alrighty then, well, have fun!" I call as he starts the boat and drives away.

Pulling off Noah's shirt, I fold it and set it on the dock, my shorts following. Brennan's eyes scan my green bikini as he removes his shirt, exposing his toned torso. This is the kind of guy I should be into. He's not bad to look at and *my age.*

Maddie seems to notice his perusal, glancing at me with a questioning look. I shrug, shaking my head. Without warning, Brennan takes off running and jumps into the water at the end of the dock, splashing us. I yelp, looking down at him, my head tilting in mock annoyance.

"You getting in?" he asks, pushing his wet hair out of his face.

"Let me just get used to it first," I say, sitting on the dock and dipping my feet into the water.

"Suit yourself," Maddie says, jumping into the water beside Brennan.

"Maddie!" I yell as she reemerges at the surface.

A deep laugh comes from behind us as Jared walks up with my drink and a couple of towels. Setting them down on the dock, he takes his shirt off before jumping in the water, too. Brennan swims up to my legs, his hands gripping the wood on either side of me.

"It's not even that cold, come on," Brennan whines, his hand sliding onto my thigh. I suck in a breath as the cold from his hand hits my warm skin, and my heart skips. I wish I could say it is from excitement, but the weight of anxiety crushes my chest.

A throat clears from behind me, and Brennan's eyes move up to the source of the sound. Before I even turn around, I know who it is.

"It's time for fireworks," Noah says.

Turning to look at him, I notice his gaze is fixed on Brennan's hand on my thigh.

"We'll just watch them from here," I tell him.

His jaw tightens as he looks at me. "Could you actually come help me with something, Kira?"

What could he even need help with?

"Now."

Sighing, I look down at Brennan.

"Sorry guys, I'll be right back," I say, pulling my legs out of the water and standing to look at Noah, anger rolling off him in waves. Without a word, he turns, walking toward the house. I have to almost run to keep up with him as we pass everyone in their lawn chairs chatting.

As we make it to the door, he opens it, gesturing for me to go inside. No one else is in here. They're all outside, getting ready to watch the fireworks. The glass door slides shut as Noah spins around to face me.

"What was that all about?" he asks, his voice low.

"What do you mean? Did I do something wrong?" I ask, knowing damn well what I was doing.

"That kid. Why were you letting him touch you?"

Irritation bubbles up in my core at his question. I knew he was jealous, but the fact that he thinks he has any claim over me is ridiculous.

"Why do you even care? You've proven you don't want me or at least won't let yourself have me, so what's the problem with me getting that pleasure from someone else?"

"Oh, I highly doubt he would be providing much pleasure," he says with a low chuckle. His eyes darken as he steps closer to me, leaning down so our faces are only inches apart.

"You've been parading around in my shirt all day in front of everyone, and then you have the audacity to let some other guy touch you," he growls.

I shudder at his statement, and the closeness of our bodies threatens to break my resolve. Behind Noah, blue sparkles paint the nearly black sky, followed by a loud bang. Keith started the fireworks.

"I'm not yours, Noah. You don't get to tell me who I can and can't fuck."

I try to keep my voice from shaking from the pure need coursing through me now. He's so close, and I'm all too aware of the few places our bodies are touching. His hand slides up my torso to my jaw, forcing me to look at him instead of the show outside.

"Are you sure about that, princess? Because I seem to remember my mouth on you just the other day."

His fingers are toying with my swimsuit bottoms, threatening to untie the strings. My breathing is ragged from need, and all I can think about is kissing him.

The sound of the sliding door breaks us from our spell. Noah takes a huge step back as I try my best to sort myself out. The light flicks on, and Jared stands in the doorway. He glances at his dad and then back to me.

"Whatever you need help with can wait. Come on, Kira, the fireworks already started!" he exclaims as he runs over to grab my hand. I follow him out, glancing back at Noah. His eyes are full of promise. This conversation isn't over.

I sit on the dock to watch the fireworks with Jared, Maddie, and Brennan. Maddie turns to look at me, a silent question in her gaze.

Are you okay?

What happened?

I nod to her, and that pacifies her for the moment. Brennan slides over to sit beside me, his hand resting on the dock on the other side of my hip. I can feel Noah's eyes burning into my back.

I turn to face him, the light from the fireworks illuminating his face. I can tell it's taking everything in him not to kick Brennan into the water. The explosions increase in frequency, signaling the grand finale. It's jaw-dropping. Keith really knows what he's doing. When the sky returns to its natural darkness, everyone claps and cheers, and I hear an engine sputter to life on the water.

"Jared and I are going to Jake's after this. Do you want to come with?"

A voice from behind me sounds before I can respond.

"No, sorry, she already promised she'd help clean up."

I turn to face him, and his body language says it all. He hands me something, and it takes me a second to realize what it is. It's his shirt. The same one I was wearing earlier.

"Really, Dad? You can't clean up on your own?"

"It's fine, I promised," I tell Jared. Even though I did no such thing. To be honest, going to that party with them is the last thing I want to do tonight.

After some more grumbling, the boys finally leave. Maddie glances between us and mumbles something about having to get home to do homework tomorrow.

The rest of the party guests have already started filtering out until, eventually, I'm left there alone with Noah.

chapter eighteen
NOAH

"You enjoy it, don't you?" I ask as soon as we're inside.

She turns to look at me, our bodies only inches apart. The defiance is visible in her eyes as she responds.

"Enjoy what, Noah?"

She isn't fooling me. She knows what she's doing. It took all I had in me not to yank that fucking kid off of her. Reaching up, I lace my fingers into her hair, tugging lightly and forcing her to look at me.

"Driving me fucking crazy."

Her eyes flutter up to mine, giving me my answer.

"Do I need to remind you who you belong to?" I ask, pinning her to the counter with my body. Her eyes are heated, but the need to defy me remains. Gliding my hand down her torso, I graze the top of her swimsuit bottoms, moving to whisper in her ear.

"Do I?" I ask again as a soft moan escapes her lips.

After a moment, she gives me a quick nod and that's all the

permission I need. My lips brand hers in a bruising kiss. She meets me with the same ferocity, her hands sliding up my neck to the back of my head. I try to remind myself that we shouldn't be doing this, I need to stop this, but those thoughts dissolve as her hand reaches for the hem of my shorts.

"Fuck," I mutter, tracing my hands down her thighs, hoisting her onto the counter.

Sliding my hands up her hips, I pull my shirt off of her, tossing it aside, leaving her in nothing but that tiny green bikini. The same bikini that's been driving me crazy all day. Our kiss deepens as I reach behind her, my fingers tugging at the strings of her top. It falls away, revealing her perfect, round tits. I can't stop myself. They're perfect.

I trail soft kisses down her neck, tasting her skin as I take one of her nipples into my mouth, nibbling, sucking, and drawing a low moan from her. The sound pushes me closer to the edge of losing control, but I hold back. I need to feel all of her.

My fingers brush over the fabric of her bikini bottoms, feeling the heat of her skin beneath. She shudders, her body responding to every touch. I slip my hand lower, pulling the fabric aside, and my fingers slide over her, already soaked for me.

"Please, Noah," she breathes, her voice shaky with need as I tease her clit. Her hips push into me, craving more, and I can't deny her. My thumb circles her sensitive spot, while my finger teases the entrance of her, coaxing soft whimpers from her.

"Greedy little princess," I tease before giving her exactly what she wants. Adding another finger, I push deep into her, earning me a shaky moan. I keep playing with her, bringing her to the edge before letting her back down again. Finally, I let her come, her pussy squeezing my fingers as she cries out. Her orgasm racks through her as I keep pumping into her.

"Fuck, Noah, I need you," she says, her eyes pleading.

God, she's gorgeous when she begs.

Removing my fingers and trailing them along her inner thigh, I lightly brush over her clit, her hips bucking into me.

"What do you need from me, princess?"

Her breathing quickens as she shifts her hips toward me, pushing my fingers that much closer to where she wants me most. I shake my head, moving my hands to grip her hips.

"Use your words."

She looks up at me, her dark eyes filled with lust.

"Noah, I—I need you to fuck me."

Those words coming out of her mouth are downright sinful, and it takes everything I have not to bend her over and fuck her right here on the counter, but if this is happening, I'm going to savor every fucking moment of it.

With a grunt, I reach under her, wrapping her legs around me and picking her up.

"Wha–what are you doing?"

"Giving you what you want," I say, making my way up the stairs to my bedroom. I lock the door behind us, setting her down in front of it. The way she's looking at me, the hunger in her eyes—I reach up and tuck her hair behind her ear, leaving a kiss right below it.

"Let me know if you ever need me to stop. I won't do anything you aren't comfortable with."

Her eyes meet mine for a moment before her hands trail down my chest, reaching for the top of my shorts again.

"I know. I trust you, Noah."

Those words hit deeper than I'm willing to admit. She trusts me completely, even with what she's been through. I push past the feelings rising in my chest, moving closer to cage her in. Her hands continue their perusal, pushing under my shorts and finding my already hard cock. She palms it, squeezing lightly, and I let out a groan, heat coursing through my body.

"Fuck, we really shouldn't be doing this," I say through gritted teeth, but it lacks any conviction.

"I know," she says, pure lust in her gaze.

Tightening her hand around my waistband, she pulls my shorts and boxers down. Her eyes widen at the sight, but she doesn't hesitate as she takes me in her hand, her tongue brushing over her lips before dropping to her knees.

My body ignites at the feeling of her hot mouth on me, licking and teasing, her hand pumping at the base. Taking me deeper into her mouth, she swirls her tongue around me, earning a low moan. She fucking knows what she's doing, and it is quite possibly the hottest thing I've ever seen.

Her eyes flutter open, looking up at me, the satisfaction there evident. She's enjoying this.

Bringing one hand up to brace myself on the door behind her, I take the other, gathering her hair at the back of her head. The way she's working me is torturous, slow, and deep, and fuck if I don't want to come down her throat, but I'm not ready for this to be over.

Gripping her hair, I guide myself deeper into her mouth, forcing her to take more of me. She moans around my cock, and that's all the permission I need before picking up the pace, fucking her mouth in earnest. God, she's beautiful like this, her lips around me. That delicious tension builds in my body, radiating through me, but I'm not done with her yet.

"I need you on the bed," I growl, pulling her off me.

Letting my cock slide out of her mouth, she looks up at me, her eyes full of need. I can't help myself. Gripping her by the back of her head, I pull her to her feet for a rough kiss.

"Bed. Now." I repeat, my voice hoarse.

She listens for once, climbing onto the dark green comforter, not taking her eyes off me.

"On your back," I say, climbing onto the bed after her. Tucking my fingers into the top of her bathing suit bottoms, I slide them down her legs. Fuck, she's gorgeous. Positioning myself between her thighs, her warm body tucked under mine, I press a kiss to her neck. I lean over her and reach for the bedside table, but she presses a hand to my chest, stopping me.

"I'm on birth control."

Looking down at her, I realize what she's implying.

"Are you sure?" I ask.

I know I shouldn't, but the idea of fucking her raw, nothing between us, is too tempting.

"Yes, I need to feel you," she says, her voice breathy.

This is so fucking wrong. I shouldn't be touching her like this, but I don't care anymore. I want her.

My lips find hers again, claiming her with all of our pent-up desire. She's consumed my thoughts ever since that night we ran into each other in the kitchen. Being with her feels fucking perfect, even if I hate myself for it.

My fingers tighten around her hips, pulling her into me. Brushing my thumb over her clit, I guide myself to her entrance, a gasp escaping her lips. Fuck, every second I'm not buried deep inside her is another blow to my already diminished self-control. Slowly, I ease myself in. The feeling is fucking euphoric as I push even deeper into her.

"Noah, please," she moans.

Sliding my cock nearly all the way out before slamming it back into her, I bury myself inside her completely. Another moan escapes her lips as I pick up my pace, fucking her deeper.

"You're taking it so well," I groan.

God, she feels so good wrapped around me, her pussy fitting my cock like it was fucking made for me. She tightens around me, and I know she's close.

Leaning down to her neck, I press a kiss there before whispering, "Is this what you wanted? My cock deep inside you?"

Pumping into her even harder, I circle my fingers over her clit, and she nods quickly, her hands sliding up over my back, pulling me into her. Her nails dig into me as I keep fucking her.

"You have no idea how long I've wanted this," she says, her voice shaky.

She shouldn't want this. She deserves so much more, but she's fucking beautiful like this, and selfishly, I don't want it to end. I know she's close, and so am I. The delicious tension builds in my core and flows throughout my body.

Reaching up to grab her face, I make her look at me. Her eyes are almost black with pure need. "You look so fucking good taking me, but I want to see how beautiful you are when you come for me."

A moan escapes her lips as her eyes lock on mine, her lips parting as she arches into me.

"Come for me, princess," I say, circling her clit with my thumb as I push deep inside her. Her pussy tightens around me as she cries out, and I keep fucking her through her orgasm as she pulls me right off that edge with her. White hot pleasure shoots through me as I finish, filling her.

I slide out of her. My eyes trail down to where we were connected, the sight of my come dripping out of her pussy satisfying that possessive urge I have only when it comes to her.

She's fucking mine.

I lay down beside her, pulling her into me. The smell of strawberries and sun invading my senses, her naked body pressing into mine. My brain flashes back to why we're here to begin with. The thought of that boy's hands on her ignites my jealousy yet again.

"So, are we clear now?" I ask.

She looks up at me, her caramel eyes fixed on mine.

"Crystal," she teases.

"I mean it, you're mine. No one else touches you." I say, my voice low. Her eyes narrow, her hand sliding down my chest.

"What about you?" she asks.

"What about me?"

Her gaze falls, avoiding mine, "Never mind, it's fine."

Fuck, does she think I'm sleeping with other people? Guiding her chin up to look at me, I brush my thumb over her lip.

"There's no one else, princess."

Her body relaxes somewhat under my touch, but something is still bothering her. "Jared can't find out. I can't do that to him," she says.

"I know. He won't, I promise," I assure her, placing a kiss on her forehead. If he found out, it would ruin everything. I can't begin to let myself think about how much this would hurt him. I'm his dad, and I just fucked his best friend. Not to mention, I'm almost certain that he has feelings for her. He's the kind of guy she *should* be with.

A better man would get up, get dressed, and tell her that this was a mistake. Instead, I pull her tighter against me as she sighs. Stroking my fingers through her hair, she falls asleep on my chest, her arm wrapped around me.

I should bring her to her room.

Who knows when Jared will be back?

But I don't.

chapter nineteen
KIRA

I WAKE UP IN THE MORNING TO THE FEELING OF A HARD BODY pinning me to the mattress. It takes a moment for me to remember where I am.

Oh my god, last night.

Rolling over, I look up to the naked man wrapped around me, his warm hazel eyes already fixed on mine. Thoughts of last night fill my mind, and I'm about to climb back onto him when I remember Jared.

Shit, is he home?

Noah must sense my panic, his hand reaching for my cheek.

"Don't worry, it's early. If he's home, he's probably still asleep," he says, his voice rough.

His fingers trace through my hair, and I lean into his touch. I need to get up and go to my room. What if he comes looking for me?

"I should go," I say, trying to sit up.

Strong arms wrap around my waist, pulling me back into him.

"In a minute, I'm not ready for this to be over yet."

His words hit deeper than I'm willing to admit. That's precisely what I'm worried about. What happens when it is over, when we go back downstairs and back to reality?

"Hey, what's wrong?" he asks, his voice barely above a whisper.

At first, I don't respond. How do I say this without sounding clingy? He nuzzles his face into my neck, kissing right below my ear, and my body melts into him.

"Tell me, princess," he orders.

"I just… I don't want this to be like every other time. I don't want you to pull away again."

He's silent for a moment, and I brace myself for the rejection. I knew it was coming. I don't know what I expected.

"That's not happening. I have no idea how this is going to work, but you're mine, and I can't stay away from you anymore."

His calloused hand caresses my face, and my heart flips, my chest filling with butterflies. I shouldn't be excited. There's no way this can work. No one can ever find out, but the thought that he wants me, only me, is enough.

"But are you sure *you* want this?" he asks.

My eyes focus on his, and I rest my hand on his bare chest.

"I've wanted this for longer than you know," I tell him.

"Fuck," he sighs before pulling me into a rough kiss. His hands slide around my body, pinning me to him. I can feel him hard against me, and all I want is to touch him, but I do have to go. The last thing I need is for Jared to find me naked in his dad's bed.

"I need to go," I mutter between kisses.

"I know."

"So let me go."

"Easier said than done, princess," he says, tracing his fingertips along my breast.

Letting out a sigh, I climb out of bed before this can go any further. A groan sounds from behind me as I walk over to his dresser, open the second drawer on the left, and pull out an old t-shirt. Smirking at him, I throw it on, heading out the door and into my room to finish getting dressed.

When I get downstairs, Noah is already in the kitchen setting up the coffee maker. He put on a pair of black sweatpants but is still shirtless, his tattooed torso on full display. My mind flashes back to that toned body between my legs, but I'm interrupted by a sound from the hallway.

Jared.

At this exact moment, I realize two things. One, I'm going to have to face him after his dad came inside me last night, and two, my clothes are still strewn about on the counter. Noah notices them at the same time I do and leans over to grab them right as Jared walks into the kitchen. He tucks them into the cabinet beneath the island, and I let out a breath.

Guilt slams into me as Jared comes over to me for a hug.

"Good morning," he says, his voice still raspy from sleep.

"More like afternoon," Noah says with a stern edge.

I look up at him, but his eyes are fixed on where Jared is touching me.

Pulling away, I change the topic, "How was the rest of your night last night?"

"It was pretty awesome. I wish you could have come!"

My eyes meet Noah's at that statement, and a smirk grows on his face. This situation is beyond fucked up.

"But, they're having another get-together tonight. Please go. I feel like we haven't hung out at all lately."

He's right. We haven't, and I feel like shit for it. I should go.

"She has to work tomorrow morning," Noah says.

"We won't be out too late, I promise," Jared tells me. It's a complete lie, but I can't keep turning him down.

"Fine, I'll go," I say with a small smile.

"Yes! I'm going to shower, then you want to go get lunch?"

Noah's body tenses next to mine, and I glance at him.

"I'd love to."

"Perfect!" Jared grins as he heads out of the room, leaving Noah and I alone. I can sense the shift in his mood before he even says anything.

"You're not going to that party tonight."

"Noah," I warn.

"I don't trust any of his idiot friends not to try something, and I don't trust him to keep you safe," he says, closing the distance between us.

"I can handle myself. I'm going."

His jaw clenches as he looks down at me. I'm standing my ground on this one. I already feel terrible enough about lying to Jared. I don't want him to feel like I don't want to be around him.

"I'll be fine, and I promise I'll call you if I need anything, okay?" I say, my fingers grazing his bare stomach. I would much rather spend the day alone with him, but I miss Jared.

His eyelids flutter closed, and he lets out a breath.

"Fine. But text me when you get there," he says, leaning down to kiss my forehead. Warmth fills my chest at the gesture. I don't think I'm ever going to get used to this.

Jared and I spend most of the day together, stopping at a little restaurant on the bay for lunch, where he gets a burger and I order pasta. The conversation is easy like it always is with him, but I can't shake the feeling of guilt that simmers low in my gut.

"What have you been up to? I feel like I haven't really gotten to see much of you lately," Jared asks with a smile, but his eyes betray him. He's hurt.

"I've just been busy with work and the pottery studio."

And your dad.

"Well, I miss you."

"I miss you too," I tell him, honestly.

Neither of us speaks for a moment, the restaurant's ambiance filling my ears.

"Kira, I have something I've been meaning to talk to you about."

Jared's eyes are still fixed on me as he seems to work through whatever he wants to say in his head. My stomach drops, and my palms start to sweat. There's no way he can know about Noah and me, right?

"Kira, I—"

"Kira!" I hear a voice shout from across the room.

Turning toward the source, I see Maddie walking toward us, with Lucy following behind.

"You didn't tell me you'd be in town today!" she exclaims as she hugs me.

"It was last minute," I say with a chuckle.

I love her enthusiasm, but right now, I can only think about what Jared was about to say.

Maddie and Lucy sit with us for the rest of the meal. We chat, and if I'm being honest, I'm glad she showed up. I don't know if I was emotionally ready for whatever Jared wanted to talk about.

The rest of the day passes without much excitement. Jared doesn't mention what he was going to say earlier, and I can't tell if I'm relieved or worried. I'm not looking forward to this party tonight, and having something off between us is not helping my anxiety.

I'm sitting in the kitchen, book in hand, when Noah walks up behind me.

"You sure you want to go?" he asks, his hand grazing the sliver of bare skin below my shirt. I shiver, leaning into him ever so slightly.

"No, but that doesn't matter. I'm going."

"You ready?" Jared calls from the hallway.

Noah's hand drops from my waist as he turns toward the fridge. My body tenses at the loss of contact, and I answer.

"Yup."

THE DRIVE ISN'T FAR, BUT AS JARED TURNS OFF THE ROAD ONTO A long driveway, I realize I haven't ever been here before. We pass the main house on the property and keep going down the drive to an old red barn, where most of the people are congregating around a fire.

I pull out my phone and text Noah to let him know we arrived. After a moment, I send him our location too. I'm not fully comfortable here, and it makes me feel safer that he knows where we're at.

"Whose house is this?" I ask, genuinely curious.

I've been to almost all of Jared's friend's houses, and this isn't one of them.

"It's a friend of Jake's. Now, come on, let's go get us some drinks," he says with a mischievous grin.

Stepping into the large barn, we locate a white cooler filled with cans of cheap beer. Jared grabs one and hands another to me. The light hanging from the barn's loft casts a warm glow onto the people in it. Looking around, I notice that I don't recognize anyone here.

Great.

"Hey, I'm going to look for Jake real quick. Are you good by yourself for a minute?"

If I were telling the truth, I would say no, but I don't want to stop him from having a good time tonight. Nodding, I give him a small smile.

"That's fine, I'll try to socialize."

Jared laughs, knowing that won't happen, and spins around, heading toward the fire. Cracking open my beer, I sit my happy ass down on a hay bale. I'm already wishing I would have stayed home. The anxiety that has been a constant since we got here is heightening by the second. I pull out my phone, reading a text from Noah.

Noah
I'm glad you got there safe.

Before I can even type out a response, another message comes through.

Noah
When will you be home?

Kira
Omg Noah, I just got here!

Noah
I don't care. Do you want me to come get you?

Laughing, I roll my eyes at his response. Truthfully, I do, but I'm not leaving Jared here by himself so early.

Kira
I'm fine

What are you doing tonight?

Noah
Sitting on the couch, waiting for you.

I'm about to type out a sassy response when a girl approaches me, her light green eyes wide.

"Hey, do you mind if I sit with you? There's a guy who won't leave me alone, and he won't take the hint. A friend is coming to pick me up, but she's still about thirty minutes away."

She looks scared, and her fear strikes me right in the chest. This is feeling too familiar.

"No, of course, come here," I say, scooting over so she can fit in with me.

She's young. Too young to be here, and definitely too young to be preyed upon by one of these assholes.

"Are you okay? Did he hurt you?"

She hesitates, her eyes puffy, before shaking her head and looking up at me. "I don't think so," she answers. My heart sinks.

"Do we need to call someone?" I ask, hoping she understands my question. The police may have failed me, but if that is something she wants to do, I will be right there with her.

She shakes her head, "No, no, it's fine. I'm fine. I'll be fine. It didn't get that far."

A small wave of relief washes over me. At least he didn't take that from her.

"It's my fault anyway. I came here with him," she says, her eyes trained on the ground.

Grabbing her hand, I meet her eyes. "No. You didn't ask for this. It wasn't your fault. Don't let anyone tell you otherwise."

All I can think about is how similar this is to what happened to me. My heart breaks for her and for my younger self. The fucking audacity of men. Rage simmers up in me, and for a moment, I want to ask her who it was so I can personally teach him a lesson, but I decide against it. Regardless of how much raw emotion there is, I still don't think I could fight a grown man.

"What's your name?" I ask softly.

"Amelia."

"Give me your phone."

She looks confused but hands it to me anyway. I go to contacts and create one for myself.

"Now you have my number. If you ever need anything or just want to talk, I'm here."

"Thank you."

Her friend shows up soon after, and I make sure she makes it to the car safely before returning to my hiding spot. I haven't seen Jared in a while, which is typical, but I'm extra uncomfortable with this crowd of people now, and I'm tempted to try to find him. Before I can get up though, he appears in the doorway of the barn, a plastic cup in hand.

"Kira! I've been looking for you."

"I've been here all night," I tell him, noticing he's a little more intoxicated than when he left.

Climbing up onto the hay bale with me, he sits down, leaning against the wall across from me.

"Are you having fun?" he asks.

I don't have the heart to tell him no, that it's actually the opposite of that. Instead I smile and reply with a small nod.

"Listen, I've been meaning to talk to you since earlier."

My heart stops, my body tensing. It can't be about Noah. There's no way.

"There's something I've really been wanting to tell you, but it's hard to get myself to actually do it."

"What's up?" I ask, trying to sound as casual as possible.

"I know we've been friends for a really long time, and you are probably one of the most important people in my life," he starts. "But lately, I've been feeling like, well..."

"You've been feeling like what, Jared?"

"Kira," he says, his green eyes locking on mine.

"I'm in love with you."

chapter twenty
KIRA

I STOP BREATHING. HE MUST MEAN AS A FRIEND, RIGHT? WE'RE JUST friends. We've always been just friends.

"Jared—"

"I love you, Kira, and I have loved you for a really long time," he says, his voice hoarse. He's been drinking, but the look in his eyes is genuine, pleading. How do I respond to that? I love him to death, but not in the way I think he's hoping.

Without warning, his hand reaches up to cup my face as he crashes his lips onto mine. It's a sloppy kiss, his tongue pushing in through my lips. I can taste the alcohol on him, and it instantly turns my stomach. That familiar fear rises inside me, and my heart starts to race.

"Jared, wait," I say, pushing him off me.

I steady my breathing, and his features quickly morph from confusion to pained realization.

"You don't feel the same way?"

It's more of a statement than a question. The hurt swirling in his eyes is evident, the alcohol enhancing the intensity of his emotions. I would do anything to make it go away.

"Jared, you know I love you…" I trail off, trying to reassure him.

"As a friend, right?" he snaps, his sudden attitude jarring me.

"I've always been there for you, Kira, through everything," he says, his voice breaking on the last word.

He doesn't even know the half of it. I am eternally grateful for everything he's done for me. He was there for me through the thick of my PTSD and depression without even knowing what caused it.

"I haven't listened to anything the guys say about you because I know you. I fucking love you, Kira."

That shocks me. What is he talking about?

"What do they say?"

"That's what matters to you?" he says, his voice louder now.

Shaking his head, he slides onto his feet, looking at me with an intensity I've never seen from him before.

"Maybe they're right," he says, turning away. "You should find a different ride home," he adds before leaving the barn altogether.

It's not until he's gone that I realize I'm shaking. He's hurt, I know that, but I've never seen that side of him, and it scares me. A tear rolls down my face as I pull out my phone and tap Noah's contact. Hopefully, he's still awake. It only rings once before he answers.

"Hey Kira, what's up?" he says, his deep voice immediately calming my nerves.

"Would you be able to come get me?"

I feel like a child having him pick me up from a party, but I don't care. I need to get out of here.

"Of course, princess. Why, what happened? Where's Jared?"

His voice grows increasingly worried. I can hear him grabbing his keys on the other end of the line.

"I'll tell you when you get here."

"Are you okay?" he asks, concern filling his voice.

"I'm fine, I promise."

"Sit tight. I'll be there in ten," he says before hanging up.

The drive should take longer than ten minutes, but somehow, I know Noah isn't going to pay attention to speed limits tonight. I head to the front of the driveway to wait for him, sitting on the stairs of the house. No one seems to be home. All of the partygoers are back down at the barn. The air is cold on my bare skin, and it feels like forever, but exactly nine minutes later, a truck pulls into the drive.

I recognize the all-black F150 that speeds to a stop in front of me, and before I can even stand, he's shutting his door and striding toward me.

"What happened?" he demands, his dark hair falling into his face as he looks down at me. His eyes roam over my body, and it takes me a second before I realize he's checking to see if I'm hurt.

"Let's just get in the truck," I say, standing up and moving toward him, trying to avoid a scene.

"Nope, you're telling me what happened. Why isn't Jared bringing you home? What the fuck is he thinking leaving you on your own like this?"

"For the last time, Noah, I can handle myself. Plus, he doesn't want anything to do with me tonight."

"Kira," he orders.

I could keep pushing. I don't know if I even want to tell him, but I need to go home, and he won't let me until he knows.

"He told me that he's in love with me," I say matter-of-factly.

Noah's jaw ticks, his posture stiffening. I might be crazy, but there's a hint of jealousy in those dark eyes.

"And what did you say?" he asks, his voice strained.

I step closer to him, resting my hand on his chest. His heart is racing, his breathing ragged. Trailing my hand down his body, I bring my eyes to his.

"I told him the truth. I told him I love him, but not like that. He didn't like it and told me to find a ride home."

His eyes narrow at that, his body tensing.

"Where is he?" he demands, stepping past me toward the house. I grab his arm, stopping him. The last thing I need is for Noah to crash this party.

"Just leave it alone. Let him cool off. He's allowed to be upset."

A long sigh leaves his lips, and he reluctantly turns back toward me, his features softening.

"But that doesn't mean he can leave you alone without a ride home."

"Just don't, please," I beg. "I already feel bad enough that I hurt him, and the worst part is, on top of not wanting him, I'm fucking his dad behind his back," I say, expressing the guilt that's been eating at me since Jared's admission. He loves me, but I want his dad. How can I do that to him?

"Is that all we're doing?" Noah asks, closing the distance between us. My back is to the truck door now, the cool metal pressed against my hot skin, his masculine scent enveloping me.

"Just fucking?" His voice is lower now as he looks down at me.

"No—I don't know, Noah," I say, my voice unsure. "Can it be more than that?"

He's silent for a moment, and my brain immediately goes to the worst-case scenario. Maybe that's all he wants. Maybe that's for the best. I've already hurt Jared enough. Before I can spiral completely, his hand reaches up to cup my face, gently directing me to look at him.

"All I know is that I'm not letting you go. You're mine."

His words stir up feelings that I'm afraid to let myself truly feel. This isn't going to end well. There's no way it can, but fuck if I don't want to be his.

He pulls me into him, his fingers lacing into my hair as he kisses my forehead. The night's emotions melt away at the feeling of him around me.

"Let's get you home, princess."

Opening the passenger door, Noah helps me up into the truck.

It's nearly pitch black outside as we make our way back home. Music plays quietly on the radio, and I can tell that Noah is still pissed. His jaw keeps clenching and unclenching, and he's gripping the steering wheel like it will run away if he lets go.

"I can't fucking believe he left you like that," he grumbles as his right-hand moves to rest on my thigh.

Letting out a breath, I look at him. For some reason, *his* anger doesn't scare me. It never has.

"Anything could have happened to you. What was he thinking?"

Jared has never talked to me like that, and he damn sure has never left me to fend for myself surrounded by strangers, but I really hurt him. I can't blame him for his reaction.

"Noah, It's fine. I'm okay," I reassure him, letting my fingers trace over the ink on his forearm.

"That's not the point, Kira. What if I didn't get there soon enough?"

"But you did."

Sighing, he focuses back on the road. "You should have stayed home with me."

I almost wish I had, but then my mind goes back to Amelia. What would have happened if no one was there for her? My stomach turns. Resting my head on the window, I'm silent for the rest of the drive.

"I'm going to shower," I tell Noah as I head inside toward the stairs. Footsteps follow me, and as I reach the bathroom door, I turn to find him standing behind me.

"What are you doing?" I ask.

"Showering."

I pause, my eyes meeting his hazel ones, and my heart skips a little in my chest. Showering with someone feels so intimate. Thoughts of Jared from earlier fill my mind, and I know we shouldn't. I hurt him. I'm still hurting him, and he doesn't even know. We shouldn't be doing this, but I can't stop myself.

"Only if you want," he adds, his hand grazing the top of my thigh. This is his way of making sure I'm comfortable, and I love that about him. He won't ever do anything that I don't want. That knowledge makes my decision even easier.

"Come on."

The bathroom is small, not leaving much room for the two of us. Noah reaches over to turn the water on before letting his eyes fall back on me.

He steps closer and slides his fingers under the hem of my shirt, looking at me for permission. I quickly nod, not letting my gaze leave his. The feel of his fingers on my bare skin ignites a desire deep within me.

"Just so you know," he starts, pulling my shirt over my head and letting it drop to the floor.

"This isn't just fucking for me."

I don't have time to process his admission before his hands are back on me, pulling my skirt down over my hips, leaving me in only panties.

Unable to take it anymore, I reach up and pull him to me, kissing him softly. He reacts, deepening the kiss and pressing his body into mine. My back touches the cold tile wall as his hand grazes up my inner thigh to the edge of my underwear. Sucking in a breath, I slide my hands under his shirt, feeling the hard lines of his muscles right as he glides his hand over my pussy, earning a whimper from me.

Breaking the kiss, he pulls off his own shirt before unbuttoning his jeans. Fuck, he's gorgeous. He runs his fingers up my legs, pulling my panties down.

"Get in before the water gets cold," he orders as he pulls back the shower curtain for me to enter.

The hot water immediately soothes muscles I didn't even know were aching until now. Noah steps into the shower directly behind me, his hand reaching around and resting on my lower belly.

I shudder, the feeling of his rough fingers brushing over me igniting small infernos on my skin. I want him, and he seems to sense it, sliding his hand up over my breasts to grip my throat.

"Already so needy," he growls into my ear, my legs going weak from the sound.

His hot breath brushes that place right below my ear as he kisses and nips down my neck. Pressing his hips into me, I can feel the hardness of him against my back as his other hand slides up to my chest, rolling my nipple between his fingers. Fuck, he knows my body so well. A loud moan escapes my lips, but I'm silenced by his starved mouth meeting mine.

The kiss is rougher this time, less controlled. I dart my tongue out, gliding it over his as his hand slides down to my pussy, his fingers dipping into my entrance, only deep enough to collect the wetness there.

"Fuck, princess, you're already ready for me," he praises as he pushes deeper, eliciting a moan from me. His fingers work into me expertly, and I lean into him, grinding my hips into his hand. I reach behind me, taking his hard cock in my hand, needing to feel him.

"Noah, I need you inside me," I plead.

He sucks in a breath as I start to glide my hand over him, brushing my thumb over the tip.

"Not until you come for me," he grits, spinning me around to face him.

Dropping to his knees, he grips my thighs, pulling me to him. Before I can register what he's doing, his mouth is on me, his tongue flat, licking my entire pussy. I yelp, tangling my fingers into his hair.

His tongue feels so fucking good as he swirls it over me, causing my grip to tighten, pleasure coiling deep in my core. He grunts, pulling my clit between his teeth. A warning. I ignore it, tugging harder.

A deep chuckle vibrates over my pussy as two fingers push into me. I nearly scream at the intrusion, pleasure shooting through my body. It doesn't take long before I'm about to come around his fingers. My eyes flutter closed as my head falls back.

"Eyes on me, Kira," he commands.

I obey surprised by his use of my name. My eyes lock on his as I tumble over the edge, muttered curses on my lips.

chapter twenty-one
NOAH

I can't hold myself back any longer—the need to be buried deep inside her overcoming me. Rising to my feet, I spin her around, pressing her against the tile wall. She gasps but doesn't fight it. It's a fucking beautiful sight, her bent over for me, water cascading down her back.

Wasting no time, I grip her hip with one hand while I guide myself to her entrance. She presses back into me impatiently, making me want to delay it even longer. I tease her, sliding my cock over her slick folds.

"Noah," she whimpers, rocking her hips into me.

The last thread of my control snaps with that plea, and I push all the way into her in one thrust. Letting out a low moan, her back arches into me. I fuck her slow at first, needing to savor every moment that I'm inside her.

I grip her jaw, forcing her to look over her shoulder at me. Her eyes widen with lust as our eyes meet, and she pushes herself onto me. A growl escapes my lips as I give her exactly what she wants. Reaching my hand in front of her, I circle her clit with my fingers as I fuck her. She feels like heaven as I pump into her. I can feel her squeezing me. I know it won't be long before she falls apart for me.

"Fuck, Noah," she moans, meeting me thrust for thrust.

Lacing my hand into her hair, I pull up so her back is pressed to my chest.

"That's it, princess, you take it so well," I whisper over her ear. "Now let go for me."

And she fucking does. A mix between a scream and a moan comes out of her mouth as she tightens around my cock, almost immediately pulling me over the edge with her. A low groan rises from my chest as I lose myself in her. Our breathing is ragged as I pull her into me, not wanting to leave her body yet.

After our shower, we're both exhausted. Kira decides it's best if we sleep in our own rooms in case Jared comes home. I know it's for the best, but it takes everything I have not to scoop her up and bring her to my bed.

Now that I've had more time to reflect on the events of tonight, the guilt is creeping in. I'm a horrible father. I could lie to myself and say that I didn't know Jared's feelings, but I knew something was happening. Anyone with eyes can see that he adores her.

He confessed his love for her tonight, and I took her home and fucked her. What dad does something like that? The situation is so messed up it's almost comical, but for some reason, no matter how hard I try, I can't stop. I can't get her out of my head.

I'm pried from sleep by screams coming from down the hallway, and I'm at the door in seconds when I realize it's coming from Kira's room. My heart sinks. She's having another nightmare. Rushing into her room, I pull her into my arms. Her body is trembling under my fingers, tears running down her face.

"Kira, baby, it's just a dream. I'm here," I soothe her, brushing my fingers over her cheek.

"No, leave her alone!" she shouts, fighting against my hold.

"Shh, Kira, it's me," I reassure, needing her to wake up. I hate seeing her like this, the twisted pain in her face as she fights against whatever is happening inside that beautiful mind of hers. How could someone do this to her? Uncontrollable rage stirs low in my chest as I think about what she told me.

I'm going to fucking kill him.

Her eyes snap open, and her muscles tense. Fear morphs into recognition and relief as she melts into my hold. She instinctively curls into me, and I pull her closer, brushing a stray hair out of her face as she climbs into my lap.

"I've got you."

I can still feel her heart pounding against my chest, and it takes everything in me not to hunt that son of a bitch down tonight.

Kira needs me right now.

"I'm sorry," she whispers, her breathing uneven. "I—I didn't mean to wake you up."

Reaching down, I lightly guide her chin up to make her look at me.

"Don't do that. Don't apologize."

Her features soften. A tear slides down her cheek as she nods at me. Without thinking, I grip her thighs tighter and stand, keeping her wrapped around my waist. One thing is for sure. She's not staying here alone. Eyebrows knitting together in confusion, Kira looks up at me.

"Noah...what are you doing?" she asks, accusation in her tone.

"Taking you where you should have been all along."

After I assure her that Jared isn't coming home tonight for the tenth time, she relaxes. He texted me soon after we left the party. He's staying at Jake's for a couple of nights, and that's probably a good thing. I'm too angry with him right now to talk to him about any of this.

He fucking left her.

I push away the anger as Kira lays her head on my bare chest. It doesn't take long before her breathing evens out, and I pull her tighter into me, placing a kiss on her forehead.

It's early, the sun not yet up as Kira and I stand in the kitchen. She has to leave early for the studio, so I probably won't see her again before my shift starts at the station tonight. I'm not going to lie. I don't love the idea of her being home alone, but there's not much I can do about it. That's the downside of this job, and that's what made it hard for Angie.

"How's he doing?" she asks, gesturing at my phone.

Jared texted me this morning to ask if Kira had made it home okay. I didn't respond. Part of me wanted him to worry. He never should have done that to her, but this morning, the other part of me—the one that loves my son to death—won out.

I keep it short and straightforward. I don't want to yell at him, but I don't know what else to say. I understand that he's hurting. I would be, too, but that doesn't give him the right to treat her like that.

"He's fine."

She nods and takes a sip of her coffee. Her eyes are focused out the window toward the lake, the early morning light casting a blue hue on her face.

"Do you think he's ever going to forgive me?" she asks, her voice little more than a whisper.

I step toward her, wrapping my arms around her and pulling her back to my chest. Pressing my lips to the top of her head, I hold her tighter.

"He'll get over it. You guys are too close for him to throw it away like this," I say, doing my best to comfort her. I know this is hard. Even though she isn't *in* love with him, she loves him. He is a massive part of her life.

Her hand brushes over my arm as she leans into me.

"I just feel bad, you know? This is his house, and he's the one staying with a friend. I shouldn't even be here."

"Don't say that. This is your home now, too. He made that choice. That's on him. Kira, look at me."

She does, tears welling in her eyes. One slips down over the freckles dotting her cheek, and I brush it away with my thumb.

"You belong here," I say, holding her face in my palm. Her amber eyes don't leave mine as I add, "With me."

Another tear falls, and this time, I lower my lips to her cheek before brushing them over her mouth. Her fingers find the back of my head as she laces them into my hair, pulling me into her. The kiss is deep, tender, and full of emotion. She's the one who brings us back to reality, her hand sliding from my neck down my chest.

"I need to leave, or I won't have time to get anything done before my students come in," she tells me, gently pushing me away.

I don't want her to go, not yet. When I don't move, she sneaks out from under my hold, setting her coffee mug in the sink.

"I'll see you tomorrow," she says with a small smile.

I follow her to the door, catching her wrist as she opens it. The chilled morning air envelopes us as I press my lips to hers once more. A giggle escapes her, and the sound sends warmth spreading throughout my chest.

"Drive safe, princess."

I watch as she pulls out of the driveway and disappears down the road. The day warms up fast as I tend to chores around the house. I check my phone several times to see if Jared has responded, but he hasn't.

I'm hopping into my truck to head to work when I see the gas gauge hovering above empty. I was already low last night before I drove to get Kira, and after that, getting gas was the last thing on my mind. It should be enough to get me to the gas station.

Pulling into the small station, I choose the only pump left. I'm grabbing the nozzle when I hear a yelp from across the parking lot.

My senses immediately sharpen, but it only takes a second to realize it was a shout of surprise rather than fear. A blonde girl who seems to be around the same age as Kira is hoisted into what I assume is her boyfriend's arms. A couple of their friends flank them. She's laughing as he holds her. They're so happy and free.

My stomach knots.

Kira and I could never do that.

"Only a couple more weeks," the girl chirps. "Then our lives officially start."

"I know, I can't wait!" another girl adds.

They must've just graduated with Kira. I don't recognize their faces. Then again, I wasn't there for them.

The excitement on their faces is evident, and I can't help but picture Kira standing there with them. It's like the universe is showing me what Kira could have, what she should have. She should be going off to college and living her life with an age-appropriate boyfriend who can hold her in public without worrying about the consequences.

Jesus, *what am I doing?*

I've known it the whole time, but I've been conveniently ignoring it as of late. Kira is only nineteen. She's so young, and has so much more to experience in life, and she can't do those things if she's stuck here with me. Kira and I won't work together. We can't. She deserves so much more than what I can offer.

I may be frustrated with Jared, but he's still my son, and the guilt of everything is weighing on me. He's in pain, and I don't want him to feel like he's alone in this.

Noah

Do you want to talk about it?

I say a quick prayer to the universe that he says no. I want to help him, but I don't know if I could talk to him about Kira right now, at least not in good conscience.

Jared

No offense, but I would rather get rejected again than talk to my dad about this.

I breathe a sigh of relief as I send him a thumbs up and spend the rest of my shift with a sinking feeling in my gut. There's no way this can keep happening with Kira.

I refuse to be the reason she gets stuck in this town.

chapter twenty-two
KIRA

As I sculpt the minuscule details of the bird's feathers, I try my hardest to control my emotions. The sun is peeking over the horizon, casting an orange tint over the studio, which is usually peaceful. Not today, though. My thoughts are racing. I keep flashing back to last night and Jared's words, the hurt on his face. What would he do if he found out about Noah and me? It would be the ultimate betrayal for him.

But I've never felt as at home as I do in Noah's arms. He makes me feel safe and secure. He's that stable rock that I've needed for what feels like my entire life. I know there's no way we can work, but I'm afraid I won't find anything like this again if we don't. It's like there are two parts of me split right down the middle, and I have no idea what I'm going to do.

I glance down at my piece. It's nearly complete. The hand is partially closed around the bird, and the details of the skin are almost lifelike. I would be proud of it, but I can't shake the feeling that it's not finished. I can't express it or figure out why, but I'm not done yet. Sighing, I pick up the project and set it on the shelf. I need to set everything up for when the students arrive in about twenty minutes. Their finished pieces are ready, and I'm beyond excited for them to see their work.

I set out the last donut as the first person walks through the door. It's an older lady named Delores. She is one of the sweetest people I've ever met.

"Are those all for me?" she calls, a wide grin on her face.

"Sure, if you're the one who tells Melinda that there's no donuts this time."

Her eyes widen as she shakes her head.

"Suit yourself. You can go ahead and take a seat at the table. Once everyone arrives, I'll bring out the finished masterpieces."

She grins at me as the door jingles, indicating more students. Maddie is the last one to walk through the door, of course. She's always almost, if not entirely, late. We all still love her, though.

"Alright, everybody, are you ready to see your beautiful creations?"

"I don't know about beautiful," Melinda chuckles.

I roll my eyes, wheeling out the shelf cart. It's a unique feeling looking at all of their art. I feel like a proud mom. I grab the first bowl. It's surprisingly even, and the colors are gorgeous, with greens and teals.

"Delores, here's yours."

Oohs and Ahs fill the room. I swear, she has to have experience with throwing because this bowl rivals my own talent.

By the time they are all handed out, everyone is comparing their work. They're laughing and smiling, and it's at that exact moment that I realize what I want to do with my life. Regardless of everything going on outside of this studio, this is one of the best feelings I've ever felt.

We all talk for a while, and most of the students sign up for the next class.

"So what are we learning next, professor?"

I chuckle, looking up at Maddie. As the last student filters out the door, I wave at them.

"Okay, now that they're gone, how is it going with the big broody DILF? Does Jared know yet?"

"Maddie!" I scold, my cheeks heating.

"Oh my god, I knew it! You fucked!"

I level a glare at her, and she tries to rein it in.

"I mean, you made love," she says, her eyes squinting as her head tilts.

"Oh god, please don't say it like that."

"But, you did, didn't you?!" accusation clear in her tone.

Sighing, I give her the slightest nod. She gasps, the sheer joy on her face a little unnerving. Her eyebrows squish together when she realizes I'm not matching her energy.

"What happened?"

I want to tell her everything. She's the only person other than Noah or Jared I trust, but I can't do it here. We need snacks and maybe some wine to get through it all.

"Do you want to come over tonight? Noah is at work, and Jared is at a friend's. Maybe we can get takeout? We can debrief then."

Her mood shifts slightly at my lack of an answer.

"Of course."

I text Noah, making sure it's okay for Maddie to come over. It doesn't take long to get a reply.

Kira

Is it okay if Maddie comes over tonight?

Noah

Sure

Sure? A one-word response? He's probably busy.

When Maddie shows up at the door at around seven with not one but two bags of takeout, I know this is going to be a good night. We get everything set up on the coffee table because there is no way I am eating at the dinner table if I don't have to. Grabbing us two glasses, I pour some of the late harvest riesling I convinced Noah he wanted. It is the best wine in existence.

"Jared told me he was in love with me," I spit out, needing to get it out there.

For the first time ever, Maddie doesn't have a response. She looks at me without blinking, her jaw nearly grazing the floor.

"Yeah, and that's not even the worst part."

"You're kidding," she says, grabbing the glass from me.

I simply shake my head.

"After his drunk confession, he tried to kiss me. I obviously stopped that and tried to politely tell him I didn't feel the same way." Sucking in a breath, I continue, "He proceeded to tell me to find my own ride home, so I called Noah. You can assume what happened after that."

"You didn't..."

"I did, but I promise it wasn't like that. I didn't do it to spite Jared. It just sort of happened, and it wasn't the first time."

"What? When was the first time?" She thinks it through for a moment, eyes narrowing. "Oh my god, was it Fourth of July?"

My cheeks heat as I nod.

"Tell me about it now. Was it good?"

"You know that's a dumb question," I tell her.

"I know, but I want to hear it from the horse's mouth!"

I decide to indulge her, not giving her exact details but letting her get the idea, and we sit there giggling and kicking our feet the entire time. It's refreshing. Life has felt so heavy lately. Hanging out and gossiping with my girl best friend makes me feel like a person again.

Maddie leaves early the next morning. It's Monday, and she has classes to attend, so I completely understand. She, however, doesn't leave without the disclaimer that I have to do better at keeping her updated with my life. I agree and make it my mission to text her more often.

Thankfully, I have the day off today, so I spend it tidying up around the house. Grabbing my Bluetooth speaker, I deep clean the living room because, god, does it need it, and I also get all my laundry washed and put away. I'm feeling quite productive when the sound of a truck pulling in draws my attention to the front door.

I watch Noah as he steps inside, setting down his bag. Instantly, his mood is off. His hand brushes over his face as his eyes slide up to meet mine. My heart skips. Even when he's exhausted, this man is handsome. He's wearing his typical uniform, a t-shirt from the department tucked into his dress pants that fit him too damn well.

"Hey," I say.

"I'm going to go shower," he sighs.

I think back to that night in the shower and have half a mind to offer to join him, but something feels off. He's never this short with me.

"Is everything okay?" I ask, closing some of the space between us.

"I'm fine. It was just a long shift."

"Oh, okay. I'm sorry," I say. "I'm going for a swim, so if you need anything, just let me know."

He nods, turning to head upstairs. I stand there for a moment, confused as hell. He's never like that. Did I do something?

I sink back into the feeling I used to get with my mom. Maybe he doesn't want me around anymore. I'm too much of a burden.

No, he just had a rough day. Not everything is about me. I hate that I even care this much. Grabbing a towel from the downstairs bathroom, I head for the dock. If there's anything that can distract me from the war of emotions spiraling in my head, it's the water.

I pull my shirt off, tossing it onto the dock, followed by my shorts, leaving me in my bikini. Without hesitating, I dive into the water, the cold enveloping me. It's almost ninety degrees outside, and the cool water is refreshing. Trying to get my thoughts under control, I sink under the surface, letting the wall of water block out the rest of my senses.

Everything is so confusing right now, and Noah is all moody, which isn't helping. Jared still hasn't texted me, and I'm worried our friendship is ruined. On top of all of that, Zach is back in town, which I've been pretending is not the case, but it's only a matter of time before I run into him again. The thought makes me sick to my stomach.

The burn in my lungs tells me I need oxygen, so reluctantly, I push off the bottom of the lake, resurfacing to the sun reflecting off the water.

"You had me worried for a second."

I jump, spinning around to face the dock. He's sitting there, close to the shore, in his uniform. His shirt is now untucked, and his pants are cuffed. Swimming over to him, I stand, only half submerged now.

"What, no shower?" I ask, gasping for breath.

He's silent for a moment, his eyes trailing over my chest before meeting mine again.

"I needed to see you."

My heart warms at his admission. The feeling of having this man's attention solely on me is intoxicating, but something is wrong. I inch closer to him, resting my hands on the dock between his legs. His body visibly tenses.

"Is something wrong? Did something happen at work today?" I ask, genuinely concerned. He shakes his head, his eyes landing on mine.

"You know I care about you, right?"

I nod slowly, my face likely showing that I don't like where this is headed. He reaches for me before thinking better of it.

"You're ambitious and assertive and the strongest woman I know. You're going to do so much with your life, but..."

With that one word, my stomach drops.

"Please don't." I can't do this right now. I am not going to sit here while he rejects me again. I knew it. I knew this was going to happen, and I'm an idiot for thinking he wasn't going to do the same thing he always does.

"Kira, I need you to listen to me."

I shake my head, refusing to have this conversation. I already know what he's going to say, and I don't want to hear it.

"Please," he begs, his hand reaching for my wrist.

Tears prick my eyes, but I don't let them fall.

"You deserve so much more than I can give you. You should be going off to college right now, starting your life, and getting the hell out of this town. You should be with someone your own age, someone who can hold you at the fucking gas station without the fear of what people think."

Where is this even coming from? He doesn't get it. I don't want any of that. I want him. I want this town. This is my home.

He's wrong.

"No."

chapter twenty-three
NOAH

"I mean, no," she says, her eyebrows jumping.

Who am I kidding? She doesn't know what she wants. She's too young. After a few years, she'll realize she settled for me and leave just like Angie did.

"Let's say we tell Jared, and he somehow miraculously is fine with it. What about five years down the road, ten? You'll realize that you want more from life than I can give you."

Saying it out loud makes me wince, but it needs to be said. There is no way that she would be happy with me in the long term. What we have right now is thrilling because it's risky, but once that's gone, she'll understand this isn't what she wants.

"You don't get to make that decision for me, Noah," she retorts, her eyes locked on mine. "How would you know what I want? You've never even asked. I don't have these massive dreams that you seem to think I do. With everything I've been through, I just want to focus on what makes me happy, and I am capable of making my own choices."

"You say that now—"

"I'm not finished. I am living my life the way I want to. This place is my home, and yeah, I'd like to go on vacation once in a while, but I love it here, and I fully plan on staying."

I never asked her what she wanted to do with her life. I mean, we talk about the things she loves, but we've never really talked about what she wants for her future.

I guess it never came up. She deserves someone who asks those questions. We're so close now, her warm, wet body between my legs. It's taking everything I have in me not to run my fingers over her bare skin.

"Fine. Tell me you don't want me," she says, wiping her cheek. "Tell me you want nothing to do with me, and I'll drop it."

I should. Even though it would be a complete lie, I should tell her that. It would be for her own good. I want her more than anything I've ever wanted in my life, but that's not enough, is it? We're at completely different stages. Her life is just starting. She deserves so much more than a single dad in a small town who barely has his own life together. I would only be holding her back.

Not to mention, Jared would never forgive me. He's in love with her, his best friend, and if he finds out there is something between us, it will crush him, which, in turn, will hurt Kira.

"Kira," I beg, my voice hoarse. I can't lie to her. "It doesn't matter what I want. What matters is what's best for you and Jared. That's all that's ever mattered to me."

"And you know what's best for me?" she asks, crossing her arms under her chest, making it even harder to hold onto my resolve.

"I don't. I just know I'm not it."

Before I can do something to make this whole situation worse, like pull her into my lap and hold her until she stops crying, I rise to my feet. I hate leaving her out here, but I'll change my mind if I stay.

When I get out of the shower, Kira is gone. Checking my phone, I breathe a sigh of relief at an unread message from her.

Kira

Going to Maddie's.

It was the right thing to do, I know it was, but the look in her eyes when she understood what I was saying nearly ended me. I have to keep reminding myself it's what needs to happen. I'm way too old for her, and any relationship between us would be doomed from the start.

None of that stops me from looking down at my bed and thinking about how Kira felt nestled in my arms the other morning. The softness of her bare skin on mine, the way she cuddled even further into me as she slept. I shake my head, trying to push those thoughts away. Maybe I can do what I always do when I need a distraction.

Grabbing two beers from the fridge, I head out the front door and across the street.

It only takes a couple of seconds after I knock for Keith to show up at the door, a confused look on his face.

"Oh god, what do you want?" he asks, his sarcasm evident.

Instead of responding, I press a bottle into his hands as I walk past him into the kitchen. What am I even supposed to say?

"Make yourself at home, why don't you?" Keith chides as I take a seat on his leather couch. He tilts his head before shrugging and sitting down in his matching recliner.

"Got the game on?" I ask with a nod in the direction of his massive TV. I've never really cared for baseball, but Keith loves it.

"Of course I do. Got some nachos in the oven, too. If you want some, you might want to make another tray."

"I'm all set, thanks."

We don't talk much throughout the game. Keith is too focused on our team winning. It's not like I could have gotten any words in any way. Keith was too busy screaming and clapping every time they made a run or cursing under his breath when the rival team did. It isn't until the bottom half of the ninth inning when he is sure that the Tigers will win, that he genuinely acknowledges me.

"Alright, tell me what's going on."

"Nothing, I just wanted to watch the game with you," I say, hoping he doesn't read any deeper into my tone. I can't tell him what's actually going through my head. There's no way he's going to understand the situation, and he's going to think I'm a perv. Anyone would. I had sex with my son's best friend. There's no sane way to justify that.

Keith levels a look at me, not tolerating an ounce of my bullshit.

"This is about Kira, isn't it?" It's more a statement than a question. My jaw tightens as I try to regulate my reaction. Does he know about

Kira and I? There's no way.

"What do you mean?"

"Noah, I wasn't born yesterday. I've seen the way you two look at each other. Not to mention, the tension between you two on the fourth was so thick, a fillet knife couldn't cut it."

Was it that obvious? I thought we were discreet, but now I'm wondering if anyone else noticed something was going on. I think about denying it again, but he knows me too well. I doubt he would believe it.

"Well, whatever it was, it's over now," I say with empty confidence. "I came to my senses and told her we couldn't do it anymore."

"God, I knew it," he says, sighing. "You're an idiot."

"I know. I never should have let anything happen between us. She's only nineteen, for Christ's sake. I feel like a piece of shit."

Keith shakes his head, and disappointment radiates from him.

"No, you dummy, you're an idiot for letting her go."

It takes me a minute to fully comprehend what he said, and even then, I'm sure I heard him wrong. There is no way he thinks that Kira and I should be together.

"Listen, in any other circumstance, I would tell you that you're a creep and need to stay as far away from her as possible, but this is Kira we're talking about here. She's different. I know you would never do anything to put that girl in danger," he explains.

"You can't be serious."

"Oh, but I am. It's so plainly obvious that she is in love with you, and I think you might love her too, or at least close to it. You've been happier than I've seen you since Angie. That shit is rare, and I know this situation isn't the most convenient, but you need to hold onto her for as long as she will let you."

"I'm not good for her, Keith. I would only hold her back."

"What the hell are you talking about? You are one of the most caring people I know. If anything, you will be there to support her in anything she wants to do."

I blanche. This is so far from what I expected from this conversation that I wasn't even planning on having. Never in a million years would I have expected Keith to tell me I should pursue something with Kira. He's crazy. Kira and I can't be together.

"Tell me what you're really afraid of," he says.

That's it, isn't it? I don't want to ruin her life. I don't want to be the one who stops her from living. But if I really think about it, I'm scared of history repeating itself. I can't get that close to someone again.

"What if *she* leaves me?" The question is so quiet I'm not sure he even hears it. I clear my throat, speaking a bit louder this time. "What if we're happy for a couple of years, but then, out of the blue, she realizes she doesn't want me anymore?"

We sit in mutual silence for a few seconds. I sound so pathetic, but it's the truth. I don't think I could survive it this time around. I loved Angie, but there's something more with Kira.

"That's a lot of what-ifs, Noah. Look, I know Angie hurt you, and fuck her for that, but you can't live your whole life afraid of letting anyone in. You deserve to be happy, and you need to accept that."

I sit in those words for a moment. None of the women since Angie have been serious, but that's because I've never felt a connection with any of them. I'd always been too focused on Jared, right?

God, I am an idiot.

"As much as I hate to admit it, I think you might be right," I mutter, looking up at Keith.

"Of course I am. Now get out of here. I have a game to watch, and you have a woman to apologize to," he says, ushering me toward the door. "And you're going to have to tell Jared."

What am I even going to say to her? I'm still not convinced this is a good idea, but Keith has a point. I've never felt this way about anyone before—this possessiveness bordering on ownership. I want to do everything in my power to keep her happy and safe.

Before I can think better of it, I tap on Kira's contact and press call. It rings so long that I'm convinced she isn't going to pick up. I mean, why would she? I was a complete asshole earlier. I'm about to hang up when a voice chirps on the other end.

"She doesn't want to talk to you."

Maddie.

At least that means she's still with her, but from the sounds of it, they aren't in her dorm room. Music thumps in the background, and I can hear people's unintelligible shouts.

"Can you please put her on the phone?" I ask, trying not to sound frustrated. I need to talk to her.

"Why would I do that? You really hurt her, you know."

The thought of Kira in pain because of me sends a deeper feeling of urgency through me.

"Please, Maddie. I fucked up, and I know that. I need to see her. At least tell me where you guys are."

She doesn't respond for a second, and the background noise dampens as if she went into another room.

"Fine, but you better not make me regret this. Kira is an absolute catch, and she deserves someone who loves her unapologetically. If I ever find out that you broke her heart again, I will personally track you down and fucking castrate you. Do you hear me?"

I rear back a little at her threat. She has every right to say that, but *Jesus Christ*.

"Loud and clear."

Maddie reluctantly gives me the address, but I'm in the truck before I can even respond. They're at a house party about twenty minutes away.

I'll make it there in ten.

chapter twenty-four
KIRA

I RECOGNIZE THE ALL-BLACK F150 THAT SPEEDS TO A STOP IN FRONT of me, and before I can even stand, he's shutting his door and striding toward me.

What is he doing here?

Maddie.

She's going to get an earful about this later. I should have known something was going on when she told me to wait out here for her.

"Go home, Noah," I order, my hand extending in front of me in a warning.

"Kira, please listen to me," he begs, his dark hair falling into his face as he looks down at me. His eyes roam over my body, and it takes me a second before I remember what I'm wearing. It's that same wrap dress from the night I kissed him.

His jaw ticks, his posture stiffening.

I have to remind myself why I'm here. He shut me out. Again. My arms cross over my chest as I look up at him.

"Why should I do that? You'll do the same thing you always do."

He towers over me, his eyes desperate. "I had no right to make that decision for you. I know that now. I'm sorry."

He pauses, stepping closer to me.

"All I've ever wanted is for you and Jared to be happy, and I'm honestly fucking terrified that I'll never be good enough for you, but the idea of not having you in my life doesn't feel like an option anymore."

Not good enough? He's more than enough. He's everything.

"Kira, I love you," he admits, "And I'm tired of fighting it."

My self-preservation instincts gnaw at me, trying to stop me from letting him in. What if he's saying this now but takes it back tomorrow? I'm not sure I can survive another rejection from this man.

Closing the space between us, I rest my hand on his chest. His heart is racing, his breathing ragged. Trailing my hand down his body, I look up into his eyes.

"One more chance. You have one chance to prove to me that you aren't going to run again," I warn, but my voice softens a bit when I add, "You are worthy of love, Noah, and I want to be the person who gives that to you, but I can only do it if you let me."

His fingers tangle into my hair, and I think he's going to kiss me, but instead, he presses his forehead into mine.

"You're mine. Forever if I have any say in it," he whispers, possessiveness seeping into his tone. His other hand slides down my body, stopping only when he reaches the hem of my skirt. I suck in a breath at his light touch against my skin. The feel of his powerful body pressed against mine makes me want to do things we definitely shouldn't. I should make him wait and brood a little longer, but I can't.

I need him.

Now.

"Prove it," I taunt against my better judgment.

He doesn't waste any time, his lips crashing into mine. His kiss is hungry, feral. I slide my hand up to the back of his neck, pulling him harder into me. He knocks my legs apart, pressing his thigh between them, the rough denim of his jeans rubbing against my bare skin. I let out a small moan as he brings his hand up to my already soaking panties.

"Fuck, princess, it's going to take all of my willpower not to fuck you right here," he says, tugging them to the side as his fingers slide over my pussy. I suck in a breath, my eyes fixed on his.

"Do it then."

The words leave my mouth without regard for the dozens of people right down the drive. Anyone could walk or drive over here and see us. I gasp as his fingers push into me, curving up at the perfect angle. He slides in and out of me teasingly as he looks down at me, his eyes dark with lust.

"Are you sure, princess? You'll have to be quiet."

Is there even any question?

"Yes, please," I practically beg as I unbutton his jeans.

He's already hard as I take him in my hand, and his lips meet mine again with a bruising kiss. Fuck, this feels so dirty, but I can't get enough of it. His hands reach beneath my skirt, sliding my panties down to my feet. I step out of them, and he takes them, tucking them into the back pocket of his jeans. Why is that the hottest thing I've ever seen?

In one fluid motion, I'm lifted into the air, Noah pinning me to the truck. His cock poised right at my entrance, he leans in, kissing and nipping at my neck. The feeling of him there, so close but not inside me, is torture.

"Please, Noah," I whine, needing to feel him.

"I love it when you beg for it," he growls. "Tell me what you need," he orders, sliding his cock over my pussy, purposely neglecting where I want it so badly.

"I need you to fuck me until your come is dripping out of me," I say, surprising myself.

His eyes flare, the desire in them all-consuming.

"Good girl," he praises as he pushes into me, the fullness making me cry out and dig my nails into his shoulders. Noah's hand grips my face, pulling me into a rough kiss as he drives into me.

I try to stay quiet, but my effort is fruitless. The feel of his hard length filling me is unmatched. He makes me feel so fucking good. If I could spend forever like this with him, I would.

It doesn't take long before I'm close, each thrust pushing me closer and closer to the edge. His thumb brushes over my clit, and I cry out. His other hand covers my mouth as he does it again, with more pressure this time. I'm so fucking close to coming when a car door slams, stopping us in our tracks.

My head shoots to the side to look down at the car. Thankfully, we're on the other side of the truck, so they shouldn't be able to see us, but Noah still sets me down, and I whimper in protest as he reaches for the driver's door behind me.

"Get in."

His tone is serious, so now is not the time to argue. I climb into the truck, sliding over to the passenger seat as Noah gets in after me, staring over at me with hooded eyes, his breathing ragged. I look down, his pants are still undone, and his cock is out.

Fuck, I want that back inside me *now.*

As if noticing my line of sight, he nods.

"Ride it."

I don't hesitate, climbing over the center console and straddling his lap. Reaching down, I guide him into me, sitting down until he's all the way in. Thankfully, the windows are tinted. No one can see us.

"Noah," I moan, rocking my hips into him.

"There you go, princess, that's it."

I pick up my pace, needing more, as he pushes my dress down and pulls one of my nipples into his mouth. Ah, the benefits of not wearing a bra. I keep riding him, the feeling of him so deep in me fucking delicious and unexpectedly intimate. Before I know it, his fingers are back on my clit, and it doesn't take long before I'm tightening around him.

"Fuck, There it is, baby, come for me."

It's too much, it's all too much. I let out a loud moan as my orgasm barrels through me. Noah isn't far behind, pumping into me a couple more times before I feel him filling me with a low groan.

We take a minute to catch our breaths, his hand rising to caress my face. It's so soft it almost makes me want to cry. The safety I feel in his arms is so complete. I know I shouldn't have feelings for this man, but it's too late. He's already burrowed so far under my skin that I'm convinced I wouldn't survive without him.

"Noah…I love you too," I admit, still panting.

He doesn't say anything, kissing my forehead before helping me off him and into the passenger seat.

THERE AREN'T WORDS TO EXPLAIN HOW MY HEART PLUMMETS WHEN we pull into the driveway and Jared's car is there. I look over at Noah, silently questioning if he knows anything. As if he can sense my suspicion, he shakes his head.

"I promise you I didn't know he'd be here. Fuck, this is the worst timing possible. Are you going to be okay?" There's genuine concern in his voice, and that fact makes me feel like I will.

"I'll be fine. Let's go before I lose my nerve," I say, my hand poised on the door handle. Noah's brows knit together, but he follows my lead anyway. Stepping out of the truck, I let him lead us into the house. My pulse is racing, and nausea swirls low in my stomach.

Jared is settled on the couch, scrolling on his phone. His head shoots up as the door opens, and his eyes immediately snap to mine. He doesn't look angry, which surprises me.

"Kira," he mutters.

"Jared," I say back, not knowing how to react.

He's going to know. He has to. I can only imagine how we look right now.

"Can I talk to you?" he asks, standing up and gesturing for me to follow him. I nod, pushing down the anxiety. He leads me onto the porch and sits on the porch swing, patting the space next to him exactly where I sat that night with Noah.

I don't sit there, instead opting for the chair across from the swing. The rough feeling of the wood against my skin reminds me that I'm not wearing underwear. A small frown crosses Jared's lips before he quickly recovers, green eyes meeting mine again.

"I'm sorry it's taken so long for me to say this, but I'm sorry for how I acted the night of the party."

"Jared," I interrupt. He was hurt, and while I don't appreciate how he treated me, I'm not mad at him. Not to mention the guilt coursing through me right now about the fact that his dad's come is dropping out of me as we speak. My cheeks heat at the sensation, and I attempt to refocus my attention on Jared.

"No, don't do that. I was an asshole, and I'm sorry. I understand if you hate me, but if there is any way you can forgive me, I would still love to be your friend. I miss you, Kira."

I glance up at the slider. Noah is watching us, far away enough not to hear our conversation but close enough to intervene if needed.

"Of course, I still want to be your friend, Jared. You will always be my best friend."

His posture softens, and his usual grin reappears on his face. It warms my heart. I missed him like this.

"I'm so glad that's over. I've been stressing out about this conversation for the past couple of days. I was sure you'd tell me to fuck off."

I squirm a little in my seat, uncomfortable as hell with the situation under my dress. I don't want to seem like I'm trying to run away, but I desperately need a shower and a change of clothes.

"I would never do that. I love you, Jared—as a friend—and I will always want you in my life," I tell him. "But I'm really tired."

"Oh, go ahead. Sorry for keeping you," he says sheepishly.

I'm officially a terrible friend.

chapter twenty-five
KIRA

W HEN I ENTER THE KITCHEN, NOAH IS LEANING AGAINST THE island, staring down at his phone. He's only wearing the pair of black and white plaid pajama pants that he went to bed in last night, and his chest is on full display. I force my eyes up to his face, and his gaze meets mine with a smirk.

Asshole. Stepping closer, I drag my nails down his torso, stopping at his waistband. Now it's my turn to smirk as his eyes darken.

"Kira," he warns, nodding towards Jared's room.

My smile quickly fades as the reality of our situation washes over me.

"We're going to have to tell him," I say.

"I know," is all Noah says.

When Jared slinks out of his room around noon, I'm outside on the porch, book in hand. Noah sat with me for a while but left a bit ago to shower. We talked about telling Jared, but I still feel like it's too soon. He's only now staying at the house again. He needs more time. Or is it me who needs the time? I shake my head, focusing back on my book.

"Morning," Jared greets as the slider door opens.

"Afternoon," I tease, grinning up at him.

He tries to meet my enthusiasm, but his smile doesn't reach his eyes.

"I hope you know that I really am sorry, Kira. It was fucked up of me to say those things to you," he says, his face genuine. "I don't want to lose you…"

"I know that, Jared," I say, standing up from my chair and walking over to him. I wrap my arms around his neck, pulling him to me. "It's okay, I forgive you."

"Thank you," he responds, hugging me tighter.

Relief stabs at me with his acceptance, but it feels artificial. The guilt over my relationship with his dad overtakes any feeling of closeness I have with Jared. If he knew about Noah and I—I can't let myself think about that right now. We're going to tell him, just not today.

The remainder of our day is rather mundane. Jared and I watch some reality TV show, and Noah makes grilled shrimp and veggies for lunch. The sun is brushing the horizon when Jared invites me to go out with him and his friends.

"Kira, come on, just this once? The guys will be here in a minute to get us," he begs with his best puppy-dog eyes from the ground next to me. "I'm going to be leaving for college soon," he adds, trying to guilt me into going.

Sitting up in the hammock, I shake my head apologetically. "I'm really not in the mood to socialize. I'm sorry." It's not a lie per se; I don't want to socialize with any of *his friends*. Ever. The thought of being in the same car with any of "the guys" makes me want to take an oath of silence and retreat to a mountaintop somewhere.

"Fine," he whines with no real disappointment. He knows I don't hang out with them by choice, though he's never understood why. Rising to his feet, he looks down at me. "Enjoy your boring night in," he says as he returns to the house.

"I love you, drive safe!" I call, using my foot to swing the hammock. "Yeah, yeah. I love you too," Jared answers. He disappears into the house, leaving me alone back here. I do feel bad that I'm not going out with him. He is leaving soon, and I will miss him so much, but there is no way I'm putting myself in a position like that right now, especially not with Zach back in town.

My skin pricks at the thought of him, and my heart rate skyrockets. I have to force myself to take deep breaths to calm my nerves, sucking in the chilly night air. I hate that he still has this effect on me. I stare up at the deep navy and lavender sky through the branches of the trees. The stars are starting to show themselves, and the sounds of crickets and frogs fill my ears. Closing my eyes, I take it all in. I'm safe here.

A shiver racks through me. The temperature has dropped significantly since we came out here. My tank top and leggings aren't doing me any favors, either. I slide myself out of the hammock and start to make my way back into the house, but I freeze. Movement flashes on the side of the house.

"Jared?" I ask, hoping to hear his voice.

Nothing.

It's probably just a deer, I tell myself, forcing the thought into my head to steady my pulse. I have to stop being so jumpy. But the unease in my chest won't subside. My eyes keep scanning the darkness, glued to the shadows that seem to pulse and shift. Something feels wrong.

I'm halfway to the deck when the silence shatters. A sound behind me, barely audible, makes my heart lurch—then a figure steps out of the shadows.

Bile rises in my throat, bitter and sour, as my eyes lock onto him. His features come into focus, and the world tilts on its axis. His eyes—nearly black, lifeless—are fixed on me with a cold, calculating stare. No. This isn't happening. How the hell did he get here? He must've come in the same car as Jared's friends.

All of the fury, fear, and disgust come rushing back, flooding my chest.

I force my breath to steady, but it comes out in shallow, uneven gasps. I can't show him how terrified I am, not now. But as I glance between him and the steps leading to freedom, it hits me: I can't run.

He prowls closer, each step measured, slow, deliberate. A predator stalking its prey. My muscles tense, my body screaming at me to flee, to do anything to escape. But I stand frozen. Every instinct in my body tells me to run, but I can't move.

"Don't come any closer," I command, putting as much confidence in my words as possible. His head tilts in response, a menacing grin consuming his features.

"Oh, that's cute," he sneers. "You think you can tell me what to do?" He reaches for my face, his fingers just inches away from my skin. My whole body recoils as I turn away, barely escaping his touch. He laughs—a low, mocking sound.

My blood runs cold, a chill so deep it sinks into my bones.

"Go ahead," he taunts, voice thick with dark promise. "Fight me. Makes it more fun."

Anger surges through me, hot and blinding. But beneath it, the all-too-familiar feeling of helplessness is creeping in, gnawing at my resolve. I feel like that scared little girl again. My throat tightens, the sting of unshed tears burning at my eyes, but I won't give him the satisfaction. I won't cry. Not this time.

"I'm not fifteen anymore. I won't let you take advantage of me again."

"Take advantage of you? You were practically begging for it."

Those words.

Those fucking words.

All of the feelings of guilt and shame and helplessness crash into me. My mom's words at the police station. The detective's questions. Maybe he's right. I was letting him flirt with me, wasn't I? I was excited to have a boy's attention for once, not only a boy but an older boy.

That's not how it works, though. I was drunk. He made sure of that. Thoughts of Amelia from the other night fill my head. Her situation was so similar to mine. Would I tell her that it was her fault? That she shouldn't have put herself in that situation?

No.

I sat there with her to make sure she was safe. I was seconds away from finding that man and ensuring he couldn't do that to any girl ever again. It isn't her fault that some guy thought he could prey on a young girl.

I may have been stupid for drinking at a party like that, but I was a kid. He was the adult. I think back to my fifteen-year-old self, just wanting to fit in, wanting to escape the shit going on at home. He saw that weakness and exploited it.

But I'm not fifteen anymore.

This man is a monster. I see that now. That's what he is to his core. An inexplicably powerful amount of anger—no, it's beyond that—pure, unadulterated rage surges through me. If this man thinks he can so much as touch me again—

His hand wraps around my upper arm, his grip bound to cut off circulation. The urge to run transforms into a visceral need to fight back. I will not let him hurt me again. My fingers curl into a tight fist, my knuckles turning white. All the hatred I once focused on myself flips.

It wasn't my fault.

It was his.

With all of the pent-up emotions swirling in my veins, I send my fist into his nose. The contact is immediate. But I'm too high on adrenaline to let the pain register. The tangy metallic taste fills my mouth. I'm no stranger to it, but this time is different. It feels good.

Zach stumbles backward, not expecting me to hit him. His face quickly morphs from shock to fury, and I suddenly don't feel confident anymore. He's bigger and stronger than me.

"You fucking bitch," he grunts, closing the space between us.

He's mere inches away when his body jerks backward.

"*You*," a voice growls.

Noah. I almost cry out in relief.

"I've been waiting for this," he says right before his fist connects with Zach's face. Unlike my punch, this one sends him to the ground. He spits out blood, bewildered.

"What the fuck, man?"

Noah's eyes meet mine for only a moment, and the violence in them makes me pause. His fist pounds into Zach's face yet again.

Is he going to stop? Do I want him to?

"Dad, what the fuck?" Jared yells, sprinting from the front yard.

Noah freezes for a second before fisting Zach's collar and pulling his face to his.

"If you ever lay a finger on her again, I will fucking kill you," he warns, shoving him back to the ground. Noah stands right as Jared approaches him.

"What the fuck happened? Zach, are you okay?" Jared asks. His concern for this monster makes my stomach twist. I have to remind myself that he doesn't know.

Noah ignores the questions, striding toward me. He pulls me into him, his hand brushing through my hair. His heart pounds as I hold him tighter, a tear slipping down my cheek. The rest of the world dampens, and it's just us. I take a deep breath, his body guarding me from the chaos. Noah will keep me safe. That knowledge feeds a confidence deep within me.

"Regardless of what happens, know that this isn't your fault," he whispers, pressing a kiss to my head before loosening his grip.

"Dad, answer me!" Jared shouts. "Jared—"

But it's not Noah's question to answer. It's mine.

"He raped me."

I take a deep breath, channeling all of the conviction I have left. "Four years ago, at a party, Zach raped me," I say as quickly as possible, hating how the words sound coming from my lips. I look over at Jared, his face flipping between outrage and confusion.

"She's lying!" Zach's nostrils flare as he yells. "That bitch is a fucking tease. She wanted it."

"Watch your mouth," Noah growls, and Zach visibly shrinks.

Jared's eyes finally meet mine, and I can tell he's trying to figure out who to believe.

"Go home," Jared says, his gaze falling on Zach. "And don't fucking come back."

I allow myself to breathe again, tears still falling as I try to process the weight of everything that's happened. Noah's arm is still around me, my back to his chest, offering the only stability I can cling to right now.

But then I hear Jared's voice—a sharp, frantic edge creeping into it that sends a shiver through me.

"Why did he know and not me?" His voice is frantic. "Wait. Why is he touching you like that?"

It's like being submerged in freezing water. My whole body tenses, a shock of guilt and confusion coursing through me. The realization hits me slowly, creeping up my spine with each word Jared speaks. It's as if the world tilts, and everything I thought was safe, secure, is suddenly spinning out of control.

"Oh my god, are you two..." he trails off, interrupting himself. "No, that would be so fucked up."

I feel the ground shift beneath me, my chest tightening with every inch of space that opens between us. I push out of Noah's arms, instinctively reaching for Jared, but he stiffens in my arms, pulling back just enough to let me hug him reluctantly. He looks so broken.

"Tell me you two aren't fucking. Please, tell me he was just comforting you because of what happened."

The words hit me like a punch to the stomach. I can't look at him. The weight of everything we've both been through, the guilt, the choices I've made—it's too much. I want to scream, to make it all go away, but I can't. He deserves the truth. He deserves honesty, even if it breaks us.

I take a slow breath, my chest tight, trying to steady myself as my gaze meets his. I can't find the words at first, but then, they slip out in a shaky whisper.

"Jared, I'm so sorry."

chapter twenty-six
NOAH

"It all makes so much sense now..." The dejection in his voice cuts deep. We did this to him. *I did this to him.* He shakes his head and pushes her away, not saying anything as he rounds the house, and his car starts in the driveway.

What kind of father would do something like this to his kid? That sweet little boy who loved working with his dad in the shop is gone. The look he gave me was far from the admiration he used to have.

I failed him.

"Hey," Kira whispers, her hand touching my cheek. "He's going to be okay." Her arms wrap around my torso, and I pull her into me, resting my chin on her hair. The scent that is so uniquely her fills my nostrils. We're going to get through this. Jared will come around. He has to.

We stand like that until Kira stops shaking. I may be worried about Jared, but she had to face her rapist tonight. Anger simmers below the surface, but I force it down. I can plot his murder later. Right now, I need to be here for her.

"Come on, let's get you inside," I say, my voice soft.

She nods, letting me lead her to the door. She still doesn't speak when we reach the bathroom, jumping at the sound of the rushing water as I fill the bathtub. Instinctively, I go for her, kneeling to meet her gaze. It takes a moment for her red-rimmed eyes to focus on me.

"It's okay, you're safe now," I reassure her, my hands resting on her thighs. She looks more like herself when she nods again, and relief creeps into my chest.

"I'm so proud of you, you know that?" I tell her, my thumb grazing over her cheek. The touch is light, but she leans into it.

"Why?" she asks, her eyebrows scrunching together.

Of course, she doesn't get it. She doesn't realize how strong she is. "You stood up to that piece of shit. That was a good punch, by the way," I tell her, trying to lighten the mood. It works, a small smile gracing her lips.

I turn the faucet off on the tub and gesture for Kira to stand.

"Do you want me to stay?" I ask, glancing between her and the water. I don't want to leave her alone here, but I don't want to push this either. There is a real possibility that she doesn't want anything to do with me after what happened, and I would completely understand if she told me to leave. I single-handedly ruined her relationship with her best friend. They both should hate me.

"Stay, please," she says, reaching for her shirt and pulling it above her head. I suck in a breath at the sight. I've seen her naked before, but this feels different, more vulnerable. As the rest of her clothes drop to the floor, she slides her hands to the hem of my shirt, pushing it up my body.

"What are you doing?" I ask, barely disguising the heat in my voice. The sensation of her hands on me is like a drug.

"I want you in with me."

It's on the tip of my tongue to tell her there is no way we're both fitting in that tub, but her eyes inform me she isn't taking no for an answer. I pull my shirt off by the collar before moving to the top of my jeans. Kira's hand stops me, her fingers unbuttoning them with ease.

If the situation were any different, I would be hauling her into my bed, the bathwater forgotten. But it's not, and we aren't doing that tonight. She needs time to process all of this.

I climb into the water first, heat spreading over my lower body as I sit at the back. Without guidance, she steps in, nestling herself into me. Her hips fit perfectly between my thighs, and she rests her head on my chest, the water sitting right below her breasts, framing them. I glide my fingers up her stomach, stopping before reaching where I want to touch her.

"Hand me the soap," I tell her.

She listens. Squeezing some out, I lather it in my hands. I wash her body, massaging her tight muscles.

When we get out of the bath, I get Kira tucked in bed and draft a text to Jared. It takes me four revisions to figure out what to say.

Noah

I know this is fucked up, and I'm sorry for not telling you. You don't have to forgive me, but please let me know you're safe somewhere?

Noah

I promise this wasn't intentional. It kind of just happened. I never wanted to hurt you.

He doesn't respond right away, and I try not to worry. He's angry, I get it. By the time I get to bed, Kira is already asleep, so I climb in behind her and pull her warm body into mine. My phone lights up, and I hurry to unlock it.

Jared

I'm fine. I'm at a friend's.

I breathe a sigh of relief as I type out my response.

Noah

Thank you. I love you.

The bubble pops up to show that he's typing, but it disappears without a response.

It's been a few days since Jared found out, and I've received very little communication from him. I didn't expect much, but his lack of response forces me to realize the gravity of the situation. We might never be as close as we were, which devastates me. It was always him and I, our little family unit. He's a part of me, and I'm not sure I can handle the thought of him hating me forever.

But all that fades when she looks up at me from the kitchen island,

and I set a mug full of coffee beside her. Her face has been buried in her laptop all morning. She's signing up for her classes for this fall. It seems like it would be a simple process, but it is *not*.

"Do you want me to see if I can figure it out?" I offer, knowing damn well I can't. Computers and I are not friends.

"Tech help from an old man? No, thank you," she says with a laugh, closing her laptop in defeat. "I'll figure it out later." She stands to bring her now empty plate to the sink. The dish clinks as it makes contact with the others, and then I'm behind her, pinning her to the counter. Her breathing picks up as my hand grips the base of her jaw. I force her to look up at me.

"Old man, huh?" I taunt.

She struggles to nod under my grip, mischief written all over her face.

The attitude on this girl.

I loosen my hold, spinning her so she's facing me. I close in, our faces inches apart.

"You're lucky I have to go to work," I growl.

Her lips part as she looks up at me, her warm eyes filled with lust. She wants the punishment. Well, she's going to have to wait. I press a soft kiss to her lips, drop my hand from her face, and grab my to-go mug.

She whimpers in response, pouting in my direction. I avert my gaze, not sure I can say no to her if she begs me to stay home.

"Maddie's coming over tonight, right?" I ask. "I don't like the idea of leaving you here alone.""

I've been trying to ignore Zach's presence in this town, but I don't trust him to stay away from her, and she is vulnerable staying home alone.

She groans in response. "Don't worry, my babysitter will be here at six. She has classes today."

I chuckle, and Kira rolls her eyes. I don't care if it annoys her. I'm going to make sure I do everything in my power to keep her safe.

The temperature has cooled off by the time I get to the station, a sign of autumn creeping in. I take a deep breath, thankful for the change in weather. I love summer, but I'm ready not to be sweating all day.

Following my usual routine, I first prep dinner for everyone while Dave talks my ear off about his family vacation coming up next month. He's taking his husband and kids to Florida for a week. I get it, though; it's exciting. I would give anything for a vacation right about now.

"Elijah is going to love the resort. They have a spa and a hot tub. Hopefully, we can get some alone time," he says, his blue eyes lighting up. I laugh.

"I'm happy for you guys. You deserve it," I tell him for probably the fourth time. I mean it, though. Dave is a fantastic person and deserves to treat himself once in a while.

I'm heading out to do some routine maintenance on one of the trucks when a call comes in.

Dispatch to station 4. A large fire was spotted in a three-story residential building downtown at the college. The address is 5655 Lakeview. All personnel requested.

The dorms?

Fuck, that's not good. Instead of going left to the trucks, I take a sharp right to the lockers. My brain switches into autopilot, pulling on and fastening my fire suit. In seconds, Dave is beside me, racing to get his gear on alongside the rest of the crew. We're not a big station, so we only have four guys on duty. If Traverse City is calling us in, it must be bad.

We all hop into the truck, me in the driver's seat. I glance at the time on the wall before we pull out. It's six-fifteen. Maddie should already be at the house.

The girls *should* be safe. I hold onto that thought because I don't have time to dwell on what could happen. These people are relying on us to help them. Flipping on the sirens, I speed out of the garage.

chapter twenty-seven
KIRA

Maddie pulls in at five-fifty with a grocery bag full of ingredients for sundaes. She hands me a carton of vanilla bean ice cream, and I hug it to my chest. It's basic, but it's my favorite. We've only been friends for a few months, but she already knows me almost as well as Jared does. I wince. I've been trying to contact him, but he's ignoring me. I brush it off.

Maddie sets her blue moon ice cream on the counter and proceeds to haul out various candies, syrups, and sprinkles. It looks like she robbed Willy Wonka's factory to get this much stuff.

"Do you have—" I start to ask as she wordlessly sets a can of whipped cream next to the other accouterments.

"What's the occasion?" I ask, mildly concerned. Something is off. She isn't her usual self.

"Trust me, we need it," she says, her voice tired. I examine her appearance. There's a slight slouch in her posture and a puffiness around her eyes.

"What's wrong?" I ask.

Her bottom lip shakes as she tries to hold in her tears, and my heart sinks. I pull her into a hug. She melts into me, a sob escaping her lips. I hold her while she cries, rubbing small circles on her back. She takes a few deep breaths and releases me.

"Lucy and I… we aren't together anymore," she explains, voice cracking at the mention of her. That is the last thing I expected her to say. They were so happy together. She notices the confusion on my face and sighs.

"Lucy isn't out to her parents."

I nod slowly, starting to understand.

"I thought I would be okay with it. It's college. We're not really around our parents anyway. But her parents visit every weekend, and I get introduced as her *friend* every time," she says with air quotes.

"I can't be someone's secret, Kira. I spent too long hiding from myself. I can't go back to that."

My heart breaks for her. I can't imagine something like that. I grab her hand, gesturing for her to look at me.

"You deserve someone who is openly proud to be with you. Maybe that can be Lucy eventually, but if not, I need you to know that you are a fucking catch, Maddie. If your person doesn't show you off, they're not good enough for you."

Tears still stream down her face as she smirks at me. "Sounds like you need to take your own advice, Kira."

I let out a breath, shaking my head.

"You know that's different."

"Is it?" she asks, her eyes narrowing.

The only difference is Jared. His anger and hurt about our relationship are valid, and I don't want to make it worse.

"Look, right now, it's still fresh with Jared, and I get that, but the same goes for you. You deserve someone who will love you shamelessly."

"I think it's time for ice cream," I announce, changing the subject.

"I second that statement," Maddie says with a small smile.

We load our bowls full of all the possible toppings. I cover my ice cream with strawberry syrup and sprinkles. If this were a fro-yo shop, the bill would be massive.

"Gilmore Girls or Supernatural?" I ask as I plop onto the couch.

Maddie grabs a blanket and snuggles in next to me, ice cream in hand.

"Supernatural. Start on season four, though. I need some Destiel tonight." That earns a giggle from me as I select the show.

We're halfway into the episode when Maddie's phone goes off. We both glance at the caller ID, and Lucy's name lights up.

"I'm not answering," she asserts, but conflict wars in her eyes.

Despite her noticeable desire to do the opposite, she lets the phone ring, not reaching for it once. When it stops, we look at each other, still silent, both jumping when it starts to ring again.

"I'm just going to tell her to stop calling," Maddie rationalizes as she lifts her phone from the table. I'm about to snatch it back, but she swipes to accept the call. She musters up as much confidence as she can before speaking.

"I don't want to talk right now."

Her face quickly shifts, though, from hurt to complete concern.

"I'm at Kira's, why? What's going on?"

Her face goes white as Lucy answers, and I catch a few words.

Fire. College dorms.

"Let me put you on speaker real quick," Maddie says.

"There's a massive fire at your dorm building downtown. It's horrifying. I wanted to make sure you were safe. They're taking people out in ambulances. Even a firefighter had to get put on a stretcher," Lucy explains.

Those words rob my body of oxygen. It wouldn't be Noah. His station doesn't service Traverse City. My heart races as I search for my phone, tapping Noah's contact as fast as possible.

It rings.

And rings.

"Hello, this is Noah. Leave a message."

Shit.

He's probably just busy. There's no reason to think he went downtown to that fire. Maddie recognizes the panic in my eyes and stands.

"We've got to go. Thank you for calling," she says before tapping the red hangup button.

"Let's go."

"Go where? We don't even know if he's down there," I tell her.

"We can see if he's at the station."

Maddie drives, and I call Noah again on the way. He's probably completely fine and going to think I'm a maniac for calling him seven times in a row, but I don't care. I focus on my breathing, telling myself that everything is fine.

When we pull into the station, my eyes scan the parking lot and land on the garage. One of the trucks is missing. My jaw tightens as I throw open the car door and make a beeline for the entrance. I push the glass door harder than intended, scaring the old man behind the desk.

"Sorry," I mutter. "I'm looking for Noah Keller. Have you seen him?"

"He's not here right now. He's on a call. There's a fire at the dorms downtown. Everyone got called in to help. Is there something I can help you with?" His voice is calm, a complete contrast to my emotions.

He's down there. A firefighter is hurt.

"No, thank you, though," I say as I whip around and sprint to the car.

"They're down there. At the fire," I rush out, my breaths coming in short bursts. I need to get downtown. Now.

"Kira, it's okay. I'm sure he's fine. Take some deep breaths. I'll get us there."

"They're not going to let us get anywhere near that scene," I say, my voice shaky.

"They're not going to have a choice," she says as she throws the car in reverse and speeds out of the parking lot.

I need to tell Jared. I don't want him to panic, but he needs to know. Pulling out my phone, I press 'call' under his name. Come on, Jared, I know you're mad at me, but please pick up. To my surprise, on the third ring, I hear his voice.

"Kira," he starts. "Listen, I don't want to talk to you or my dad right now. Please stop calling me."

On any other day, those words would have broken me, but I can't focus on them right now.

"Jared, wait," I say before he can hang up. "It's your dad. I mean, It's probably nothing, but his crew is at that fire downtown right now, and apparently, it's really bad." I ramble, trying to get my point across. "Maddie's gir—ex-girlfriend called and told us that she saw a fireman hauled out on a stretcher."

There's no response on the other end, and I'm convinced he hung up until he mutters a whispered curse.

"Where?" he asks, his tone hard.

"The dorms at Northwestern," I answer. "I just thought you should know about it."

"Thanks," he grumbles, and a tone indicates the call has ended.

I'm pretty sure he's going to hate me forever.

As soon as we even get close to downtown Traverse City, the roads are blocked. Traffic is stopped, and they're directing cars away from the college.

"We're going to have to go on foot," I tell Maddie.

"Already on it," she says, pulling onto a side street and shoving her car into park. We waste no time, stepping out and jogging toward the chaos. We're about five blocks from the college, and even from here, the blaze licking up over the top of the building is visible.

"He's okay, Kira, I'm sure of it."

I nod, but there's no way she can know that. This has always been a risk for him. He puts his life on the line to save others. My heart rattles in my chest as we jog down the street toward the danger.

We're stopped in our tracks by flashing blue and red lights. It's a roadblock, officers stationed on either side. I suck in a breath. There's no way they're going to let us through.

"Follow me," Maddie says, guiding me into some trees on the side of the road. I catch a glimpse of the bay in the distance as we stumble through the brush. My heart races as we give a wide berth, sticking to the trees for longer than is likely necessary. Thankfully, the officers' main goal is to stop cars from driving through their barricade, so they don't notice us.

He's going to be okay. Everything will be okay.

I let out a shaky breath as we pop back out onto the street. I'm overwhelmed by the sheer size of the scene in front of me. The entire building is on fire, flames spilling out all of the windows, and I can feel the heat radiating from it. There's a crowd of people, many of them students, watching helplessly as it all unfolds. I push through them.

Where is he?

I scan the slew of firefighters, trying to see if he's there with them. My eyes land on one of the men, not Noah, but Jeff. One of the firemen from Noah's station. He's part of the team keeping the crowd at bay.

"Jeff!" I call, trying to project my voice as loudly as possible.

His head spins around, his eyes softening in recognition. He bounds toward me.

"What are you doing down here?" he asks.

"Where's Noah?" I ignore his question. I need to know that he's alright. He has to be alright.

His face hardens, and he takes a moment to respond as his eyes flick to the burning building.

"Inside."

chapter twenty-eight
NOAH

Thirty Minutes Earlier

"Where's Dave?" I ask, concern lacing my voice.

The fire burns hot, the flames licking up the side of the building. We've rescued almost all the students left inside, but this fire hasn't been easy. Our running theory is a possible gas leak on the lower level.

"I don't know, I can't find him either!" Jeff shouts over the sound of the blaze. "The last time I saw him was when he ran back inside."

A weight lands on my chest. That was almost twenty minutes ago. That's too long. One of the other crew's men already had to be rushed to the hospital due to smoke inhalation.

"Last one!" an officer calls as he carries a woman out of the building. She's covered in burns and looks to be unconscious. She doesn't look much older than Kira. That could have been Kira. *She's at home,* I remind myself. *She's safe.*

I eye the entrance to the building, smoke billowing out of the doorway. There's not enough time. It doesn't matter; he's part of my crew, and he's making it out. I pull my mask onto my face and stride toward the door. A hand lands on my chest right as I reach it.

"No one else goes in," the man orders, his gloved hand still on my chest. I don't recognize him. He must be from one of the other departments.

"One of our officers is in there," I tell him. I'll be damned if anyone tries to tell me to abandon one of my men.

"Doesn't matter. I was ordered not to let anyone else enter. The structure isn't safe."

I cringe at his statement. I know it's protocol, and he's just doing his job, but I'm not leaving Dave in there.

"Fine," I say, backing away with my hands raised.

The officer nods as he watches me. He won't budge, and I need to find a way in.

"I need a favor," I tell Jeff.

"Sure, anything. Did you find Dave?"

I shake my head. "He won't let me in," I say, gesturing toward the officer guarding the door. "I need you to distract him."

We're quickly running out of time.

The conflict in his features makes me nervous, but he sighs and finally nods. He runs toward the man, saying something that I can't hear. The man nods and follows Jeff over to the truck.

Now is my chance.

To avoid suspicion, I walk to the entrance. I'm feet away when a voice booms behind me.

"Noah, what are you doing?"

It's Al.

His eyes level me, but I only have time to look back at him with a chin dip as I disappear behind the flames. The heat is immediate. I scan the inside of the building. Where the fuck could he have gone? Debris blocks the path to the left hallway, so I head right.

"Dave!" I call as I look into the first room.

This building must have at least fifty dorms. He could be anywhere. Not finding any trace of him, I continue down the hall. A thud sounds in front of me as pieces of the ceiling hit the ground. My pulse quickens, but I try to control it. There's only so much oxygen in this Air-Pak, and I need to conserve as much of it as possible. There's a high chance that Dave will need it.

I continue through the hallway. Dread fills me, spreading further with each empty room. What if I'm too late? Opening the last door leads me to a stairwell.

"Dave, where the fuck are you?" I call, listening as hard as I can for an answer. Sweat drips down my back as I climb the soot-covered stairs. The door for the second level is being held open by what looks like an end table from one of the rooms.

Always have an exit strategy.

"Dave! Can you hear me?" I yell through the haze of smoke.

I listen, needing to hear his voice. Sirens blare from somewhere outside, and the fire is so goddamn loud.

"Help! We need help!" I hear a scream down the hall, but it's not Dave. It's a woman's voice. I charge toward the sound, looking into each room before I freeze. Wearing an officer's gas mask is a woman in her early twenties. She's huddled down in the corner, her arms and hands badly burned. She sobs as I enter, making an effort to stand.

"Please, he needs help," she begs.

I follow her line of sight, and my heart stops when I see it. Dave is on the ground, unconscious, a beam pinning his leg to the ground.

"Shit, is he breathing?" I ask as I kneel to check his pulse. His heart rate is faint, but it's there.

"Yes, I've been sharing the mask with both of us. I couldn't leave him here," she cries. "But, I can't get him out."

"You did great," I tell her. "Can you walk?"

She looks at me, nodding frantically.

"Okay, good," I pull my mask off, putting it over Dave's face.

"What's your name?"

"Susan," she answers.

"Okay, Susan. I'm Noah. Hold this mask while I free his leg," I explain. She obeys, watching as I analyze the situation.

The beam must have fallen when he was trying to rescue her. It's large, but I should be able to move it.

Wrapping my hands around the burnt wood, I lift it as high as possible, exposing his leg from below. The awkward angle of his foot tells me that something is likely broken. Channeling all of my strength into moving the beam, I toss it to the side, and it lands a few feet away. Dave stirs at the sound, and his voice is music to my ears.

"What is going on?" he asks, looking over at me.

The sounds of the building falling apart around us fill my ears.

"You're hurt, and we need to get out of here. Now," I explain, my voice hoarse from the smoke.

He nods, still dazed. His screams drown out the sirens as I haul him onto my shoulder. I wince, knowing that he is in excruciating pain, but he must pass out again because he goes silent.

"Let's go," I tell Susan, leading the way.

I glance in the direction I came from, grateful to see the door still open. Holding Dave's legs with my right hand, I slowly navigate the stairwell, trying my best not to irritate his injury. The heat is suffocating now, and I'm running out of oxygen. We round the corner, and my heart drops when I look at what was our exit.

Flames burn high on the other side of the door that leads to the first-floor hallway. I try the door, but it doesn't move. Debris is probably blocking it. I try again, sending my body weight into the metal, but it doesn't budge.

"Are we stuck?" Susan cries as I rethink our plan.

This can't be the only exit. I try to remember the building's layout from the map we reviewed before we entered. There should be three stairwells—two on either side and one toward the center.

"Do you know how to get to the main staircase?" I ask, hoping she lives here or at least visits often.

She's silent for a moment, my question processing in her mind.

"The one by the elevators? Yeah, I do."

"Can you take us there? That might be our only way out," I say, hoping and praying that that exit is clear. I follow Susan, moving as fast as I can without passing out. The smoke is starting to get to me. We trudge up the stairs and through the hallway on the second floor.

"It's right over here," she yells, pointing to a set of metal doors. I step before her, pushing the doors open with my shoulder. We carefully head down the steps, avoiding the rubble and quickly reaching the door to the main lobby. I see daylight through the glass, and I almost cry.

I shove open the door, stepping into the flame-filled room as a deafening sound booms from our left. The force throws my body to the side, and a shooting pain moves up my arm as we land.

I fade in and out of consciousness, focusing on the flashing blue and red lights outside. *Go! Get out of here!* I want to yell, but I can't. It's like I'm not physically here. Susan appears in the corner of my vision, her hands ripping at her mask. She slaps it onto my face as tears stream from her eyes.

God, this is it, isn't it? This is the end. Dave isn't going to make it to that Florida vacation. I'm never going to see Kira or Jared again. My son is forever going to resent me for what I did to him, and I won't have the opportunity to apologize or even explain myself. My body feels weak, my vision fading.

You are worthy of love, Noah, and I want to be the person who gives that to you.

Kira's words replay in my mind, and I grab onto them.

I'm not done fighting.

I suck in air, and my body shoots up as Susan yelps, her hands dropping from my face.

"Jesus, I thought you were dead!"

The fear in her eyes proves her point, and I work to stabilize my vision, everything wobbling.

"Not yet," I grunt. "Let's go," I say, heaving Dave back onto my shoulders. A sharp pain radiates through my wrist, but I push past it. Our path is far from clear, but the sight of the door gives me the edge I need.

I step around the pieces of building littering the floor, trying my best to keep my balance, the mixture of a lack of oxygen and the hit to my head making it hard to focus. We're feet from the door now, and I look to Susan.

"Go, we'll be right behind you!"

She nods, ready to get out of here. I'm at her heels and feel my legs about to give out. I know I won't be able to stay vertical much longer. I take the last few steps, emerging into the clean air. I stumble, falling to my knees as I lay Dave on the grass.

Paramedics stride toward us, and I know I must have a concussion because I think I see Kira right before my vision goes black.

chapter twenty-nine
KIRA

"Noah," I scream as his body goes limp. I duck under the caution tape, needing to run to him, but arms wrap around me before I can go anywhere.

"Kira, you can't go over there," Jeff says, his grip tightening as I squirm against him. A sob escapes my chest as I call his name again.

"Hey, it's okay. Let them do their job," Maddie says, looking toward the EMTs. My hand covers my mouth as tears stream down my cheeks. I watch as they hoist him up onto a stretcher, his body moving like a rag doll. He's going to be okay. He has to be. He's still unconscious when they wheel him over to the ambulance.

"I'm going with him," I grunt as I pull out of Jeff's grasp.

"Kira," he scolds, but I'm already halfway to Noah, leaving Maddie with Jeff.

My heart plummets as they load him in the back of the truck.

"I'm coming," I demand, my voice cracking.

One of the paramedics, a man about my height, opens his mouth like he's going to protest, but something on my face changes his mind.

"Get in," he orders.

I listen, not wanting to give him any reason to kick me out.

"All set?" His colleague, a woman who looks to be in her forties, calls over to him.

"Yup, let's go," he says, stepping up into the ambulance with me.

The sterile scent invades my senses as I try to calm my breathing. He's right there, his face bruised and bloody. I want to touch him, but I don't want to get in the way of the man currently working on treating him across from me. The siren blares as we start to move.

Please wake up.

From what I can tell, his heart rate seems normal; the little monitor beeps steadily. He puts a mask over Noah's face, probably for oxygen. No longer able to stop myself, I reach for Noah's hand, giving it a squeeze. I relax for a second, remembering that day downtown at the bookstore, his rough hand as it brushed mine. I almost break down again, but I steel myself. I can't be a sobbing mess when he wakes up *because he will*.

It doesn't take long before we're pulling into the hospital, and my heart rate spikes again. What if they don't let me stay with him? I can't leave him like this.

"Dave," Noah mutters, his voice hoarse.

I bite back a sob, relief flooding my veins.

"Oh my god, Noah," I cry.

"Kira? What's going on? Where's Dave?"

"Sir, you were injured in a fire. We need to get you inside, okay?"

"Where's Dave, the man that came out with me? Where is he?"

The fear in his voice crushes me.

"I'll find out, okay?" I tell him.

He nods, wincing in pain.

The staff instructs me to sit in the waiting room as they bring Noah back to work on him. I tried to fight them, but they explained that I could see him after treatment and I would only get in the way.

My phone vibrates in my pocket as I sit on the cold plastic chair. Shit, Jared. My hand still shaking from the adrenaline, I swipe to answer, bringing the phone to my ear.

"Kira, I'm here. Where are you?"

I should have called him in the ambulance.

"We're at the hospital," I say softly. "He's okay, at least I think he is. Jared, he—"

"I'm on my way," he says before hanging up.

I push away the hurt of that action. He has the right to be angry with me.

"Kira?" an older man asks. With his stout frame and sandy gray hair, he looks familiar. Where do I know him from?

"I'm Al, Noah's boss, for now at least," he explains. "Jeff told me you'd be here."

Right, Al, the fire commissioner. He sits down on the chair next to me, and I'm sure I look like a mess, my face puffy from crying.

"He's going to be okay, you know," he soothes, his hand resting on my shoulder. I nod, forcing myself to believe him.

"Do you know anything about Dave? Is he okay? And the woman?"

"The woman seemed okay when they took her. She was badly burned but conscious. Dave, on the other hand… Let's just say he's in worse shape than Noah."

"But, he's alive?"

Al bobs his head and sighs. "He wouldn't be without Noah."

"Jesus, Kira," Jared's voice is filled with concern as he rushes over to me. I stand, unsure if I should hug him, but he beats me to it, pulling me to his chest. I inhale his comforting scent, my nerves immediately calming.

I sniffle, trying to keep the tears at bay. I need to be here for Jared, not the other way around. Wiping my cheeks, I back away, looking up at him.

"They're checking him out right now. They said they'd tell me when we could go back and see him."

Jared doesn't respond as he sits across from us.

"I'm going to check on Dave. Let me know if we get any updates," Al says, gesturing to my phone in my hand. He gave me his number so we could keep in touch.

We wait for what feels like hours, and I am all too aware of my surroundings.

Jared's knee bouncing relentlessly, machines beeping in distant rooms, and the ticking of the clock all add to my anxiety.

The tension between us grows by the second, and it's getting to the point where I can't take it anymore.

"Jared," I start, needing to clear the air.

"Not right now," he says, his jaw tightening. His usual easy-going demeanor is replaced with a coldness that I'm not used to from him.

"Please, let me explain," I beg.

"Miss Williams?" a doctor calls from the doorway.

I shoot up, wasting no time as I rush toward him.

"Is he okay?" I ask as Jared steps up behind me. My chest pounds as I wait for his response.

"Yes, he's going to be fine. He has a sprained wrist, a concussion, and he inhaled a lot of smoke, but he should be good to go home tomorrow."

I let out a breath, my hand on my chest.

"When can we see him?" Jared asks.

"Right now, if you'd like. He's awake."

"Yes, please," I say.

We stop at the door to Noah's room, and I look up at Jared.

"You can go first," I tell him, taking a seat in one of the chairs lining the hallway. He deserves to talk to his dad without me breathing down his neck.

"Thanks," he says as he steps into the room.

The words are muffled, but Noah's voice soothes the remaining anxiety in my chest. My phone buzzes in my pocket. I check my notifications seeing a text from Al.

Al

Dave is going to be okay. His leg is broke in multiple places, and they had to intubate him because of the smoke, but they think he'll make a full recovery.

I breathe easier with that knowledge as Jared emerges from the room, the heavy door clicking as it closes.

"He's all yours," he says. "I'm going to head out. Let me know if anything changes." His voice is reserved, and I realize how badly I want the old Jared back.

I don't respond as he disappears down the hall.

"Noah?" I say as I enter the small room.

"There's my princess," he says.

My heart stutters at that. This man can make me swoon even when he's in a hospital bed with tubes in his nose. His left wrist is wrapped with compression tape, and a cut above his right eye adds to his rugged appearance.

"Come here," he says, gesturing to the hospital bed.

"I can't lay there with you, Noah. They're going to yell at me."

He tilts his head at me as if to say, *since when do you care about getting in trouble?*

I roll my eyes at him but obey his request anyway. I climb into the small bed as carefully as possible, not wanting to hurt him. He hisses as I lean into his ribs, and I instantly pull back, but he wraps his arm around me, pulling me closer.

"It's fine. I'm just a little sore," he explains, running his fingers through my hair.

I lean into his touch, my heart melting at its intimacy. He pulls my head to him, pressing a kiss to my forehead.

"You scared the shit out of me, Noah," I scold, my voice breaking on his name. He holds me while I cry, rubbing my back.

"I know, princess. I'm sorry."

I nestle my face into his chest, breathing him in.

"But I'm okay, I promise," he tells me, guiding my face to look at him. "Now, when was the last time you ate?"

I look at the clock, noting the time. He's not going to like my answer.

"Eight-ish hours ago," I say in more of a question than a statement. His eyes narrow on me as he presses the call button on the bed.

"Noah!" I gasp.

A nurse steps into the room, his eyes briefly grazing over me before speaking. "Is everything okay?"

"Yeah, could I get some food sent up though? Maybe some chicken tenders or something?" Noah asks like he's ordering at McDonald's. The nurse chuckles, looking at him with amusement in his eyes.

"Of course, coming right up!"

He returns with two orders of chicken tenders, and Noah and I eat together. The nurse eventually tries to get me to leave, citing "visitor hours are over," but he ultimately caves, my stubborn attitude coming in handy for once.

"Have you heard anything about Dave?" he finally asks me.

The concern in his voice is audible, and it breaks my heart.

"Yeah, the doctors said he will fully recover." I leave out the bit about him having to be intubated and his shattered leg.

His chest sinks under me as he exhales.

"You saved his life," I tell him, in complete awe of the man holding me.

"That's my job," he says, brushing it off.

"That doesn't make it any less impactful," I tell him.

"He would have done it for me."

I sigh, knowing that he won't accept the compliment. Instead, I run my fingers over his jaw, swinging my leg over his body to straddle him.

"Now, don't fucking do it again," I say as I brush my lips over his. He chuckles at my demand, his breath hot on my neck.

"I can't promise I won't," he says, nipping at my skin.

And even though it scares the shit out of me, I'm okay with it. It's who he is.

It's why I love him.

chapter thirty
NOAH

"You should be at home resting," I say, looking over at Dave. He's hobbling beside me in a cast and crutches. He's still in pain, that fact evident by the way he winces with each step. It's only been a few days since the fire, and the brace on my left wrist reinforces that.

"I told you, I'm just visiting," Dave answers.

My eyes narrow on him and my intuition tells me something's up. I open the station door for him, and he enters. I follow close behind him, my senses on high alert. The room is dark, which shouldn't be the case, and I don't see anyone. What is going on—

"Surprise!" All the guys shout in unison, or at least as close to that as they can get. A banner that reads 'congratulations' hangs over the doorway to the kitchen.

"What is this for?" I ask, confusion written on my face.

"We got a new fire commissioner," Jeff explains, giving me that notorious Jeff look that tells me he knows something I don't.

My brows knit together as I step further inside. Glancing over my shoulder at Dave, I give him a questioning look. A smirk is all I get in response. What do they know that I don't?

I scan the room, looking for Al, but I don't see him.

"Where's Al?" I ask Jeff.

"Oh, that's right. I was supposed to tell you that he wants to speak with you in your—I mean his office."

I'm not sure I like the direction this is taking, but I listen anyway, walking through the kitchen to the back office. He's seated at his desk, exactly where I expect him to be.

"Jeff said you wanted to see me. What is all of this?"

"Just a welcome back party."

"They said there's a new commissioner," I deadpan.

A smile grows on his face, his gray beard stretching.

"There is. I'm looking right at him," he says.

I shake my head. "I already told you I'm not the right guy for the position. There's got to be someone else better suited."

I'm not trying to be humble or fish for compliments. It's the truth. I don't deserve that position. I'm not Al.

"Who are you kidding, boy? You are the only one suited for this position. Everyone knows it," he says, his hands waving in the air for emphasis. "What is stopping you from accepting that?"

I can't help but remember them. That kid's parents. The look on their faces when I had to tell them that their son wouldn't make it. I don't deserve that role because I didn't save him, and a better firefighter would've. Al must see the pain on my face because he sighs.

"Noah," he starts.

"Trust me, it should go to someone else," I interrupt.

"Will you shut up for a minute?"

That stops me in my tracks. My jaw tightens as his face softens.

"I need to tell you something."

I stay silent, not wanting to be scolded again, and at my lack of response, he continues.

"It was 1991. I was an experienced officer at that point, and the call sounded routine—a car accident on US 31. The driver was drunk and had swerved into oncoming traffic. When we got there, the scene was horrific. The drunk driver hit another car head-on, and in the process of trying to avoid the collision, the other car was upside down on the side of the road. When I got to it, I knew it wasn't good. The woman in the driver's seat was unresponsive."

He pauses, taking a breath.

"There were two kids in the backseat: A five-year-old and a ten-year-old. They were conscious and screaming for help. I don't think I'll ever get their voices out of my head."

He clears his throat, his eyes welling with tears.

"She didn't make it, did she?" I ask.

He shakes his head. "No. And the kids didn't have any other family.

They were put into the state's custody. The point is, we all have a story like that. We all have a ghost that follows us around our entire career. That's part of the job. It's what keeps us striving to do better. You did everything you could to save that kid. Sometimes, things happen for no good reason. It's out of our control."

His words hit deep. Logically, I know I did everything I could, but what if someone else could have done more?

"You earned this job. Not to mention what you did for Dave. You saved his life when you were told not to. Now, I can't force you to take the job. You can say no, but then you'll have to explain why to all those men out there, and they'll be even harder to convince than me."

God dammit, he might be right. What is my life amounting to if not this? Being a firefighter is part of what makes me who I am. I don't have plans to stop anytime soon. These guys are like family, and I would do anything to keep them safe. Maybe it's time I let myself have something for once.

"Fine, I'll do it."

"That's what I thought," Al says with a cocky grin. Misty-eyed, he claps his hand on my shoulder. "Now let's go. You have a promotion to celebrate."

When we finally head back to the party, we're met with nearly the entire crew eavesdropping outside the door.

"What is there to eat? I'm hungry," I say, brushing off the emotions still warring inside me.

I'm the new fire commissioner.

"Well, *boss*, we have the most delectable walking tacos in the state," Dave says.

"I knew you were in on this," I accuse.

I find Kira on the back porch when I get home. She's on the phone, and I think Jared is on the other end. I'm glad he's not shutting her out like he is me. She doesn't deserve it.

"What do you mean he was arrested?" Kira asks. "What for?"

My eyes shoot to hers, and her face goes white. I rush over to her, trying to listen to the other end of the call. So help me, god, if that boy got arrested, but it is Jared's voice on the other end.

"It was a fourteen-year-old girl. Her parents filed charges against him," he explains.

She takes a couple of deep breaths, her hand shaking as she tries to hold the phone.

"Thank you for telling me," she says, her voice cracking.

She hangs up the call, and her eyes, filled with tears, meet mine. Without a second thought, I pull her into me, running my fingers through her hair.

"Talk to me, princess. What happened?" I ask as I move my hands to her back.

Her jaw clenches as she looks at me, a mixture of emotions swimming in those brown eyes.

"They arrested him. Zach. He raped another girl," she explains as the tears flow freely down her face. "She was only fourteen."

My grip tightens around her. I should have killed him. She wipes her tears, frustration creeping onto her face.

"I should have tried harder. I should have fought that detective. Then he might not have been able to hurt that girl."

"Kira, don't blame yourself for this. None of this was your fault. It's not your responsibility to protect the public from that asshole," I tell her, needing her to hear me.

"It's not your fault," I repeat.

She nods into my chest, taking a moment before looking up at me. She's so beautiful, even like this.

"You're right. I won't let him have that power over me again." She sniffles, and I wipe the tear that falls.

"That's my girl."

She smiles up at me, and my heart melts. She is so resilient. So strong.

"Well, how was your day?" she chuckles through her tears.

I eye her, and she knows exactly what I'm thinking.

"I will be okay, I promise. I just don't want to think about that right now."

"Well, it wasn't too bad considering you're looking at the new fire commissioner," I say, finally feeling the pride that comes with that statement.

I still don't entirely feel like I deserve it. Al is a fantastic boss, and there's no way I can compare to him, but I am confident I will do everything possible to be a good leader to our crew. For the first time in a long time, I'm moving forward instead of staying stagnant.

"That's amazing, Noah," Kira squeals, her face lighting up.

The admiration in her eyes almost brings me to my knees. I run my thumb over her lips, comprehending just how lucky I am. Unable to resist, I press my mouth to hers. Her lips are soft, and the kiss is slow. I grip her jaw with my hand, kissing her harder. Her hand comes up to my chest, pushing me back.

"We need to celebrate. Let's go out to dinner tonight," she breathes.

I groan, mourning the loss of her kiss. I would much rather stay in. I can think of plenty of ways to celebrate with only the two of us, but something in her eyes catches my attention.

"If you don't want to, I get it. People might judge," she says.

Does she think I don't want to be seen with her? If so, she's crazy. I grab her chin, forcing her to look at me.

"I would love to get dinner with you," I tell her. "Now go put on one of those little dresses and meet me downstairs in fifteen."

A blush creeps onto her cheeks, and she nods.

chapter thirty-one
KIRA

Jared leaves for college today. I want to be excited for him, and I am, but the amalgamation of guilt, sadness, and anxiety completely overpowers any enthusiasm I have. What if he never fully accepts his dad and me? I wouldn't blame him if he didn't, but I miss how things used to be between us. We were close, and losing that feels like losing a part of myself.

"Can you pass me that sweater, please?" Jared asks, pointing to a black and gray hoodie he's had since freshman year.

It's weird to see his room like this, devoid of his usual mess. An ache grows deep in my chest. I don't want him to leave with this huge rift between us, but I don't know how to fix it.

He stuffs his remaining clothes into the last box, and I open the door for him, following him out to his car. I want to say something, anything, but I can't get myself to.

"Listen, I wanted to talk to you," Jared says, his eyes not meeting mine.

My heart drops. Here it comes. He's going to tell me we can't be friends anymore. He is the closest thing I have to family, and he's going to tell me he wants nothing to do with me.

"I wanted to apologize for how I reacted when Zach showed up that night. I shouldn't have just let him go like that. Hell, I'm sorry I didn't realize something was up sooner. I wish I could have been there for you when it first happened."

"Jared, you don't need to apologize," I try to reassure him.

"No, you deserve an apology. I'm sorry I didn't kick his teeth in when I had the chance. I'm sorry I let that happen to you when we were younger. I should have been there."

I want to go to him, to hug him, but I'm not sure that's what he wants from me right now.

"It wasn't your fault. I'm sorry I didn't tell you sooner. I was scared, and I know it sounds stupid, but I felt embarrassed," the words leave my lips before I realize what I'm confessing.

I felt ashamed, as if I had done something to deserve it. I know now that I didn't, but that feeling still lingers. I have to remind myself that it's no one's fault but Zach's.

"I'm sorry too," I continue. "I should have told you about Noah and me right when it happened. I hate that I hurt you, and I hate the fact that I drove a wedge between you two."

"Kira," he stops me, his fingers wrapping around my wrist. "I'm not upset with you. Do I wish you would have told me sooner? Of course, but I see how much you love him. I can't hold that against you."

"Talk to him then," I beg. "Please." That has been the most

challenging part of this. Jared still won't respond to any of Noah's calls or texts. He specifically picked a time to stop by when his dad wouldn't be home, and now he's leaving for college and—

"I just need some time, okay?" He explains, his voice soft.

I take a deep breath and nod. I need to be patient. He'll come around. He has to.

As Jared's car disappears down the road, I focus on the hope blooming inside me. He said he needs time, so I'll give it to him.

I step into the studio around noon. Darla sits behind the counter and greets me with a warm smile, gray hair sporting its usual purple streak.

"Hey Kira, I hate to ask, but do you think you could take over the register for a minute? I have to run some errands."

"I would love to," I tell her, setting my bag behind the desk. "Just show me what to do," I laugh.

I haven't run the checkout here yet, and it's a bit different from the grocery store. She's patient with me as she explains how to enter the products. We sell pieces from a couple of other artists, so we have to make sure they get credit for their sales. She's showing me how to take the payment when a younger couple comes into the studio.

"Good afternoon. Let me know if you have any questions or need help with anything," I say as they begin to look around.

It's not long before they're heading up to the register. The woman looks at the mug she's holding, and her eyes light up with excitement. "We were here about a month ago for the Cherry Festival, and I saw this mug. I talked myself out of it but regretted it right after we left, so I told him we had to come back up here," she says, gesturing toward the man.

I return her smile, noticing it's one of my pieces. It's a wide mug glazed with a blend of oranges and pinks. It reminds me of how the sun looks as it sets over the lake at the house.

"I'm glad you love it," I say as I enter the product into the register and select my name as the vendor.

"Your total will be $42.40," I tell her. She hands me the cash, and I wrap the mug and pack it into a paper bag. "Have a great rest of your day," I tell them as they leave.

"Okay, you're hired," Darla says. "When can you quit at the grocery store?" I expect humor in her eyes, but there's none. She's serious.

"I thought you couldn't afford an employee," I say.

"Well, I can now. Plus, you need to know how to run the store if you're going to be part owner."

My eyes widen, and my brows shoot up. What is she talking about? Noticing my bewilderment, she continues.

"Kira, you are the only person who cares about this place as much as I do. It's been growing, so much so that I can't do it all by myself anymore," she tells me, her eyes soft. "Now, when can you start? I know school is coming up, and I don't want to take you away from that, but you can work as many hours as you'd like. You can also do school work here during your downtime."

I probably look like an idiot, my mouth opening and closing like a fish. This is my dream. To be able to co-own a pottery studio in Traverse

City, it's everything I've ever wanted.

"Um, I just have to give Rob a two-week notice, but I can see if he'll let me leave sooner," I tell her, still uncertain.

"Perfect, now I have to go. I wasn't lying about those errands. Are you good to handle the store for a little bit?"

I nod, unable to keep the grin off my face.

Darla is gone for a little over an hour and a half, and in that time, we get four more customers. I'm pretty confident in the checkout process now, and all I can think about is how this is my new reality. Darla takes over again for me, and I wander to the back of the studio.

It's still on the shelf where I left it. I take the piece down and set it on the cool metal table in front of me, removing the plastic bag I used to keep the sculpture moist. The hand grips the tiny bird, holding it in place. I stare at it, feeling the same sense of wrongness wash over me. The bird looks powerless, the fingers pinning its body down. It's trapped.

Images of that night flood my mind: his arms lifting my body as I try to scream, his weight on top of me, the way he caged me in. He took my power from me, and I let him, even after that night. I let myself believe it was my fault, that I did something to deserve what happened to me. I listened to my mom and the detective, and who could blame me? I was fifteen, and they were people that were *supposed* to keep me safe.

I read somewhere that one in five women report having been sexually assaulted. That's tens of millions of women in the United States alone. Tens of millions of women that had their power taken from them. A familiar anger burns deep within me. It's a distinctly feminine rage, and I let it consume me. I didn't deserve what happened to me, and neither did any of those other women.

I'm taking my power back.

I look at the sculpture, the bird looking up at me as if asking for help. I oblige. My fingers dig into the soft clay, a renewed purpose guiding my hands.

It still needs to be fired and then glazed, but I'm content with my progress as I place the piece back on the shelf, sans bag this time. I say goodbye to Darla before leaving the studio, and the air is cool as I step outside. My car is parked only about a block down, so I take my time breathing in the city as I walk. This is one of my favorite times of year here. Summer is still hanging on, but there are hints of fall in the cooler nights and shorter days.

I look at all the shops, passing the bookstore that Noah and I went to together.

It's surprisingly quiet for the city tonight, with only the sounds of cars passing by as I walk. There's a gallery nestled right next to it, and I study the paintings through the windows. They're beautiful, and I admire the talent it takes to create masterpieces like that. I've tried painting, and it is not for me. Something about a blank, flat surface causes my brain to short-circuit.

I'm so enchanted by the artwork that I almost miss the small paper taped to the window.

NOW ACCEPTING NEW ARTISTS

We have two open spots and are now accepting new submissions of two-dimensional and three-dimensional pieces.

The new artists will be featured at our fall gala the first weekend of October!

There's no way they would pick me, but something is telling me I need to do this. Opening up my mail app on my phone, I type in the email provided on the flyer.

Here goes nothing.

chapter thirty-two
NOAH

THE PALE YELLOW OIL SLIDES DOWN THE FUNNEL AS I POUR THE remainder of the quart into the engine. It's surprisingly warm for an October afternoon, and the breeze from the open garage door brings in the fresh autumn air.

Kira's gala is tonight, and I want everything perfect for her. Hence, the black dress pants and button-down shirt, which make me feel like I'm going to prom all over again. The Nova is getting similar pampering to ensure she's ready for the event, and the routine brings me back to a memory from almost ten years ago.

"Hey Jared, buddy, can you come help me with something real quick?" I call, my body hunched under the hood of the car.

A stampede of footsteps comes rushing in from the hall, and a head peeks around the corner. Bright green eyes find mine.

"Do I have to?" He whines, pushing his bottom lip out in a pout.

I don't know what happened. It seems like just yesterday, he was begging to work on the car with me. I guess he's getting to that age.

"I can help if you want, Mr. Keller," a small voice says from behind him.

Jared brought a new friend home today—Kira, I think her name is. She's quiet, but they already get along like two peas in a pod. Jared takes the opportunity and bolts.

"Thanks, Kira. I'll get Guitar Hero ready while you help," he says as he spins around for the living room, leaving me alone with this twelve-year-old girl.

"Call me Noah, and that's fine. You don't have to. I can do it myself," I tell her, not wanting her to feel uncomfortable.

"It's okay, I want to," she says as she enters the garage. "What do you need me to do?"

"Could you hold this light for me? I can't see into the engine to change the spark plugs."

She nods, grabbing the flashlight from me and turning it on. It illuminates the engine block, giving me a far better view of what I'm working with.

I crank the ratchet, loosening the spark plug.

"Thank you for the pasta tonight, Mr. Keller. It was really good," she says, her appreciation clear in her tone. "I never get to eat stuff like that."

My brows pinch together, trying to figure out what she means. It was only Alfredo with broccoli. Jared always complains when I make it.

"Oh, why not?"

"Mom says it's too high in carbs, and I already need to lose weight," she says matter-of-factly.

I freeze, looking at her. It's not my place to correct someone else's parenting. Hell, I'm a single dad who has no idea what he's doing, but this girl is thin. If she lost any weight, I'd be concerned for her health.

"Well, feel free to come over anytime, and I can make it again," I tell her.

She smiles, and something about it breaks my heart.

I shake my head as I screw the oil cap back on. That was a long time ago. It was my first inkling that her home life wasn't a good situation. From then on out, I encouraged Jared to invite her over as much as I could, and at some points, she was at our house more than she was at her own.

As I reach up and grab the hood, slamming it shut, my eyes land on the last person I expect to see.

"Hey, Dad."

Jared stands in front of me, dressed in a pair of nice jeans and a blue button-down similar to mine. I want to hug him. I haven't talked to him since everything that went down with that piece of shit, Zach. Instead, I grab a red work rag and wipe off my hands.

"Hey, what are you doing here?"

"I was in town for Kira's gala and thought I'd stop by," he shrugs. I can tell there's more than what he's saying, but I don't feel it's my place to pry.

"Well, how has school been?" I ask, desperate to know what his life has been like these past few weeks. I hate the fact that we aren't talking.

"It's good. I honestly love it," he says.

"Good," I say, a tiny bit of relief warming my chest.

He nods, and silence stretches, surrounding us. I'm not sure how to handle this new awkwardness. Jared always was the one to fill any lull in conversation, but now he's looking at me like he's not sure what to say. It kills me.

"Jared," I start, but he already knows where I'm going.

He shakes his head, stopping me.

"Listen, Dad, I came here because I needed to get some things off my chest," he says, a pained expression on his face. When I don't say anything, he continues. "Finding out about you and Kira the way I did was fucked up. It was probably the deepest feeling of betrayal I've ever felt."

"I'm so sorry—"

"But I've been thinking, and it sort of all makes sense now. Kira is a wonderful person. She's strong, independent, and caring, and as much as I hate to admit it, you are exactly what she needs. You make her feel safe. I can see it in her eyes when she looks at you."

He sucks in a breath, his eyes softening.

"And she's what you've needed since mom."

His words hit deep, and my mind struggles to reconcile them with his anger when he found out. Is this some kind of fucked up blessing he's giving me?

"I guess what I'm trying to say is…I'm not mad at you. Yeah, I'm still a little hurt that you guys didn't tell me, but I understand it now. Seeing the way she reacted after that fire…She's in love with you," he tells me. "Now, as her best friend, if you break her heart, so help me god—"

I can't help but laugh at his threat.

"Oh, I know. You don't have to warn me," I tell him with a grin.

"Good," he says, his lips turning up at one side.

Seeing that hint of happiness slip onto his face dissolves the weight resting on my chest. He's okay. I didn't fuck him up completely, and he doesn't hate me.

"You want a ride to the gala?" I ask, gesturing to the Nova.

"Are you kidding me?" Jared deadpans, and my heart drops out of my chest for a full minute until he adds, "Hell, yeah."

WE APPROACH THE GALLERY IN STYLE, WITH THE WINDOWS DOWN and the music blaring. It's been a long time since we've done something like this together, and it's refreshing. Only a couple of spots are left in the parking lot, and I take the one closest to the building, which still leaves us a decent walk away.

I hold the glass door open for Jared, who enters. The large room is full of people. Some hold glasses of champagne as they analyze the artwork, while others are in small groups, talking amongst themselves. I scan the room, looking for Kira.

My eyes land on her right as she looks up and sees Jared and me. Her eyes widen the slightest bit, and her lips curve into a smile.

The warm glow of the lights illuminates her exposed skin in the deep-cut emerald dress she's wearing. She looks exquisite, with her honey-brown hair falling over her shoulders.

"Kira!" Jared calls as he runs up to her.

She giggles as he lifts her into the air. I can't help but laugh. This is how it should be between them. It's how it's always been. I let them have their space, looking at all the artwork. The walls are filled with intricate paintings. There is a grouping of landscapes, and I recognize all of the exact locations. They're of Traverse City. My favorite is the peninsula, a view from one of the wineries.

As I wander, I take in more of the pieces. They're all made with different materials and have different subjects. I've never been a big art guy, but I'm starting to think there is something to this. I stop when I see what looks like the piece Kira was working on all those months ago. It's an outstretched hand, and in its palm is a beautifully colored goldfinch. Only one claw is touching the hand, the other frozen in the air as the bird takes flight.

I stare at the finished sculpture, and all I see is her and the confidence and freedom she's found for herself. She's come a long way from the scared girl she was when she first moved in, and I'm so fucking proud of her. My eyes find her again. She's still talking to Jared, and their conversation looks so easy.

"Hey, big guy," a voice from beside me says.

I turn to face Maddie as she hands me a glass of champagne.

"Do you have artwork here?"

"God, no. I'm just here to support our girl," she explains, following my gaze over her shoulder to Kira.

I nod, watching as Kira moves on to talk to a couple looking at a large portrait.

"I wanted to thank you," Maddie says softly.

"For what?" I ask, wondering if I'm forgetting something.

"For taking care of her," she rolls her eyes as she looks at me.

I laugh, shaking my head. "You don't have to thank me for that."

She opens her mouth to respond but is interrupted by a girl, who I assume is Lucy, wrapping her arms around her waist.

"Come here, my mom wants to show you something," she says as she pulls her away. Maddie looks at me, an apology on her face as she follows Lucy.

Unable to wait any longer, I make my way to Kira. She's facing away from me, looking up at the landscapes I admired earlier. Silently, I slip my hand around her waist, pulling her back into me.

"Hey, princess," I say, loud enough for only her to hear.

She can't help but lean into me, her hand covering mine.

"You and Jared came together?"

The hope in her voice tugs at my chest, and I love how much she cares about my relationship with my son.

"Yeah, we did."

"So, you two are good now?" she asks, needing more reassurance.

"Yes, we're good."

She lets out a breath that sounds suspiciously like a sob, so I turn her to face me, her eyes meeting mine.

"I'm so proud of you," I tell her, meaning it with everything in my being.

A blush creeps across her cheeks as I run my fingers over her back. I want to bring her home and show her just how proud I am.

It's clearing out in here now, and the scheduled end time for the gala has already passed.

"Jared's taking your car. You're riding with me," I tell her, her amber eyes reflecting the need in my own.

Not ten minutes later, I hold open the door for her as she slides into the Nova. The slit in her dress shows the perfect amount of skin as I sit down next to her, the engine roaring to life. She's beyond beautiful as she looks back at me, her gaze heated.

Without warning, I crash my lips onto hers. She lets out a small moan as I lace my fingers through her hair.

"Noah," she chides as she breaks the kiss.

I shake my head, pressing my forehead to hers.

"I'm done waiting."

epilogue
KIRA

THREE YEARS LATER

I never expected Noah to want to leave the state of Michigan, let alone the country, but here we are—at an absolutely gorgeous vineyard attached to our hotel.

In Italy.

I sip my wine as I take it all in. The view is jaw-dropping. Rows of grapevines stretch over the hilly landscape, and a couple of old cottages pepper the horizon.

"What are you thinking about, princess?"

I look up to see Noah in his button-down shirt, gazing over at me like I'm the only thing in the world.

That will never get old—having this man's full attention on me. We've been together three years now, and I still crave it.

"Just about how I might be ready to head back to our room," I tell him, sliding my leg between his under the table.

He laughs, brushing his hand over my bare thigh under the table. Heat spreads up my leg as his eyes darken.

"Still impatient, I see," he chides, but there's no weight to it.

He wants this just as much as I do.

Pushing the door open to our room, Noah leads me inside. As soon as it clicks shut, he's on me, my back against the cool metal. I gasp at the sensation, but the sound is cut off by his lips on mine. The movement is rushed, almost frantic.

I reach up to his waistband, needing to feel him, but I'm stopped by his hands on my wrists.

"Not yet. Not until I'm done with you," he growls, and I feel it in my chest as he pins my arms above my head. I'm surrounded by him. My breathing is ragged, and all I want is to touch him.

His lips trail over my jaw as his other hand grazes up my thigh to the hem of my dress. I suck in a breath at the sensation, leaning into his touch.

I need him.

"Noah, please."

He pulls away, his eyes filled with heat as they meet mine.

"My little princess is so impatient," he chides as he hits the edge of my panties.

His eyes still don't leave mine as he pushes them to the side, his fingers sliding over me, feeling how turned on I am.

"This all for me?" he asks, already knowing the answer.

I nod, needing more of his touch.

Suddenly, his arms wrap around my thighs, hoisting me into them. In moments, he's dropping me on the end of the bed, peeling off his shirt. His familiar tattooed body sends a wave of warmth through me.

This is all mine.

He's mine.

His hand moves to the back of my head, his fingers lacing into my hair as his lips crash into mine. I soak it in as I kiss him back. He wants me. He knows everything about me, and he still wants me.

His kisses quickly move lower, grabbing my lace panties and sliding them down my legs. His hands grip my hips, pulling me closer to the edge of the bed.

"Fuck, you're so beautiful like this, all spread out for me," he groans.

Before I can say anything, his mouth covers my pussy, his tongue gliding over me. All I can do is moan, loving how he feels on me. I reach for him, tangling my fingers into his hair as he explores every inch of me with his tongue.

"You taste so fucking good, princess."

My cheeks heat at his praise, pleasure already building deep in my core.

"Noah, you're going to make me come," I moan, teetering on the edge.

He groans into me, the vibration of it sending shockwaves through me. He keeps devouring me as he pushes two fingers into me, expertly navigating my body. It doesn't take long for me to come apart for him.

"Good girl."

His hands slide up under my dress.

"Off. Now."

I don't hesitate, sitting up and pulling it off. I'm completely bare for him now.

His hands go to his belt, unbuckling it and pulling it off with one hand. The sight is borderline pornographic. I sit up, crawling over the bed to him. His rough hands grip my jaw as he kisses me, slower this time—more intentional.

My fingers find his waistband, unbuttoning his jeans and pulling them down, exposing his hard length. I look up at him, our faces inches apart.

"Lay down," he breathes over my lips.

I think about denying him, pushing his limits, but I need this too much.

He climbs up onto the bed after me, pushing my legs open as he towers over me. I reach for him, pulling his lips to mine.

I can't wait anymore.

"Noah, please, I need you," I beg.

He finally gives in, pushing into me in one deep thrust. A loud moan escapes my lips at the intrusion, but I love it. I run my nails up his back as he pumps into me.

I'm already so close, and I can tell he is too with the way he's breathing. Knowing I can do this to him is such a powerful feeling. My eyes squeeze shut at the pleasure flowing through me.

He keeps fucking me as he reaches up to cup my cheek. "Look at me."

I do, and the emotions swirling in his eyes nearly end me.

"I love you," I whisper as I arch into him.

"I love you too, baby. Now, come for me," he commands, his eyes not leaving mine.

And I do, pulling him over the edge with me.

FRESHLY SHOWERED, I PULL ON ONE OF NOAH'S SHIRTS. HE MAKES fun of me for never wearing my pajamas, but I don't care. I'll never stop stealing his clothes.

I still can't believe we're here, in Italy, even as I gaze out over the vineyard. I'm perched on the balcony, wine glass in hand. The sun is hovering just above the horizon, and the fresh night air wraps around me as music plays from somewhere in the distance.

It's like I'm standing in the middle of a painting.

Strong arms snake around my shoulders, pulling me into them. Noah presses a kiss to my head, and I lean into his touch. His warm body surrounds me, and I breathe him in.

"Already ready for round two?" I ask.

A low chuckle erupts from behind me as his hand slides up my neck to my jaw. He pulls me to look at him, and I think he's about to sass me back, but he presses his lips to mine instead.

I melt into him.

He breaks the kiss, looking down at me, his hazel eyes searching mine.

"Kira," he starts. "I never would have thought this is what my life would look like. After Angie, I had fully accepted the fact that I was most likely going to be alone, but then you came along."

My heart is pounding in my chest.

Where is he going with this?

"You are everything I've ever wanted, and my life doesn't exist without you."

My heart warms at his admission.

Reaching into his pocket, he drops to one knee.

No way. There's no way.

There, between his thumb and index finger, is the most beautiful ring I think I have ever seen.

"Kira, will you marry me?"

My heart races as I look down at him, tears threatening to stream down my face.

"Noah, oh my god," I cry, grabbing the ring. "How much did you spend on this thing?"

The diamond is huge, nearly the size of a pea, and it sits atop a simple gold band.

"That's what you're worried about?" he laughs as he looks up at me from his position on the ground. "So, is that a yes?"

Wait, I didn't say yes?

"Of course it's a yes, Noah. I've wanted this for way longer than I should have," I tell him as I slide the ring onto my left ring finger. It fits perfectly.

He rises to his feet as he holds my hand in his, inspecting the new addition.

"Do you like it?" he asks, genuine concern in his eyes.

"I love it. You picked perfectly."

The pride that flashes on his face makes my heart skip a beat. His hand reaches for my face, and I lean into him.

"I can't fucking wait to call you my wife."

dear reader,

First, I want to thank you for even deciding to read this book. I never thought I would be able to call myself a published author, but here we are!

The setting of this book was super important to me. I've never read a book set in Traverse City, and it's one of my favorite places on the planet, so I made it happen.

This book is and always will be my baby. I fell in love with Noah and Kira as soon as I put pen to paper. Kira's story has elements to it that are very similar to my own, and I know that's the case for so many other women. I wanted to show those people—and myself—that healing is possible.

You can take your power back.

-Sarah

about the author

Sarah was born and raised in Michigan and spends most of her days cycling through various hobbies. She lives with her partner, Hannah, and two dogs, Beck and Gracie. She also co-owns a spicy book business called Pages & Peonies.

Visit the business page at: pagesandpeonies.com or scan the code below.